# BOLL WEEVIL

## A NOVEL

# JAMES RADFORD

© 2019 James Radford
ISBN: 978-1-54397-792-9

Boll Weevil
Written by James Radford
Photography by James Radford
Cover design by Kristen Sharp Pastras

Biscuette Books
www.biscuette.com
www.jamesradford.com

*To the places*
*I miss every day*

# BOLL WEEVIL

# PROLOGUE

THE COURTROOM was still. The opposing lawyer had finished his closing remarks, and now Michael watched him step quietly back to the defendant's side of the room. Michael pushed out his chair and stood. He lingered there for a moment, unmoving, listening to the sound of his own breathing, looking down a final time at his notes. He heard the faint rustle of some papers from the gallery, heard someone cough a sort of nervous, unnecessary cough. His scalp tingled, blood and adrenaline rushing to his brain. He took slow, deep breaths to contain and to channel the great nervous energy that now boiled inside him. He buttoned one of the buttons on his suit coat, worked his tall, lanky frame to the front of counsel's table, looked up at the judge and nodded. "Mr. Drummond," said the judge. Michael turned and faced the jury. He knew they were watching him, reading his every movement.

Over the course of the previous weeks, he had methodically presented to this jury every fact, every piece of evidence, to show what happened on the day that Malcolm Everett died and Kecia Everett lost the use of her legs. He had presented the doctors who operated on Kecia, the coroner who examined Malcolm's body, the terrible photographs of the accident's aftermath. He had presented Malcolm's mother and father, who choked and stuttered their way through an account of Malcolm's character and the loss to their family. He had presented their pastor, their friends and co-workers, to describe the impact on their community. Now, he needed to ensure the jury understood the import of their task; he needed to ensure they delivered the verdict justice demanded.

He braced himself and prepared to speak.

"Ladies and gentlemen," he said. "Thank you once again for your service these two weeks. We have brought you from your homes, from your work, from your families, to sit and listen to the evidence and to decide the terrible dispute that has brought on this trial. The decision you make today will have an enormous impact on the Everett family, on this community, and on the law. Please never doubt the profound importance of your service. It means a great deal to me, it means a great deal to my clients, and I sincerely thank you.

"You have heard the evidence. You have heard how the 18-wheeler—owned and operated by Darby Tobacco—plummeted through the rainy night down the Dixie Beeline, exceeding the speed limit by some twenty miles-per-hour, a ten-thousand gallon tank of sulfuric acid hitched behind it. You have heard the testimony of the driver, who had not slept in nearly twenty-four hours, whose brain was buzzing with Mini-Thins, those cheap gas-station stimulants. You have heard him testify that he knew it was against regulation to drive in such a state, yet he did it anyway, because his dispatcher was screaming at him, demanding he get the chemical to the plant on time. You have learned that the driver dozed off, that he woke suddenly to the sound of a blaring car horn, realized too late that he had veered into the oncoming lane, twisted the wheel, overcorrected. The momentum from the trailer was too great, of course, and the truck twisted into an L." As he said this, he held his hands forward, his fingers pointed toward the jury, then turned them at his wrists, ninety degrees to the side, to demonstrate the trailer's movement. "The trailer lunged forward, perpendicular to the road, like a gigantic scythe." He moved toward the jury box as he spoke, the plane created by his hands a simple model of impending doom.

"You have heard from the dispatcher. You have learned that Leon Darby himself insisted that the driver get the chemical to him right away, desperate to cook another batch of preservative to prevent the harvest-time tobacco leaves from spoiling.

"You have learned of the first collision—with the Rushing family—before the Everetts' vehicle was hit. You have seen that the

Corolla driven by Jacob Rushing was struck with such great force that it ripped through the entire upper half of the vehicle, yet kept moving toward the Everetts."

At this, Michael detected defense counsel shifting in his seat. It almost caused him to smile. He could feel Darby's expensive Atlanta lawyer steeling himself, ready to object the moment he discussed any further the details of the Rushings' death. He glanced over and met the eyes of Tyler King, Darby's personal lawyer and local counsel, now glaring at him. Judge Roundtree had forbidden Michael to describe the injuries to the Rushings, horrific as they were. "This is not about the Rushings," the judge had ruled. "Their case has settled and is a separate matter. Describing their injuries may confuse the issue and prejudice the jury." So, Michael had said all he could say. He had described the physical impact the truck had on the Rushings' vehicle as evidence of the truck's speed and momentum.

Even still, as he stood there, relishing the nervous silence from the defense table, he could not prevent himself from recalling the things he knew about the Rushings. He imagined the horrible resignation that must have entered the mind of Jacob Rushing as he watched the trailer lunging toward his car. He wondered if Jacob was conscious in the moments before the trailer smashed through the top of his vehicle, whether he was able to take a final look at his young wife before the trailer decapitated them both. He wondered if Jacob had a moment to be grateful that his two-year-old son was lying down asleep in the back seat, so that the trailer might pass over the little boy's reclining body. He wondered if the little boy had seen the twisted, headless torsos of his mother and father, slumped onto the dashboard, when he woke from his slumber.

He took a moment to collect himself.

"You have heard, ladies and gentlemen, the testimony of Kecia Everett." He gestured toward his client, a young black woman, the tone of her skin a shade darker than his own, sitting to the side of counsel's table in her wheelchair. She had once been carefree and beautiful, you could tell, and the shadow of her former vivaciousness occasionally showed as a vague impression upon her now scarred and solemn face. "Malcolm had been driving the pickup home from Vidalia. They'd just seen a movie, something that she would like, a romantic comedy. Malcolm must have seen the chaos unfolding before him, he must have seen the trailer smashing through the Rushings' Corolla, because he made the split-second decision to maneuver the pickup right, off the shoulder and into a shallow ditch that ran alongside the road. He knew it was their only chance to escape. And they almost did escape. The back end of the trailer smashed into the rear of the pickup, split it in half. The truck bed separated from the cab. The separated cab rolled forward, jumping end over end through the air, smashing head-first into the ground three full times before it finally came to rest on its roof amidst the tall, dry grass inside the ditch.

"Malcolm's airbag dispatched. The seatbelts kept him and Kecia from flying through the windshield. But the impact had been so great, so sudden, that the safety devices could not save them. As the noise subsided, Malcolm's lifeless and broken body hung suspended by the seat belt. The impact of the cab slamming into the dirt forced the steering column forward, crushing Malcolm's trachea, collapsing his lungs. Kecia hung there also, her pelvis crushed, her face shredded by the glass and debris that flew through the cab in those terrible seconds. When she came to consciousness, she was so badly beaten that she could not muster the strength to unbuckle the belt and free herself. She hung there, trying in vain to awaken Malcolm with her shallow cries. The one thing she recalled was the little digital clock on the dashboard, which had somehow survived the crash, reading 10:10 when she came to. As she slipped in and out of consciousness, she looked at that clock, watched the minutes pass slowly by, each one seeming like an eternity, wondering if anyone would ever come, until finally, at 10:22, she heard the sirens and knew help was on the way."

Michael looked out at the jurors. Collectively, they were serious, disturbed. He saw a profound sadness on the face of one old man. Two women were crying quietly, dabbing their eyes now and then with Kleenex.

"Ladies and gentlemen, there is no question that Darby Tobacco is liable for Malcolm's death and for Kecia's injuries. The only question is: what is the appropriate measure of damages?"

The events that led him to this moment flashed before his eyes. The case could have been settled had Darby offered the Everetts fair compensation, had the company offered them something akin to what it had offered the Rushing estate. The Rushing child's grandmother had retained a very good personal injury attorney from Macon, and Darby's insurance carrier had agreed to pay the full five million of coverage offered by its policy into a trust for the child's benefit. But when it came to the Everetts, the carrier had been far less generous.

After weeks of negotiations, they finally offered $750,000 to settle Malcolm's wrongful death claim, and $500,000 to settle the claims for Kecia's injuries. Michael had said no. He had insisted on the full five million. He felt insulted and enraged at the insurance company's position—that the earning potential of a black farm worker from Goshen County, Georgia, was inherently limited, that Malcolm Everett would probably never have earned the type of money they were offering in settlement even if he worked until he was 80 years old. The carrier argued that $500,000 would be more than sufficient to compensate Kecia. Public assistance would cover most of her medical bills, they said. And Kecia, like Malcolm, lacked great earning potential. Her pain and suffering? Too speculative to determine.

The racial bias angered him, sure; but what enraged him more was the carrier's belief that it could buy this young lawyer off. The total settlement being offered—$1.25 million—would have been far and away the largest Michael had ever brokered. It would have afforded him a fee of $416,000—his one-third contingency—and changed his life. The insurance carrier knew this, and Michael knew they knew it, and he could not countenance such a result.

When he gave the final *no*, and returned to his office to prepare for trial, there had been a moment of sickening in his gut. The decision to turn away such a large payday ate at him; it worked against his conservative, risk-averse core. But he had calmed his nerves with the dual knowledge that (a) he owed a sacred duty to his clients to pursue everything to which they were entitled, and (b) the risk he was taking was a reasonable one, a manageable one, and one whose outcome he could control.

As he stood, preparing himself to ask this jury for a great deal of money, he allowed the inequities that had brought him here, the carrier's underestimation of his own tenacity, to spin in his mind. This was something he had planned on doing. He had become a master of controlling his own emotions, of disconnecting himself from the most gut-wrenching of circumstances, in order to analyze rationally and to plan. Yet, he also knew that some outpouring of emotion was necessary, that it would be needed to persuade the jury to give him what he asked for. So, he had decided early on that before he presented his damages case, he would dwell on the things that moved him, he would let his emotions boil inside him, he would channel them, and he would release them at the right moment. Now, as he looked out over this Goshen County jury, this box full of his countrymen, he took a final silent breath and prepared to let his emotions loose.

"My friends," he said. "You have heard the arguments of defense counsel. You have heard him say that the Everetts cannot prove their earning potential, the dollar value of their lives. You have heard their entreaty to deny your emotional reaction to these events, to deliver a justice that is cold and impartial.

"And it is true, we *will* never know what young Malcolm might have accomplished. I look at the photos of this young man"—he gestured toward an array of photographs displayed on an easel in front of counsel's table—"and I think of my own life. I wonder, if I had died some years ago, would they say the things about me that these lawyers are saying about Malcolm Everett? Would they say, this young black man would never have amounted to anything? Would they say my life is not that valuable?

"Would they say that of my children? I think of my little girl. I look in her eyes and I imagine all she might accomplish, all she might become. I imagine her as a great artist, as an engineer, as a lawyer, as the President of the United States if she wants to be. And as I listen to these lawyers attempt to devalue Malcolm Everett's life, I wonder, will my child be valued by others as I value her? Will her potential be limited by others' expectations of her, because of her race?"

His lip trembled. He paused for some time, took careful, measured breaths.

"I pray the answer is no. And I have faith that, in this community, this place where I was born and raised, you all will agree with me. We are not that kind of community. We are a community that believes people have dignity. That life is priceless.

That *all lives* are priceless. That we were all created in the image of God, our maker, and that in his eyes we are equal."

He knew he was giving some of these jurors more credit than they deserved, that many of them almost certainly held far less egalitarian attitudes when it came to race, at least subconsciously. But he also knew that most racists are anxious for an opportunity to prove they're not, and this would be a good one. He also knew the reference to God would help. Michael knew that, here in Goshen County, he could get away with invoking the Lord's name in court, and his skin tingled with excitement as the words came from his mouth.

He turned toward the defense attorneys sitting at the table across the room. "And for *these* men"—he pointed accusingly—"to suggest that this young man could not possibly amount to much, because of where he was born, because of the circumstances of his birth, because of struggles he had in his younger years, *because of the color of his skin*. That is something that we will not tolerate!" His voice rose as he spoke. Spittle jumped from his lips. His hand and his body began to shake with apparent rage.

"Objection, your Honor! Objection!" The attorneys from Atlanta were caught off guard by this pouring-out from Michael Drummond, who had been so mild-mannered, so matter of fact, so rational, during the evidence phase of the trial.

Judge Roundtree banged his gavel. Michael forced himself into a calm. "Counsel," the judge said. "This is getting a little out of control. Let me caution you to stick to the facts."

Michael stood there for a moment, breathing long, dramatic breaths, his chest heaving in and out, still staring at defense counsel. He created the impression of a man who was unstable, who might explode at any moment, yet who was laboring to control himself, to contain his righteous indignation. He slowly drew his finger back down to his side.

Michael continued, equally passionate, but quietly and calm. "Do not let these men deny you the emotion, the outrage, you feel in your hearts. That feeling you got in your chests when you listened to this young woman describe her life apart from her husband, a life spent confined to a wheelchair, a life in constant pain—those are the pangs of justice, tugging at your heart. That is your conscience, demanding that you right this wrong. Justice is not cold, my friends. Justice is an all-consuming fire.

"These plaintiffs' lives are not commodities that can be valued, bought, and sold. These are flesh and blood people. The value of their lives is far more than can ever be arrived at in a court of law. Even still, I will ask you to try your best. Accessing everything you know about good and bad, right and wrong, justice and injustice. I ask you to endeavor to come to an award that is fair and just.

"What we ask, ladies and gentlemen, is one million dollars to represent each horrible minute that Kecia hung there in the truck, next to the lifeless body of her beloved, her entire world disappearing in front of her, as she waited for help to arrive. That is twelve million dollars, a reasonable, indeed conservative, verdict under these circumstances, and one to which my clients are entitled.

"Thank you."

With that, he returned to his table, sat down, and waited.

# 1

DANIEL RILEY loved the Chicken Pit, where he ate his lunch nearly every day. Today, he had invited his wife to join him. Now, he sat across from her at a little square table, gesticulating wildly, periodically running his fingers back through a section of straw-colored hair, describing his allegedly heroic performance at that morning's deposition. Amber Riley was a lovely, olive-skinned woman whose friendly round face and calm, thoughtful eyes made her appear to listen carefully even when she was just being tolerant. She munched on her salad and nodded at appropriate moments, raised her eyebrows occasionally, and said *oh really* and *wow!* when such an expression was warranted.

"It's unbelievable," he said. "So many lawyers still don't know how to conduct a cross-examination. Asking all these open-ended questions, letting the witness just ramble. I was in that deposition for less than an hour, and I had the witness basically confessing every element of the claim! You have to ask *leading* questions—that's what these other lawyers don't understand. You *tell* the witness what happened, based on what you already know, and *then* you ask them to confirm. And if you ask in the right way—quickly, before they realize what's going on—and you make the question seem innocuous, like it's not going to hurt them, they will almost always say *yes*! They're just so eager to get out of there sometimes, they'll say yes just to get it over with. And then they're stuck with the answer! Oh my God, you should have seen their attorney, he looked miserable. You remember this case, the one I was telling you about?"

"The one with the teacher, who they accused of coming to work drunk?"

"Ha! No—but that case is crazy, too. No, this is the false arrest case, where the cop busted into the kid's birthday party, at the jumpy-house place, and arrested the dad? Totally had the wrong guy. Complete case of racial misidentification. White cop. Black dad—looked nothing like the guy the cop was looking for. Actually jumped into the ball pit chasing my poor guy! Carried him right past the piñata and the birthday cake in handcuffs before his lieutenant came along and made him let my guy go. And this whole time, until today, the city's been defending him! Saying he acted reasonably, making up all this bullshit about the dad acting suspicious—*furtive*, they said. But I destroyed them! The asshole was basically begging for forgiveness by the time I was done with him!"

The murmuring sound of the dining room dipped suddenly, and there was a brief, uncomfortable silence as those at the surrounding tables turned to look at Daniel, who was now cursing in a room full of polite businesspeople and several young children. He looked at Amber and sank his head into his shoulders and showed his teeth in an embarrassed expression and gradually, the murmur of the room rose again.

He realized he was speaking more rapidly, and louder, than usual, and he knew why. It was because he was nervous. He was nervous because there was a difficult, indeed outlandish, subject that he needed to broach to his wife, something that had nothing to do with this particular tale of litigation. He was doing all he could to distract himself from the topic that was foremost on his mind, or perhaps he was hoping that he could slip the topic gracefully into the cavalcade of words now pouring from him, and she would be less disturbed that way.

He took a moment. He reached into the red plastic basket on the table and lifted the fried chicken sandwich to his mouth and took a long, lingering bite, closed his eyes, relished the buttery texture of the bread, the sultry flavor of the peanut oil-soaked chicken, the tang of the pickle. He chewed slowly, and the sensation of the flavor rushed to the forefront of his brain, cleansed the chaos of words and ideas that had been there, allowed him to collect himself. He took a long sip of lemonade from the straw in his Styrofoam cup, swallowed, took a deep breath, then turned his attention back to his wife.

"I talked to Michael Drummond for a while this morning," he said.

"Oh really?" she said. "How is he? How is Jackie? I haven't seen her in ages, seems like."

"It really has been a while. They're good. Really good, actually. *I* called *him*, to tell you the truth. There was an article about him today in the *Fulton County Daily Report*. Last week, he won some huge verdict down in Goshen County."

"Oh! I can't believe he's still down there. How much was the verdict?"

Daniel looked cautiously, theatrically, from side to side, leaned in close. "Twelve million dollars," he said, quietly. "And the verdict was against Darby Tobacco. So it's totally collectible. They've got the money to pay. Insurance, too."

Amber sat back in her chair and her eyes opened wide. "Wow," she said. "Good for him. Good for Jackie."

"Tell me about it. There'll be an appeal, but. . . getting a jury verdict overturned isn't an easy thing to do. Odds are pretty good they'll get paid within the next year or two." There was a tinge of sadness in Daniel's voice as he spoke.

"You wishing you could find a case like that?" Amber said.

"Of course," he said. Then there was a pause. "Do you ever think about moving back home?"

She laughed, looked down into her salad and ate.

He remained purposefully straight-faced, waited for her to look back up, then met her eyes with a serious, weighty expression. She stopped mid-chew, caught off guard by his look. She looked away, back down toward her food and began carefully, slowly to finish chewing. She swallowed, cleared her throat, looked back up at him and said, "do *you* ever think about it?"

He raised his eyebrows dismissively, fiddled with a napkin in his hand, took another bite of sandwich. "Michael told me about some things," he said as he chewed. "About Darby. About some changes that could be coming to the county. There could be a good opportunity for us there."

"What kind of opportunity?"

He looked back into her eyes. "A political opportunity."

The curiousness on her face melted into disappointment.

"There's an election next year," he said. "Leon Darby has been County Commissioner for decades now, and there are reasons to believe people are finally sick of him. I think maybe we could beat him."

"What do you mean, *we*? Is Michael planning to run?"

"No. I think maybe I should run."

She put her fork down into her salad, put her elbow on the table, put her face into her palm. Daniel watched her, guilt forming inside him. Her salad now looked sad and disheveled. Some honey-mustard dressing had congealed upon the plastic lid. The fork lay there amongst the greens alongside a crumpled napkin.

"And practice law, of course," he said. "It was Michael's verdict that made me start thinking about this in the first place. There wouldn't be a lot of competition down there, ya know?"

"You should have led—and then stopped—with the law part," she said, her face still in her hands. "You lost me with the running for office part." She took her hands away, looked him in the eyes. "I hoped you had gotten that out of your system for a while."

He looked away, a bit ashamed. He knew how badly he screwed up the last time he ran for anything.

Daniel Riley and Michael Drummond's life trajectories met at some point in high school and ran along parallel tracks for a while thereafter. They had known one another—or at least known *of* one another—from very early on in life, as two kids growing up in tiny, rural Goshen County. As young boys, they played on the same t-ball teams, went to the same public elementary school and occasionally played together on its rusty playground. But throughout most of their childhood, they had been separated in most regards by those most powerful separators of people in the small-town South: race and money. Daniel was white and the son of a prosperous farmer. Michael was black and lived with his mother, who struggled to make ends meet with an hourly job at the Wal-Mart Distribution Center. But they shared in common a similar, far-off, vaguely-defined goal of success and greatness, and they realized this about one another on the first day of high school, when the two of them were the sole sign-ups for Goshen County High School's policy debating team.

A professor and debate coach at Mercer University in Macon had decided to retire to the country and bought a small farm in Goshen County. Unable to get the debating bug out of his system, the professor volunteered his time and some of his money to start a team at Goshen High. In the years prior to Daniel and Michael's arrival, the team struggled to gain traction. In fact, there was quite a bit of skepticism and even resistance among both students and members of the administration when they learned what exactly policy debate was. It was an unusual sport in which teams of two competed against one another in extraordinarily fast-paced matches of words, ideas, and research at tournaments throughout the Southeast. Over time, the sport had evolved to favor the team that could make the most arguments and present the greatest amount of evidence within the confines of its strictly time-limited speeches. So, competitors were encouraged to speak as quickly as possible, at an almost robotic, auctioneer-like pace, moving rapidly from topic to topic, the goal to overwhelm and even confuse the opponent. Competitors and judges took notes in a meticulous sort of shorthand—they called it the "flow"—a single column of paper or computer spreadsheet devoted to each speech, tracking the arguments made and evidence presented, plotting out the response to each point in an adjacent column. To those who knew it, practiced it, and loved it, policy debate was intellectually stimulating beyond any other thing. But to someone untrained in the art, debate rounds were almost completely indecipherable—it was chaos, nonsense. In a conservative, agriculture-centered place like Goshen County, it was almost comically bizarre, too useless even to be real.

To Daniel Riley and Michael Drummond—ambitious, testosterone-fueled teenagers longing for intellectual challenge and eager to make use of their wits—it was a godsend. Over the course of their freshman year, the two spent countless hours together in the school library, across from one another at laptops, researching topics ranging from U.S. foreign policy in South America, to the Supreme Court's federalism jurisprudence, to assisted suicide, to queer theory, to critical feminist studies, to Ayn Rand's theory of objectivism, to political elections in the U.S. and abroad, to any other topic on which people might disagree. They absorbed an enormous amount of knowledge, at a rate only possible in the still-forming teenage brain. By debating one another, and debating other students from other Georgia high schools at weekend tournaments, they sharpened their skills, they learned to think critically, strategically, and they learned to present their points persuasively, even while delivering them at hundreds of words per minute.

They made a great team. Daniel was brash, cocky, verbose. He was known to crack jokes during speeches, to taunt his opponents in cross-examinations, to laugh out loud to demonstrate how stupid he thought an opponent's point might be. It was obnoxious, but often effective, if only because it wore on the confidence of the other team and caused them to lose faith in their own position. Michael, on the other hand, was polite, calm, rational. He said little in the opening moments of a round, offering simple smiles and courteous handshakes to judges and opponents alike. He was a great researcher. He spent far more time than Daniel did reading every possible publication on key topics, clipping the most critical information into briefs, organizing briefs into accordion files so they could be quickly accessed and presented in the course of a debate round. His quiet likeability helped to smooth things over with judges who might otherwise dock points for Daniel's antics.

It also helped that both boys had lovely South Georgia country accents, an asset to their persuasiveness and something rare in the world of competitive policy debate, which tended to be dominated by private schools and well-funded public schools in and surrounding Atlanta.

By the end of their sophomore year, Goshen County Riley-Drummond, or "Goshen RD" in the shorthand of debate tournament tabulation rooms, had developed a reputation as one of the best in the state. Their junior year, they won the Georgia State Championship tournament, upsetting teams from wealthy institutions with staffs full of experienced coaches. Their senior year, they qualified for the national tournament, held that year in Washington, D.C., and advanced to the quarter-final round, beating teams from elite prep schools along the way, the children of great lawyers, politicians, and diplomats from all over the United States. They each accepted full scholarships to join the University of Georgia's nationally competitive debate team. Their first year of competition showed much of the promise of their high school careers. They consistently finished tournaments with winning records and advanced to breakout rounds, beating good teams from Northwestern, Dartmouth, Harvard, Emory, and other powerhouse schools. But they began to drift apart.

At the time, there was a struggle brewing within the intercollegiate debate community about the role of race and class in the activity. Scan the room of people at any given debate tournament, or peruse the roster of teams competing, and it was undeniable that the vast majority of competitors were Caucasian. There was a healthy smattering of Indian and East Asian mixed in, a sprinkle of Latino, but very few African-American students, and virtually none from a background like Michael's, virtually no one else competing at a high level who was raised poor in the rural South and was here now by virtue of untold hours of work and the help of God's grace. There was a growing sentiment among the few black and brown voices within the community that the activity was structurally biased. That, because of the highly technical, frankly unnatural speech style, and the necessity of resources—for travel, for research databases, for coaching salaries—the activity had evolved to be dominated by moneyed, mostly white, institutions. The case of Goshen County High School was truly an exceptional one. There were exceedingly few opportunities for lower-class, minority kids to participate at a high level in high school debate, and as a result, few made it to college debate. This was far more than just an academic problem—college debate, and the community of people who competed in it, had grown to be a mafia of sorts, a closely-connected network of highly competitive intellectuals who helped one another to enter the ranks of elite law schools, elite law firms, think tanks, political campaigns, and big business. In other words, debate had become a gateway to political and economic power that few minorities could ever hope to access.

From Daniel's perspective, Michael had become swept up in this discussion, and it had distracted him from competition. Michael became interested in an experimental debating paradigm in which the competitors shifted the focus of the debate from the usual issues of government policy, to theoretical issues about how arguments were presented, how competitive debate was structured, and which team could present the best solution for making debate a more accessible, socially beneficial forum. Daniel didn't like this. He and Michael had been tremendously successful, with the potential for even greater success, at traditional policy debate. He viewed this new, critical focus as sacrificing personal success for some nebulous, far-off social good. He often made the argument to Michael that the way to help minorities to win was to be a minority who won. Of course, Daniel had no idea what he was talking about, having never been in a position to have to overcome any bias or adversity in his own life, and it was this inability to appreciate Michael's perspective that eventually pushed the two apart.

Both young men continued to debate throughout college, but they found different partners. Each did what he wanted to do— Daniel found a like-minded, policy-focused kid from Woodward Academy, and the two of them plowed forward, with some success, on the national circuit. Michael recruited Jacqueline, a girl he met in his African-American Studies class—an education major from East Atlanta, someone with no prior debate experience—to join

18

him, and the two of them pursued a project to critique what debate had become. They refused to speak at the breakneck speed that had become the activity's feature, objecting in the middle of an opponent's speech that their speaking style was excluding Jackie from participating, which was true. They urged judges to abandon the "flow" in deciding the round, and instead to listen to the arguments presented as a layperson might, to assess the earnestness with which arguments were delivered, to assess the social value of choosing one team over the other. They actually had quite a bit of success in this manner, both in terms of winning debates and encouraging other schools to follow their lead. They won no championships, but they felt good about what they were doing. And along the way, they fell in love.

Whereas the two friends diverged in their academic paths, they made similar decisions when it came to love. Michael went to Emory Law School, which he chose in large part because Jackie wanted to go to Atlanta to teach and be close to her family. Daniel stayed at UGA in Athens for law school, in large part because Amber, his girlfriend since high school and three years his junior, was there now working on her art degree.

Once law school was finished, Michael asked, and Jackie agreed, to return to Goshen County, where Michael wanted to build a practice and, in his words, get at the root of things.

Daniel took the opposite approach. He had done well in law school and took a job at a large commercial firm in Midtown Atlanta. Over the course of four years, he cranked out billable hours and put a healthy sum of money in the bank. Soon after their son Jonathan was born, he decided he was done with Big Law. He found work at a small litigation boutique in Rosewood, the little north Atlanta municipality they called home, and built his practice there. The change gave him more time with his family, and it also afforded him the freedom to consider a thing that, in his mind, had always been his destiny: to run for political office.

Daniel had always been honest with Amber about his ambitions, and she had encouraged him. They had been living in Rosewood for only about three years when he saw what he believed to be his first great political opportunity.

The Rosewood Town Council was a small and informal body, yet an important and influential political forum. Rosewood was an affluent community of well-educated people, home to many who were considered leaders in law, government, business, and medicine. In recent decades, Rosewood had become a model for other metro Atlanta governments, with thoughtful, effective policies that were studied and emulated by other communities wishing to share in the town's success.

An aging Council member, one Bob Robbins, had gotten himself into some hot water. Bob's granddaughter Sophie had set him up a Facebook account. She uploaded her very favorite pictures of him: there was one of him sitting on a couch with all his grandkids in front of the Christmas tree; there was one of him holding up a big bass he had caught in Lake Lanier; there was one of him and his wife, with the caption "Grandpapper and Granny" written below. Sophie showed her Grandpa how to "friend" his grandkids, his cousins, his nieces, his nephews, and the like. She showed him how to see their photos and send them messages. Bob's friends and neighbors received notice of Bob's friend requests. He connected to pastors, schoolteachers, housewives, his business associates, his fellow councilmembers, his former classmates from high school and college. It was neat.

Councilman Bob was a heterosexual man, and he had heard about the things you could find on the internet. So, that evening, when Sophie went home, he settled into his easy chair and typed "nude women" into the bar at the top of his screen. Unbeknownst to him, he had typed this text into the "status update" bar, rather than the "search" bar, and his naughty query was broadcast to all his loved ones, like this:

Bob Robbins [picture of Grandpapper and Granny]: nude women

He did not realize this, of course. But he did realize that the search had failed to yield any naked ladies, so he tried again, this time finding the correct field, the "search" bar. And this time, to his great delight, he found endless images of busty, nubile young women. Next to their photos, there were boxes that said "Add Friend," which sounded quite nice. He requested their friendships and, to his further delight, they all accepted.

Bob had no concept that these young ladies' profiles were facades designed to lure poor men like him into giving private data to Russian email marketers and Nigerian scam-artists. With every notification that a promiscuous young exhibitionist had accepted his friendship, he reacted not with skepticism, but with unabashed joy. If he felt anything like regret, it was only the regret of knowing that these enthusiastic women had been here all along, and he had been missing out because he hadn't taken the time to learn to use the computer.

Bob encouraged his new friends with his masculine wiles. Beneath an image of a dark-haired beauty, bending forward into the camera as she pushed her breasts into the frame, Bob wrote "young lady, you are truly blessed." In another image, a tall woman in a men's dress shirt and a frilly thong stood straight-legged, bending over at her hips into a 90-degree angle, her blonde hair hanging toward the ground, her round bottom protruding: "I have always been a leg man," Bob wrote, "but you might turn me into an ass man!" Under an image of two buxom, underwear-clad playmates, laughing and giggling as they smooshed their breasts together, Bob wrote simply, "bad girls!!!"

Bob didn't know, of course, that his every mouse-click, his every "like," his every naughty comment, was broadcast to his entire network of friends and neighbors. The pillars of the community, and often their young children, watched with a mixture of horror and fascination as Bob's commentaries appeared on their screens, one followed by the next. They'd see an image of a smiling Bob, surrounded by his grandchildren in front of a Christmas tree, beside the text, "nice titties!"

After a little while, someone wrote below the big-butt blonde, "Mr. Bob, you might want to change your privacy settings." Someone else wrote, "Councilman Bob, did you get hacked?" Bob's eyes squinted with confusion, then widened with terror, his jaw going slack. He realized that, somehow, through some unknown magic, others could see his dirty deeds. His heart sank. He lost his erection. He slammed the lid of his laptop closed. He threw it across the room. He sat there in his easy chair gasping for air, his heart pounding.

Closing the laptop didn't make the comments disappear. His words remained on everyone's screens throughout the evening and well into the next day before he finally called his grandson, embarrassed and ashamed, to help him make it go away. In the course of a single evening—in the course, really, of a few minutes— his posts had created such uproar, such glee, such scandal, that any reasonable person would have concluded that his tenure as Town Councilman was over.

Yet, no one emerged to challenge him. Even though many of his so-called friends avoided him in public, even though he gained the image of a pitiful, somewhat loathsome figure, no citizen stepped immediately forward to contest his seat on the council.

Daniel saw a perfect opportunity, a political office free for the taking.

Daniel planned a campaign that would focus heavily on Bob's internet foibles. He ordered yard signs, paid a web designer, cajoled a few friends into positions in the campaign organization, and spent weeks drafting the speech he would give at the meeting of the Rosewood Business Association, where all the movers and shakers could meet their presumptive new councilman.

The evening of the announcement before the RBA was forever burned into his memory. "My friends," he had said to a crowded, curious audience. "I know many of you are searching for a dignified alternative this election. I know many of you have been embarrassed, as I have, by the behavior of our councilman. Our community is too good for that type of behavior. We are looked to as role models throughout Atlanta and throughout the state. I am here to offer the dignified alternative you are seeking, and I look forward to serving you." He went on like that for some time, speaking a little bit about himself, but mostly waxing poetic about how shameful Councilman Bob was.

In retrospect, it had been a terrible, stupid speech. As he came off the stage and moved through the crowd at the RBA meeting, no one seemed eager to shake his hand or speak with him. People became uncomfortable as he approached. He received polite, but apprehensive nods of greeting. He witnessed people actively moving away from him. And the behavior of the electorate, throughout the remainder of the campaign, mimicked their behavior on that evening.

Daniel had failed to appreciate the deep and abiding loyalty that many in this community felt toward Bob Robbins. Even as people mocked Bob in private, they respected him at heart. The Robbins family had stuck by Rosewood during a difficult time in its history. In the early 1980s, Rosewood was hit hard by the economic recession. Businesses closed and people lost their jobs. Tax revenue declined. Garbage collection was reduced to once every other week. The police force was cut in half. Crime increased. The town's affluent residents, and then its middle-class, fled to the suburbs. Many of the town's largest homes were abandoned or sold off at discount prices to be converted into multi-tenant rentals. The town became a shell of its former self. Its restaurants became vacant storefronts, its bookshops replaced by ramshackle convenience stores selling cigarettes and lottery tickets.

Yet as their neighbors fled, the Robbins family and a handful of others stayed. These families developed a bond. They bought up abandoned homes and other distressed real estate, maintained them, ensured they had decent tenants who would take care of the property. They continued to patronize the few restaurants and retail shops that hung on, offering a lifeline to local business. They kept their kids in the schools, served on the school board and the town council when nobody else wanted to. They kept the place from dying. Bob, a younger man then, had been elected to the Rosewood Town Council without contest. The Council had made wise decisions during the years that followed. They sold off some old city property for revenue, took advantage of municipal bond programs, and gave heavy tax incentives to businesses willing to set up shop downtown. They spent wisely, avoiding public works boondoggles and investing in basic infrastructure—good sidewalks, well-repaired roads, public squares free of trash. They made good hires at the police department, at public works, and in the City Manager's office. Through a combination of the council's decision-making, and the economy's eventual recovery, Rosewood came back to life over time. Many believed, and rightfully so, that Rosewood owed its recovery to the good work of people like Bob Robbins, who had continued to invest in the town despite its hardship.

Daniel did not understand or appreciate this history, and it showed. He had openly derided a respected, foundational figure. He had called the man "undignified." It made him appear foolish, vainglorious, and opportunistic. After he gave his speech at the RBA, it was too late to turn back. When his yard signs, for which he had expended over one thousand of his own dollars, arrived on his front step—Daniel Riley, A *Dignified* Alternative for Rosewood—he almost cried. The website he had paid a pretty penny to have designed bore the same terrible motto, emblazoned into a flashy logo. He had irretrievably marked his candidacy as mean-spirited, nasty, and uninformed. He received emails with subjects like "Shame on you" and "Who do you think you are?"

The voters of Rosewood were naturally suspicious of a young man like Daniel Riley, who had been here for such a short time, yet presumed to unseat a long-time incumbent. If only Daniel had understood this, he might not have run at all. Or, if he had decided to run, he would have given Bob a certain level of deference even while opposing him. But he had lacked the foresight, or the experience with political campaigns, to understand this. By failing to do the hard work necessary to understand the history of Rosewood, by failing to study the data that would drive the election, by a sheer failure of humility, he had doomed himself. He had been defeated by a margin of nearly four to one.

Amber pulled out her phone, looked at it for a few seconds, tried to distract herself, to calm the distress now stirring inside. When Daniel invited her to lunch, he'd said he had something exciting to talk about, and she thought it would be something nice—a surprise vacation, maybe—but instead he was proposing to resurrect one of her most unpleasant recent experiences.

"I have to go," she said, not looking back up at her husband. She stood and turned toward the exit, then turned back suddenly and met his eyes. There was a spark of hope in his expression, as if he thought this would be the moment where she said, "I trust you honey—I'd follow you to hell and back." It made her feel a little bad, but not too bad, as she prepared to deliver her actual line. She pointed down to the remainder of her meal and said, "Can you throw this away for me?"

"Sure," he said.

"Thanks. Love you," and then she left.

She walked out the back door of the restaurant into the hot summer air, reached into her purse and pulled out a pair of sunglasses—thick tortoiseshell frames—and put them on her face. She walked along the sidewalk toward Rosewood's town square, listening to the gentle click of her heels on the concrete. She felt regret at having put on the heels, at having made herself look nice for Daniel. When he told her he had something exciting to talk about, she hadn't realized he was upselling what he knew would be a difficult, distressing idea.

She approached the center of the square, and the crackle of the fountain in the Rosewood wishing pool grew louder, a pleasant, watery hiss beckoning her forth. She sat on the concrete lip of the pool, twisted her torso, put her hands on the warm surface, looked down into the water. The water spewed from the fountain and splashed endlessly down into the pool, creating a soothing white noise that calmed her racing mind. Droplets of cool water splashed out onto her arms and face. She took a deep breath, inhaled some of the mist rising off the surface.

She looked around at Rosewood's thriving town square. The little coffee shop, the boutique where she admired expensive leather boots and chic handbags each October. The pristine sidewalks, the bright summer flowers hanging in baskets from the lamp posts. It was all so very nice. This is where she had imagined raising her family.

But maybe it was time to go.

She had been embarrassed during the course of Daniel's doomed campaign for Town Council, and that feeling had lingered long after it was finished. They hadn't been in Rosewood long when he announced, and they had only just begun to develop a set of close friends. The campaign had turned once-pleasant gatherings with these new friends into exercises in anxiety, for her at least. She dreaded the moment when the topic of the election would come up—and it inevitably would, the proverbial elephant in the room— and she would have to act optimistic and hopeful, or at least watch Daniel act optimistic and hopeful, when in fact she knew the effort was over before it had hardly begun. It felt like falling on her face, only in grueling slow motion, a long, drawn-out pratfall, surrounded by an audience of the people she most wanted to impress.

No one in their social circle had been outright ugly to her— maybe some at the fringes, but no one she considered a friend. Most of their friends were near their age, parents of young children, and fairly new to Rosewood themselves. They had not felt the outrage toward Daniel that many of the town's older residents had. But even among these friends, there remained something under the surface, something she could see in the subtle expressions on their faces, a bit of incredulity toward Daniel, a bit of pity toward her. Maybe it was all in her mind—Daniel had told her it was. But it *was* in her mind, and it had stayed there long after the election was over, and she had not been able to shake it. She had wondered how it might affect their son, whether he'd somehow be judged according to the sins of his father.

The ordeal had impacted their marriage. Although Daniel masked it well with his usual exterior of exaggerated confidence, she knew the election injured his self-esteem. She tried time and again to get him to talk about what had happened, to be honest about his mistakes, and he gave lip service to the idea that he had misjudged his opponent, but he avoided the reality that his own hubris had been to blame. He would insist that the timing had just not been right, that it was always hard to beat an incumbent when the economy was good, that people just weren't paying close attention to the race, that he hadn't invested enough money in yard signs, and a number of other explanations that did not involve him being too cocky and trying to insert himself into a position that he had not earned. This refusal to face reality, this resistance to her attempts to help him, became a glaring symptom of a pathology that existed at his core—the conviction that he was smarter than everyone else, that he somehow held the path to enlightenment, that his primary struggle in life was to make those around him understand this fact.

It was becoming more and more difficult every day for Amber to accept this as a fact of her life. He was quite clever overall, it was true. And he was loving, generous, and loyal as a husband and a father. But oftentimes, he behaved like a fool, and refused to see it, and forced her to make the choice to go along with his foolishness or else confront him, which never yielded anything other than a bitter argument, and she sometimes wondered if she could take this for the rest of her life.

Truth be told, all of this had caused her to pine for change, for the opportunity to start over somewhere else, to see if a new landscape might be the medicine their marriage and her life needed. But she'd been thinking Savannah, New York, New Zealand even, somewhere exciting and distant, not back home in Goshen County, Georgia. And certainly, she had not envisioned relocating for the purpose of another political campaign.

She looked into the pool and allowed herself to remember, for a moment, the happy parts of her childhood back home. She remembered traipsing through acres of woodland with the other children, hunting arrowheads by the creek, playing hide-and-seek in the cornfields, singing learning songs with the other students in her tiny grade-school class. Those were things little Jonathan might love as well.

She allowed herself to remember the reasons she fell in love with Daniel in the first place, and therefore the reasons she would even consider following him back home. As a young person in Goshen County, she had been different, awkward, in need of someone who appreciated her, and Daniel had embraced her fully, precisely because of her difference. And unlike some of the other boys who had appreciated her, who wanted her, she actually wanted him back.

It had not been anything dramatic that separated her from her peers—not a physical handicap or a confused gender identity or even a striking birthmark, nothing like that. She was shy, but not painfully so. Her outlook and interests were just unusual for the society. The things so many of her peers seemed to find interesting—cheerleading, hanging out in the Hardee's parking lot, getting their hooks in some boy on the football team, getting passed-out drunk at a bonfire—struck her as boring. She was fascinated primarily with art.

Goshen County High School offered art as an elective, and she was one of many who took it, but she was the only one who came to school early to sit in the art room and work on prints and collage, the only one who skipped break and lunch to sit in the classroom and flip through big hard-cover books on Egon Schiele and Jeff Koons and Yayoi Kusama (she wondered today who had donated those books in the first place, and thought how grateful she was to that mysterious person).

She loved music as well, and not especially the type that formed the soundtrack to teenage life in Goshen County. She escaped often into corners of the internet devoted to unusual music, and she discovered things that moved her—minimalistic electronic music built on clicks and pops and driven along by heartbeat-like bass thumps; odd women like Bjork and Tori Amos and Kazu Makino who crooned heartful mixes of desperation and joy; angular, jarring rock music build around odd time signatures by bands from Athens with names like Cinemechanica and We Versus the Shark.

There was, actually, quite of bit of the—let's say local—music that moved her as well and provided her a rare, unexpected opportunity to enjoy social gatherings. She had once allowed herself to get dragged along to a bonfire party out on some piece of property, and there was this kid who had an amplifier and an enormous set of sub-woofers behind the seats of his F-150, and he had played bass music by the likes of Kilo Ali, 69 Boyz, and Quad City DJ's all night, and she'd found herself affected by the way the bass drum was pitch-shifted and arranged into a melody that you could feel in your chest. The bass melody drove the song more than the vocals, which functioned more like staccato rhythm sections than any kind of poetry. She started going to parties regularly, for this reason alone, to hear this type of music, played on woofers deep enough to capture the full range of bass intended by the artists. Field parties were the best places to listen to music like this, she decided, with open air to give the long, deep waves of bass room to stretch. Still, she never socialized more than necessary, just looked for a good spot on the tailgate to sit and sip on a beer and listen. She knew the other girls found her weird, and offputtingly quiet, and she noticed when they whispered together while glancing in her direction, and she'd be lying to say it didn't hurt her feelings.

There was another thing that separated her from her peers, and that was money. Goshen County had plenty of wealth. Darby Tobacco was a major employer, and there were numerous families with stakes in its business, still others employed in upper and middle management. There were successful farmers, real estate developers, professionals who worked somewhere beyond the county but lived here and made the long commute each day. There was old money wealth still left over from the days when cotton was king. Amber's family was not dirt poor, but they were also not as fortunate as some. Her father had been a farm mechanic who unfortunately developed a drinking problem. Her mother divorced him, and he moved out to Swainsboro, and Amber never saw much of him, nor did he contribute much in the way of child support. Amber's mother worked as a teacher's assistant at Goshen County Elementary School, and it didn't pay much, but it was a steady, reliable job, so nobody went hungry. But there was no extra money for Amber to have a car, or to buy whatever trendy clothes the other girls were wearing, or to go on weekend jaunts to Jacksonville. Any extra money, she had to work for. She held a job working the drive-through at Hardee's for a while, swept the floors at the Jessup tobacco warehouse, was a check-out girl at the grocery store. Few other girls who looked like her held jobs like this. So, she felt excluded. This was perhaps part of the reason why she spent so much time absorbed in music and art, because they were escapes available basically for free and amazingly, thanks to books and the internet, right there in Goshen County.

Daniel didn't fit in, either. But while Amber retreated into her difference, Daniel flaunted his. She watched him, from afar at first, with interest and admiration. He was aggressive about his nerdiness, taking on roles nobody else wanted—captain of the debate team, editor of the high school newspaper, president of the Progressive Students Alliance (something she was pretty sure he had made up himself and of which he may have been the only member)—and using them to insert himself into the life of the community. He was the kid who talked a lot in class, debated the teachers, declared himself a "liberal" in a place where the term had a distinctively pejorative flavor. He wrote most of the articles in the paper, often editorials in protest of some school rule, sometimes news coverage of his own achievements on the interscholastic debate circuit. His close friendship with Michael Drummond was ubiquitous and, she thought, itself some act of rebellion.

In short, Daniel had been interesting. He had been different than anyone else she knew in Goshen County. In the same way that she'd been fascinated by the paintings in the art books and the strange music online, she'd been fascinated by Daniel Riley, who was smart and unusual and actually fairly good-looking. The art classroom was right next to the social studies classroom that served as the headquarters for the school paper and the debate team, and she decided one day to start wearing a push-up bra to school, and to sort of linger around in the hallway whenever she knew he would be passing by, and as it turned out, that had worked. Guys are so simple-minded, even the smart ones.

Daniel spoke to her whenever they crossed paths. He started sitting next to her in class. She texted him playlists of some of the more interesting music she discovered, and he was genuinely interested in it. He started offering her rides to school. One day, they'd been sitting in the old pickup his father had given him, in the parking lot before school began, listening to some lovely electronica through the AUX cable, and they'd both been caught up in the sound of the music and the smell of one another, and they'd met eyes and leaned in and kissed and sat there intensely making out to the music well into first-period. This scene repeated itself innumerable times after that and led of course to sex and, eventually, to love.

Amber spent so much time on the Riley farm that Daniel's parents became like a second family to her. Her moments of greatest joy, even to this day, had been riding on the Rileys' four-wheeler, on the back with her arms around Daniel at first, but later on by herself, zooming along the length of empty cornfields in the wintertime, exploring the woods along deer and cow paths, finding ramps and slopes to launch her into the air. She loved the power the engine and the enormous tires afforded her, relished the feeling of speed, the wind in her face, her dominion over the landscape. Never before had she fully appreciated the wonder of the country's expanse, never before had she realized how open and free it all was. The power of the vehicle to bring so much of it to her, so quickly, all at once, to allow her to frolic on the earth like a bird might frolic in a windstream.

This is what Daniel meant to her, and this is what Goshen County was to her.

Amber pushed her arms off the wishing pool. She took a last look into the water, then spun around toward the old Reynolds Shoe Factory building, a historic structure that, unlike most of the other buildings in the Rosewood square, had never been properly renovated. She rented a little room on the second floor for use as an art studio/office. She worked on paid graphic design gigs there, but also spent quite a bit of time working on passion projects—paintings, prints, collage. She could see into the window of the room from here, could see the back of a large canvas she'd started earlier that week but not found much to do with. A warm breeze passed over her face. It caused something unexpected, something precious, to rise into her skull. It was that rare and valuable thing that always seemed to appear, without prior announcement, at times of struggle: artistic inspiration.

She walked quickly toward the Shoe Factory. Time was moving, and she had no guarantee how long this bout would last. She opened the heavy glass and steel door of the old building and vaulted up the steps, taking two stairs at a time. She took off her heels and flew down the hall to her studio, where she opened the door and stepped into the warm room, the summer rays pouring in through the windows. She stepped over to the window, briefly looked out upon the town square, upon the wishing pool where she'd just been standing. She moved to the back of the cluttered room, shuffled through a stack of large canvases. She grasped one by its sturdy wooden edge and drew it out with her arm. She held the canvas up before her, its top edge almost touching the ceiling. She admired the muscles of her arm, flexing as they balanced the weighty canvas in the air. She looked at the painting closely. There was a vast field of green, rising up to the center of the canvas. The expanse of green was textured heavily, interspersed and blurred with grey, white, yellow, even blue. Above the green was a field of grey-blue, with suggestions of wispy white clouds. The painting created the impression of, but did not demand, a field full of vegetation with a rich cyan sky above. It could also be read simply as Amber Riley's vision of green and blue, two skillfully blended colors displayed for their own sake.

She took from her easel a canvas covered in geometric black and white, set it to the side, placed the green and blue canvas there in its place. She pulled over a wooden rack, atop which sat a palette of sturdy resin covered in many colors of paint. She swirled her brush in a jar of cloudy mineral spirits, tapped out the brush on the edge of the jar. She took her brush to the palette, drew paint from a little pool of white, a little pool of red, a pool of black. She gathered a small bit of yellow. She brought the brush to the left side of the canvas, into the field of green. She made a few gentle strokes there, brought the brush back to the palette to gather the right colors, took the brush to the canvas once again. She concentrated on that single spot and the minute details of the thing she was creating there. After some time, she put the brush down onto the pallet and raised her finger to the spot on the canvas. She smudged with her thumb, blended the edges of the new shape with its surroundings.

At some moment, she was finished. She sat back on her stool and examined her work. There was the smallest impression of two figures emerging from the field of green. Their contours were decidedly human, but their action was uncertain. The two figures seemed to struggle, also to embrace. They remained distant impressions on the landscape, both part of and apart from the green. A scattering of black and grey and red and yellow surrounded them, a certain chaos, an interruption to the serene colors around them.

Amber admired what she had done. She put down her brush. She took her phone from the windowsill where she had set it down and sent Daniel a text. She wrote, "I'm willing to go down there and meet with Michael and Jackie. I'm willing to hear what they have to say about all of this."

He didn't respond right away. She put down the phone and began washing her brushes out in a jar of thinner. Then she heard a ding. She looked at the phone and saw his response: "This weekend?"

# 2

DRIVING into Goshen County was like entering some strange, yet deeply familiar alternate universe. The Riley family entered the border to this universe when their Ford Explorer exited Interstate 16 onto the ramp for State Highway 319, a road known locally as the Dixie Beeline. Past the exit ramp, they passed an old, empty Stuckey's convenience store, its sad sign still announcing Pecan Logs for $1.99. They drove along the Beeline, and the interstate soon faded from the rear view. Shortly, they entered a realm of pasture land, acre after acre of lush, green fields as far as the eye could see, clusters of cows bumbling about in the distance, eating their grass, oblivious to the cars speeding along the Beeline.

Then, about a quarter-mile of trees, and on the other side, from nowhere, a strange little town square emerged. A freshly painted wooden sign said, "Welcome to Goshen County's Historic Downtown." It was hard to discern what was so historic about it. There were two rows of dilapidated storefronts, one on each side of the Beeline, almost completely empty. In the summer light, you could see through the dusty glass windows into the barren, abandoned bodies of the properties. Mack's General Store was still hanging on for dear life, probably still selling small hardware, rodenticide, and chicken feed to nearby farmers. The Humble Pie restaurant was still there, right next to Mack's. It was an eternal mystery to Daniel how the place stayed in business. Here it was, nearly dinnertime on a Friday, and there were a total of two cars parked in the spaces in front. Daniel peered into the windows as they passed. The lights were on, there was steam rising off the food on the buffet, but he could otherwise discern no human activity.

Across from the Humble Pie was the handsome white-stone Goshen County Bank & Trust building, built in 1923 according to an etching in its cornerstone. Some years ago, the bank had abandoned its flagship structure and moved its operations to the new commercial district on the east side of the county. Yet, the building looked shiny and clean, like it had just been pressure-washed, a contrast to the neglected structures that surrounded it. Along the edges of the building were rows of bushes that looked manicured and well-cared for, surrounded by a lawn of recently cut, vividly green grass. In this lawn was a flagpole, atop which hung a gleaming American flag. The walkway leading to the front door appeared to be made of newly poured concrete. Daniel eyed the sign above the front door, freshly painted and stately looking, similar to the new sign welcoming them to historic downtown. It said, "Michael Drummond, Attorney at Law, P.C." That brought a smile to his face.

Just past the strips of storefront was the little post office, a freestanding structure that, when open, contained the county's lone federal employee, reliably behind the counter each weekday from nine to one.

As they passed downtown, Daniel looked into his rearview mirror at the square's most intriguing feature, the weird, crooked monument to the boll weevil. There it stood, in a grassy median that split the Beeline briefly in half, right in the center of the rotting town square, a little metal insect with a long, protruding snout, perched atop an iron stake, poking out from a crumbling marble column.

Beyond the old downtown, on the north side of the Beeline, were a series of Victorian homes, some of them pre-Civil War, lavishly maintained, with expensive cars and pickup trucks parked in pristine tar driveways in deep front yards. On the south side of the highway, directly across from these fine homes, was a tall hill of dirt and brambles that ran for nearly a mile, a barrier that blocked any view of what lay beyond. Beyond that hill, Daniel knew, were ramshackle houses, broken streets, and poverty—the "black side of town"—a place he seldom saw, and then only briefly, during his childhood.

Past this were miles and miles of farmland, seemingly never-ending fields of tall, ripening tobacco stalks, weeks from harvest, punctuated occasionally by a driveway or fence line. The stalks obscured the horizon in all directions, a rich green palette on either side of the grey line of road, the entire scene haloed by the perfect blue of the cloudless sky above. Daniel accelerated the Explorer through the parted sea of the stalks. The sound of the tires on the road grew softer, muffled by the leaves on both sides. It could make one feel cocooned—or trapped, depending on your perspective—surrounded by all that tobacco, concealed from the world beyond.

Finally, they emerged from the stalks, drove through several more yards of pasture, and came upon the county's new commercial district. First, there was an industrial area that housed an animal feed manufacturer, two towering grain bins, the John Deere dealership, Will King's chemical plant and, dwarfing all the rest of it, Darby Tobacco's enormous warehouse and distribution facility. Past that were a couple of fast food restaurants, a Huddle House, an Applebee's, a Ford-Chevy dealership, and a strip mall with a Piggly-Wiggly, a furniture store, and something called the Social Butterfly. Past that was a new, good-looking six-story red-brick building. A sign of thick plastic, hoisted atop a brick column in the lawn, displayed the modern-looking red logo of the Goshen County Bank & Trust (now GCBT).

Across the road was the new government complex, two structures, linked by a breezeway, built of the same color bricks as the new GCBT building. The tallest of the two structures was the Goshen County Courthouse, which had a marble staircase leading to two tall front doors. The other, smaller structure had a parking lot full of brown police cruisers in front, "Sheriff's Office" emblazoned in yellow on their sides. On one corner of that building were glass double-doors that led to the Sheriff's administrative offices. In the other corner was a small staircase leading to a single door. A little sign out front read, "County Commissioner's Office." Daniel glared at it as they passed.

Immediately beyond that was the second ramp from Goshen County onto I-16, the one they would have taken had they wanted to miss old downtown, the old Victorian homes to the west, and all the farmland between there and here. They passed under the interstate and into more country, another expanse of farmland. After a little while, the GPS on Daniel's phone announced that they were approaching their destination. Soon, they could make out the contours of a white home sitting atop a grassy hill in the distance. Daniel slowed as the Drummonds' driveway grew nearer. As he prepared to turn into the drive, he looked ahead at the "County Limits" sign, only a few yards beyond. "They're really out here on the edge of the county, aren't they?" he said.

As Daniel drove the Explorer up the winding tar path through the front pasture, Amber gazed up at the house, curious and apprehensive.

She saw a wide front porch of glimmering white wood, obviously brand new, columns of vivid burnt orange bricks supporting a rooftop covered in light charcoal-colored shingles. The front door was new, too, an ornately molded affair with three squares of frosted glass buttoning down the center. The porch attached to a lovely old single-story farmhouse, its shell made of freshly painted wood, or maybe new white siding, looking somewhat out-of-place, but proud, in the presence of its newly-constructed porch.

Amber broadened her focus, placed the home in its context, surrounded by acres of pristine, unplowed grassland. It was beautiful.

Daniel pulled the Explorer up next to the house and cut the ignition. He looked at Amber and smiled, "We're here." She looked at him, raised her eyebrows briefly, only to acknowledge that yes, they were, in fact, here, then looked away. She was excited to see the house, to see Jackie and Michael again, but she didn't want to show it. She wanted him to know that she remained unconvinced that they should be here for any reason other than a friendly visit.

Jonathan—four years old, a disheveled mess of dirty blonde hair springing from his scalp, a chubby face soiled by gas-station snacks and dirt—had unbuckled his seatbelt and began bouncing around inside the car before it even came to a stop. Now, he leapt out the door and ran toward the home. It pleased Amber to see him so excited, but she didn't let that show either. With some effort, she kept her expression pleasant but neutral, constraining the smile that otherwise threatened to form. Daniel and Amber followed Jonathan along the walkway, up the front steps, and onto the porch, which seemed even more expansive now that they were standing on it. Amber looked up at the outdoor ceiling fans, which blew a wonderful breeze down upon them. She looked over at the oversized chair-swing hanging on the right side of the porch, swinging gently on its own momentum. She imagined herself sitting there, drinking a mojito, reading a paperback. The smell of new construction, of fresh paint and wood chips, of fresh lumber and the sweat of builders, still permeated the air.

As Daniel reached for the bell, the blurry impression of Jacqueline Drummond formed in the frosted cubes of the door.

Before he had a chance to push the button, the door opened, and there she was, as striking as Amber had ever remembered, an enormous smile on her face. She was wearing a white, crumpled-cotton peasant dress, which hung casually off her shoulders. The dress was tied delicately in the front, just below her throat. The sleeves reached her forearms, cutting off just above her wrists. The hem was short, exposing her smooth knees and her slender legs. Her feet were bare. Amber felt suddenly warm inside. She herself smiled, sincerely and gratefully, unable to resist the impulse triggered by Jackie's warmth.

Jackie's dark skin was a stunning contrast to the white of her dress. It reminded Amber of the first time the two met. It had been at Amber's bachelorette party, the week before her wedding. Jackie, as the girlfriend of one of Daniel's groomsmen, had been invited to come along. It was a winter wedding, and Jackie had worn a long, bright pink pea coat that Amber recognized from the most recent edition of the J. Crew catalog. The coat was striking against Jackie's skin, then as now. Jackie had been tall and slender and intimidating. In Amber's estimation, she looked like a London fashion model. But she had been friendly and cordial, and she didn't sound like she was from London. She spoke like she was from Georgia—not the syrupy small-town drawl that Amber knew so well, but something related, vowels drawn out the way she was used to, certain words internally abbreviated, the final syllable of some words clipped off for the sake of brevity. Amber knew she had made a friend after they drank several glasses of champagne, and Kilo Ali's "Love In Your Mouth" came over the limousine speakers, and Jackie knew every word. They had laughed and fallen all over one another as they sang together to the raucous, obscene music of their childhood.

Jackie stepped out of the doorframe and hugged Amber tightly. Michael appeared behind her. He looked at Daniel and issued a gentlemanly smile. The friends shook hands and embraced. The moment crackled with promise.

The friends sat on the front porch, eating dinner and drinking beer, watching Jonathan and little Zoe—only two and newly mobile—play in the enormous yard. The orange sun hovered above the tree line in the distance and warmed their faces. It was early August, and the air was hot, but an occasional breeze blew past them, as if somewhere in the distance a storm was moving in. There was pan-fried bass seasoned with basil and lemon juice. In the center of the table was a great ceramic bowl brimming with a salad of black-eyed peas, wine vinegar, chopped onions, tomatoes, bell pepper, and parsley. They passed around a warm, cloth-covered basket full of sweet cornbread, and aromatic steam rose into the air whenever someone pulled back the cloth.

Amber wanted very much to broach the subject of Michael's trial and the verdict. After all, it was ostensibly the thing that led Daniel to reach out to his old friend and sparked the idea to come back home. But her Southern manners told her it was rude to talk about money in anything other than a roundabout way, so she resisted the impulse. She strategized for ways to lead the conversation naturally to the subject.

"I'm so jealous of this porch," she said. "I just love it. Was it here when you bought the house?"

"Lord, no," Jackie said. "You should have seen this place. I nearly had a fit the first time Michael brought me here. The house hadn't been lived in for years, it was falling apart. The plumbing didn't work, the cellar was flooded. There was a big ol' bump in the kitchen floor where a tree root was growing up! There was a porch, but it was a rickety wooden thing—I was afraid to even step on it, it looked so rotten. It was a mess." Jackie took her knife to a formation of soft butter, brought it back to the triangle of cornbread in her other hand, worked the knife into a slice in the center of the bread.

"We had been renting a little house closer to town. It was nice enough, and rent was next to nothing, but it wasn't exactly my dream home. We were there for about three years, then Michael's practice started to pick up, and we decided to look for a home. There were several nice, new houses built in that new subdivision off County Road 11, and *that's* what I was thinking. But I let Michael talk me into buying this old thing and fixing it up. It's taken a while to get it into shape, but . . ." she looked up from the cornbread, which she had been buttering profusely as she spoke, and issued a lovely, pleased smile—"look at us now!"

"Cheers to that," Daniel said, raising a bottle, and they all toasted.

Jackie's discussion of the house seemed a good enough segue to the topic of money, Amber decided. "So, Michael," she said, a hint of humor and mischief in her voice, "did you build this porch before, or after, you got your verdict?"

Michael kept his eyes fixed on a piece of fish, which he was picking at with his fork, but a smile formed on his face. "Well," he said, still looking sheepishly down at his plate, "I paid the deposit before the trial, just hoping I wouldn't lose it." Now he looked up, met Amber's eyes with a friendly expression. "But now I'm pretty sure I'll be able to pay for it."

"Counting your chickens before they'd hatched?" Daniel said. "That's out of character for you."

"To tell the truth," Michael said. "The chickens still haven't hatched. Darby's filed an appeal. I'm not too worried about it getting overturned, but. . . Anyway, we were doing ok even before the Everett trial. And construction is a whole lot cheaper out here than what you're used to in Atlanta. Jackie had been wanting this porch for a long time, and I had put her off as long as I could.

"Actually. . ." he looked over at Jackie, then back to Amber. "I signed the contract for the porch just so she'd stop bugging me about it, and I could actually focus on the trial!"

"Hush!" Jackie said. "Don't listen to him." She looked at Michael with a flirtatious smile. "Pass me some more of that salad, you knucklehead."

"Well," Amber said, "it sounds like y'all really have made a place for yourselves here. I'm afraid I wouldn't fit back in. Actually, I *never did* fit in here. But it sounds like that hasn't been a problem for you."

"Oh," Jackie said, now giving Amber a serious look. "I imagine you'd fit in better than we ever did. I've finally gotten comfortable here, but I wouldn't say we 'fit in.' We stick out like sore thumbs here. I'll give you an example. Just last year, I tried to enroll Zoe in the daycare at the First Baptist Church—which we all know is the nicest one. Do you know they tried to ghost me, hoping I would go away? I filled out the application online, they set up a time for me and Zoe to come in and look at the facility, and when we showed up, you could tell from the moment the white lady who runs the place put eyes on me that she thought she had made a mistake. She looked so sick and worried, and you could tell she was sort of half-trying to be friendly, but also half-wanting me to see how uncomfortable she was, like maybe I'd realize this just wasn't the right place for us. She was so nervous, so quiet as she walked us through the place. She just wanted the whole interaction to be over. To tell you the truth, I kind of wanted it to be over, too.

"But I wasn't about to let her scare me away. That's the best daycare in the county by far. I was anxious about it, of course—all the other little children were white, so I knew Zoe would stand out. But I didn't think she'd be mistreated. Most of the staff were black—and let me tell you, they all gave me funny looks as well—but that gave me some assurance that she'd be alright. So I sent in my deposit and waited to hear back on a start date.

"Well, of course, no one ever called me back. I called several times myself, I sent emails. And I realized pretty quickly that it was no accident that nobody was returning my messages. So the day the school year was to start—which was my first day back to work at the high school—I just showed up with a check for tuition and a bag with diapers and a change of clothes. And that same lady acted shocked as hell to see me. But I just smiled and acted like nothing had ever happened and told them thank you, and I left. And Zoe's been there ever since. They've eventually relaxed, and everything is fine. I've been extra nice—bringing everybody cookies now and then, gave them all a nice cash gift at Christmas time. But it was tough at first."

"That sounds awful. Were there no other options?"

"First Baptist is the cleanest, it has the largest staff, they've got a big playground, big bright classrooms, an actual curriculum. Zoe's already learning shapes and colors and letters and numbers. Some of the other daycares are run out of people's houses or in storefronts. I went to this one place, supposedly the 'best' lower-income place, and in the main room where the kids were hanging out, there was a huge television on, just blasting cartoons, the kids all glued to the screen. It was more like a warehouse than a school, to be honest. I'm not about to put my little girl in one of those places, not when I can afford better. And if someone don't like it, fuck 'em!"

The table burst into laughter.

"I've been dealing with that type of thing since we first came here. Let me tell you, restaurant service is a trip. Now, that's changed over time, because we've been here for a minute and most everybody knows us, but I remember the first time we walked into Humble Pie, over there near Michael's office, lady was just as short with us as she could be. And I could see the tellers clamping up the first time or two I walked into the Bank & Trust, and I'm just there to make a deposit. There are still some good ol' boys around here who will openly scowl at us, or spit on the ground from their truck or whatever when we walk by. I mean. . . It's not the 1950's, but it ain't all good, neither."

She took a bite of black-eyed pea salad, looked into the yard, and thought for a moment. "It's hard," she said. "But I'd rather fight than flee any day. And that's what I intend to teach my daughter as well."

There was a moment of pause and reflection, as the friends ate and drank and thought about what Jackie had said. Breaking the quiet, she continued, "Speaking of fighting. . ." She looked to Amber with a conspiratorial expression, then to Daniel. "I hear Daniel's thinking about challenging ol' Leon Darby for his seat."

Daniel looked over at Amber, met her eyes, a request for permission on his face. Amber returned a noncommittal, neutral expression. She looked away, shifted nervously in her seat, picked at the label on her bottle.

"Some of the things Michael told me," Daniel said, "led me to believe Darby might be vulnerable. I've got a little experience under my belt after running for town council back in Rosewood. I came up short, but I learned a lot from it, I think." He looked over at Amber, hoping for some confirmation, but she was still fidgeting with her bottle, the label now almost completely removed. "Anyway, it's just an idea."

"Frankly, I think it's a wonderful idea!" Jackie said, her face beaming.

Amber's expression changed from neutral, even downcast, to intrigued. She saw that Michael was smiling a crooked, bemused smile. She saw that Daniel's eyebrows had risen almost to his hairline.

"I've been trying to convince Michael to do it," Jackie said. "But he won't budge."

Michael shook his head, shifted in his seat, grunted. "It wouldn't be as easy as you think," he said, looking out into the yard. "Darby is vulnerable, but. . . someone with roots that deep has a lot of advantages you wouldn't even think of, no matter how people might feel about him personally. And he has some very specific advantages over me," he said. "Due to historical reasons that I don't think I have to explain." Now he turned his gaze to Jackie, held it there firmly. "More importantly," he said, "I don't want to run. My practice is finally starting to grow into what I want it to be, and I have no intention on getting distracted by a fool's errand like running for office. It wouldn't be good for me, and it wouldn't be good for our family."

Jackie rolled her eyes, traded looks with Amber, turned to Daniel. "But you want to, don't you, Daniel?"

Daniel laughed a nervous laugh. "I guess I do," he said. "Ever since I was a kid, I wanted to be in office. Maybe it's a stupid dream, but it's a persistent one. And coming back home to do it, running here in the place I know best. . . It feels like the right thing."

Jackie looked to Amber. "How do *you* feel about it?"

Amber took in a deep breath, released an audible sigh. "To be honest, I can't believe we are even talking about it. The idea of uprooting our family, leaving our lives behind, starting all over again here. . . . I can barely even process it." She looked to Michael, "do you think he could actually win? Would it be a fool's errand, like you say?"

"I shouldn't have said that," he said. "There is an angle. There's an opening. But it's far from a sure thing."

"Don't you want to tell us, honey-pie?" Jackie said, teasingly, looking expectantly at her husband.

Michael returned her gaze, sighed, then nodded compliantly. He pushed himself up from his seat. "Let me grab another beer," he said.

"Leon Darby has had his hands around the necks of these farmers for decades," Michael began, extending his thin, muscular arms, shaping his long fingers into a strangling gesture for effect. He was opening with a dramatic line, using severe body language that he knew would capture the attention of his audience. He had been hesitant to open this line of conversation, but he couldn't avoid it now, so he figured he might as well make a good presentation. "During the Everett litigation, we conducted discovery on Darby's business. We had to fight to get down to the level of detail we did, and we had to agree to keep most of it confidential. So . . . I'm really not supposed to be telling you any of this. . ." He halted, looked off into space for a few moments.

"I think maybe you should keep drinking," said Daniel.

He did, draining the last of his bottle. "Well, here we go," he said and banged the empty bottle down on the table. He cleared his throat, put his elbows on the table, and leaned in, scanning the others one-by-one. "Did you know that over one-half of the farmers in this county are caught in long-term contracts with Darby Tobacco, and that he basically tricked them into signing them?"

Daniel and Amber each shook their heads no. Jackie sat listening, because of course she had heard this already.

"Darby Tobacco was Leon's father's business. Under his father, before Leon took over, it was basically just an auction house-slash-distributor. They owned a couple of warehouses and some trucks, and farmers would bring their harvest yields to the Darbys' warehouse, and they would hold auctions there amongst the various buyers—mostly cigarette manufacturers—and then Darby Tobacco would handle delivering the product.

"The family made good money this way, but Leon was more ambitious. He wanted to control the entire tobacco economy. So, the first year after he took over the business, rather than just warehousing the harvests and taking a fee, he offered to outright *buy* everyone's harvests. The business had plenty of cash and a good line of credit, so he was able to do it. He paid just slightly below the market rate, which everyone agreed to because it eliminated the risks of auction and the costs associated with distribution. Everybody was pretty happy about it.

"Of course, before he had offered to buy all those harvests, he had worked out a deal with an ultimate buyer. He had a direct line to this company over in North Carolina that sold discount cigarettes in the grocery aisle—Delicious Smokes, they were called, I shit you not. Well, Delicious had agreed to buy all Darby could get, at just slightly higher than the market rate, because again, they were eliminating risk and costs by doing so. He, in turn, made a nice profit."

"I remember when this happened," Amber said. "My dad worked summers at the Jessup tobacco warehouse, which I guess competed with Darby. I was real little, but I remember my mom telling me there wasn't any work for him because everyone had already sold their harvests. I had no idea why, though."

"It had a big impact on the local economy," Michael said. "And with him buying so aggressively, a lot of farmers who hadn't been growing tobacco started growing it. And everyone thrived for a while, because each year, he was just buying, buying, buying. He basically created a guaranteed, risk-free market for the crop. Before too long, nearly three quarters of the farms in the county were growing mainly tobacco, all in reliance on the idea that Darby would buy their yields, no questions asked. For nearly a decade, it worked very well for everyone, and it made Darby very, very popular. His operation was the lynchpin of a strong tobacco economy. That's when he ran for Commissioner. Unopposed, of course, and he won."

"Hold on a minute," said Amber, looking off to the end of the yard, where Jonathan was scaling a fence that separated the manicured lawn from the acreage beyond. "Johnny, stay where we can see you!"

"Ok!"

"Sorry," she said. "Go ahead. I'm intrigued."

"So anyway, the bubble burst in the mid-90's, when the anti-tobacco litigation hit. You probably remember when you stopped seeing Joe Camel on billboards, and you started seeing TV ads showing tar-covered lungs, tracheostomy victims, deformed babies. Basically, America realized all at once that the tobacco industry had been selling them poison, and lying about it, and the cigarette business took a big hit. U.S. demand crashed. And of course, so did the market price for tobacco. There was panic in Goshen County."

"I remember that, too," Amber said. "I was in high school. It was all anybody could talk about. I had this history teacher who would just rant, nearly every day it seemed like, about free market capitalism and how America was becoming a socialist economy, and it all related to the government taxing and regulating cigarettes."

"Right. Exactly. That was the sentiment around here. It was already a conservative place, so the idea that everyone's lives were being ruined as a result of government bureaucrats was almost too easy to sell. And that's what Darby did. He fanned those flames, while also presenting himself—the figurehead of the county's precious tobacco economy—as the only savior. And boy, did people drink it up. They trusted him, and he took advantage of it. He met with each individual farmer and offered them what he presented as their only salvation, a deal that would keep them solvent for decades to come, at great risk to himself, he said. Darby Tobacco would offer the farmers a guaranteed price, over a long-term contract—twenty years in some cases—if the farmers would promise to stay in the tobacco business and to sell their yields exclusively to him for that period of time. This 'guaranteed price' was based on a highly depressed market value, of course. But, he convinced them, the market was about to sink even further, or perhaps vanish entirely, so this deal was actually quite merciful. It was the only way to save their livelihoods and their culture.

"Now, there were a few who said no, a few who got out of the business altogether. Some who went back to peanuts, which were big before Darby's contracts came along. But most bought into what Darby was selling. I think they felt trapped. Every warehouse, every facility, every truck, much of the land, was dedicated to tobacco and owned or controlled by Darby. Finding another buyer would be difficult. Getting another crop to market would be a challenge with Darby in control of the entire farming infrastructure."

"That's hard to believe," Daniel said. "That people would take such a terrible, long-term deal, rather than just switch to another crop."

Michael said, "It is hard to believe. But I think there was a cultural element to it as well, which Darby knew and exploited. People just didn't want to change. And their pride and their resentment made them easy to convince that signing on with Darby was akin to battling against these evil outside forces. They felt like someone was plotting to destroy their way of life, and Darby promised to save them.

"Meanwhile—and of course Darby knew this would happen— the cigarette business eventually rebounded. Exports to China alone have more than made up for the loss in U.S. sales. And now, with vaping, U.S. demand is picking up as well. Darby has gotten richer and richer, of course, while the farmers have struggled to make ends meet."

Michael watched the reactions on his friends' faces. He could tell they were processing this new, highly interesting, information.

"And?" Jackie said, expectantly. "What's happening now that makes all this relevant?"

"Right," Michael said, and looked at Jackie, a little annoyed that she had interrupted what he considered to be a profound, thoughtful silence in the wake of his narrative. "Another renewal term is coming for a batch of those contracts. People are fed up, and there are hold-outs. There is a yearning, I have gathered, for a change. For an alternative to Leon Darby."

Daniel was grinning enormously. Amber looked over at him, saw this, then turned to Michael. "Wait a minute," she said. "How does Darby's seat as Commissioner have anything to do with this? Whether he is County Commissioner or not, he still runs his business, and the farmers are still under his thumb. I don't see the connection."

Michael smiled a calm, knowing, satisfied smile. "I like to save the best for last," he said. He relished the intrigue on his friends' faces.

"What changes everything," he said. "Is the cannabis law."

"The what law?" Daniel said, and looked over at Amber, who returned his quizzical expression.

"A buddy of mine from law school is a state legislator. There's a bipartisan conspiracy brewing between the metro Atlanta caucus—mostly Democrats, a lot of them African-American—and a group of farm-country legislators—including Goshen County's own state rep, Ed Gardner—to legalize marijuana in Georgia. Not some half-ass medical oil deal, either. Complete commercial legalization, on par with Colorado, California, and all the rest."

"That can't be," said Amber.

"It can. Think about it. There is no way the law can resist the economic pull of commercial marijuana for much longer. There is enormous, growing demand for the product, with all these other states legalizing. Meanwhile, agriculture states like Georgia, with the infrastructure and the know-how to facilitate a robust farming operation, are missing out. There is massive money to be made. It's going to seem very sudden, but—mark my word—in the next legislative session, the General Assembly is going to pass a law making it legal to grow and sell pot in Georgia."

Michael laughed at the dumb surprise on both Daniel and Amber's faces.

"But here's the catch. Under the law that is likely to pass, as a compromise to hold-out conservatives, counties can elect to remain dry. With Darby as our sole Commissioner, he will have the absolute power to prohibit the growing of marijuana here. And I think there is a good chance he will exercise that power, because nothing would be a greater threat to his business. And *that* is the thing that might finally loosen his grip on office."

There was a long, ponderous silence, which Michael finally broke with, "anyone want another beer?"

"Yes," said Daniel and Amber, in tandem.

Daniel scooped up empty bottles and dirty plates and followed Michael into the house under the pretext of helping him to tidy up. He lined up the bottles on the kitchen counter and stacked plates in the sink while Michael disappeared into the restroom. When Michael emerged into the kitchen, Daniel pointed to the empty bottles and said, "y'all got recycling out here?"

Michael chuckled, shook his head. "No," he said. "All goes to the landfill." He opened the refrigerator and clanged out several more bottles of beer. He turned and handed one to Daniel. "Opener's on the counter right next to you," he said.

Daniel grabbed the opener, pried the top off his bottle, handed it back to Michael. "Maybe we can change that," Daniel said. He leaned back against the counter, settling in for a chat.

Michael took the signal, set the wives' beers down on the kitchen table and pulled out a chair. He sat, opened his bottle and took a drink. "You think so, huh?" he said. "That's not going to be as easy as you think. Closest recycling facility is in Macon. We don't have the equipment for it. Or the demand, frankly. You've got a lot to learn if you're serious about running for office here."

Daniel nodded, looked away, a little embarrassed. "You know," he said. "I never fully understood why you came back here. I would've thought that you of all people would have been glad to escape."

"Why me of all people?"

Daniel stuttered. "I mean, given your background, given all that's wrong here. I imagine you could've had any job you wanted out of law school. I pictured you taking a federal clerkship, then going to some elite firm. Or Department of Justice. I could hardly believe it when I heard you were coming back."

Michael thought for a moment, then looked his friend in the eye. "I came back here because I love it here," he said. "I love the open country. I love the food. I love the people I grew up with—the poor people. I love the quiet, the view of the full field of stars at night. I realized during law school in Atlanta how much I had taken it all for granted. Yes, there are problems here. Big problems. But I've come to view them as *my* problems. This is my home. I could go to Atlanta and make a bunch of money, join some do-gooder political organization and go to cocktail fundraisers and draft legislation. Or I could come here and help *my* people, one on one, as a lawyer and an advocate. That's where my obligation lies." He took another drink. "That's how I've come to see it, at least."

Daniel nodded slowly, quietly, taken aback by his friend's earnestness. "Has business been good?" he said, finally.

"It has, actually. One of my professors back at Emory had been a small-town lawyer back in the day. He gave me two pieces of advice: take out an ad in the Yellow Pages—which apparently people still use—and go to church. Which is what I did. I took out an ad for DUI defense and divorces, the two most in-demand attorney services, and I went to church every Sunday, passed out business cards to everyone I met. And for a while there, I was defending drunk drivers and arguing child support at dirt cheap prices, day after day. Drafted a few wills, too."

"Wow," said Daniel.

"Let me tell you, it was a weird feeling—I had spent the previous two summers working an internship at Tibley & Turner in

Midtown, sitting in a high rise, mingling with business-suit wearing social climbers and bank executives or whoever, and that's what I knew of practicing law. When I first came back and started doing this kind of work, I really did second-guess myself. It felt almost wrong going from Big Law to becoming, I dunno. . . a country hustler."

They both laughed at this line.

"But it's what the people here needed. And I learned how to practice. After a while, it started to pay off. I was getting acquittals and winning custody fights and building a roster of satisfied clients. People began to hear about me, and I think it became pretty apparent pretty quickly that I was the best lawyer anywhere within a 50-mile radius. I started getting calls for car accidents, workplace injuries, wage and hour disputes. This big personal injury guy in Savannah hired me as local counsel in a couple of cases he had here. By year three, I was making good money. And then, there was the Everett case. Which, assuming the appeals go our way, will make it all worth it, financially speaking."

Daniel nodded, looked about the kitchen, built the courage to pose his next question. "What would you think about partnering up again?" he said. "We could be Drummond & Riley."

Michael looked at Daniel, looked away, down at the bottle in his hand. "It's an idea," he said. He looked back up at Daniel. "You sure this is what you want to do, though? Come back here?"

"Yeah," Daniel said. "It is. Ever since I was a kid, all I've wanted to do was run for office. Running in Rosewood was a mistake. I'm not from there. I had no stakes in the place. Nobody who mattered knew me. I don't talk like the people there. This is the place I know. My family has been here for generations. I feel like myself here. Like I can breathe."

Michael thought for a while. "But you've been gone a long time. I know you're from here, but your potential constituents might not see it that way. They might see an opportunist. Someone who abandoned the county, but came back because he couldn't make it elsewhere."

"That's harsh," Daniel said.

"I'm just being honest with you. I know you well, Daniel. And I know your eyes can be bigger than your stomach sometimes. I don't want to see you move your family here and then realize it's not what you thought it was going to be. What if there's someone else out there with the same idea? Who sees the same vulnerabilities in Darby that I see? What makes you think you're the candidate that can beat him?"

"Is there anybody else?"

"I have no idea. But there could be."

"Are you sure it's not you? Michael, if this is something you want to do yourself, I'll support *you*. Hell, I'd move down here just for the chance to help you run. That would be almost as exciting as doing it myself. And hell, you might have a better chance to win than I do."

"It's definitely not me. I'll be straight with you, my biggest struggle as a business has been that virtually no white people in the area will hire me. I've got more education, and greater skill, frankly, than any of the white lawyers here, but even still. The farm-owners, the white-run businesses, they go with their own. This little place has been so isolated for so long. It has been very, very slow to change. If I can't get their business, I have no confidence I could get their votes. I like to think I pick my battles wisely. And this one, I'm staying out of."

"But you would support me if I ran, wouldn't you?'

Michael hesitated. "Of course I would," he said.

Daniel processed his friend's hesitation. "Even if I didn't run," he said. "I think we could do well as a team again. As a law firm. Maybe having me around could help you with your little problem? We could start bringing in clients from both sides of the Beeline."

Daniel did not expect the expression that formed on Michael's face. It was almost as if Michael was laboring to keep his expression blank. He looked annoyed, with a hint of anger behind his eyes. Finally, he took a drink, wiped him mouth. "Starting a brand-new law practice, especially in a place this small, is a big haul," he said. "I've got plenty of work for myself, but not enough to spread around. I'd be happy to give you an office and put your name on the door—there's lots of space at the old Bank & Trust building, and rent is cheap—but I couldn't pay you a salary. It would have to be an eat-what-you-kill type arrangement. If you're comfortable with that, we could give it a shot."

This sounded fine to Daniel. But he was taken aback by how unenthused Michael seemed. He could sense that he had offended him somehow. "Ok," he said. "Well, let's keep talking about it, can we?"

"Sure," said Michael, now seeming to wind down. "The door is always open." He sighed, picked up the bottles from the table. "So what happened in that election in Rosewood, anyway?"

In the diminishing light of the evening, Jackie and Amber sat side by side on a pair of cushioned chaise lounge chairs, watching the cars pass by in the distance along the Beeline and the children still rolling about in the yard.

"Do you miss it here?" asked Jackie.

"Honestly," said Amber. "Not really. I mean, sometimes I do. I miss all *this*," she said, gesturing toward the sky and scanning the expanse around them. "But I've never wished I could come back.

Until Daniel got this wild hair about running for Commissioner, I never imagined we would ever live here again."

"Tell me about it. You think I ever pictured myself living someplace like this? I still can't believe I let him talk me into it."

"Are you happy here?"

"Sometimes I am, sometimes I'm not. I love this house. I love that Zoe will grow up in all this nature. That's something I never had, growing up in Atlanta. But, man—and no offense, I hope—it is so trapped in the past. There is so much casual racism here. I guess Michael's thing is that we're here to change that. But it hasn't changed yet, and it's hard for me to imagine it changing enough, and in any time, for me, or even for my kids, to benefit from it."

"Who do you hang out with?"

"Well. . . you know I've been teaching at the high school. And they needed a coach for the girls' basketball team, and I played in high school myself and was pretty good, so I've been doing that. And there's a couple of cool ladies who work at the school, and we cut up together. Some of the girls' moms and I get along pretty good, and we have a good time on road games and whatnot. But there's definitely this undercurrent that we're different. With the white ladies, it's because of race. With the black ladies, it's because of money—which I have and they don't. So I've never been invited to dinner or drinks at one of their houses. . . and I've never felt comfortable inviting anyone here. I don't want them to think I'm showing off. Or holding myself out as better than them. So yeah, it's a little lonely." She shifted her side, gave Amber a loving expression.

Amber smiled a big smile. "You remember my bachelorette party?" she said. "You remember what we were listening to in the limo that night?"

"Um, yeah," said Jackie, grinning. "If you're thinking about what I'm thinking about."

"Am I thinking about what you're thinking about?"

"If it starts with"— she sang—"'I met this girl in Atlanta / she let me play in her miz-outh,'" then yeah.

Amber burst into laughter, put her hands on her face, embarrassed but elated. Jackie cackled.

The laughter eventually faded into a moment of quiet. Finally, Jackie looked at Amber and said, "Can I be completely vulnerable with you for a moment? I would love it if y'all came here. I could use a friend."

Amber searched for the right words to respond. She was about to speak, when Jonathan appeared suddenly at her side, Zoe stumbling behind him. "Mommy, look!" he said. She turned to look down into her son's hands, which were cupped carefully around some precious object. The boy parted his thumbs ever so slightly, and a soft yellow glow rose from his palms. Amber could see a little black lightning bug crawling around in the cave of her son's enclosing hands.

"Wow!" she said and looked at him with an exaggerated expression of wonder. A smile grew on the child's face.

"Look, they're everywhere!" he said.

Amber looked out over the pasture. The sun had disappeared behind the tree line, and hundreds, maybe thousands of fireflies had taken to the air, their soft bioluminescence flashing on and off, on and off, filling the landscape with magical light as far as the eye could see. She felt the warm country air circulate through her nostrils and fill her lungs. A breeze wafted over her face. She felt it on her scalp, under her hair. Then, in a single moment, an orchestra of animal sounds erupted into the night sky. Frogs bellowed, cicadas cackled, crickets chirped, owls hooted. She had almost forgotten how loud the nighttime cacophony could be. She watched the children run back out into the pasture to catch more fireflies. She listened to the sounds of the summer night and realized that she did sort of miss this place.

That night, after the Rileys had departed and Zoe had passed out from exhaustion, Michael and Jackie stood side by side at the sink, washing dishes. They had a brand-new electric dishwasher, but hand-washing the dishes together in the evenings had become a daily ritual of cooperation and a time for conversation.

Jackie was gathering pieces of silverware and dropping them into the bowl that once held the salad and which was now filling gradually with water from the spout, a crown of suds floating atop. "That was so much fun," she said. "Do you think they'll actually do it?"

"I don't know," said Michael, neutral and non-committal in his expression, scrubbing a wooden salad-grabber with a sponge. "I wouldn't be surprised if Daniel completely changed his mind by the time they got home."

"Why do you say that?"

"He's impulsive. Has lots of big ideas that he doesn't think through fully. Hopefully Amber will talk some sense into him."

"Well I, for one, hope they do it. Wouldn't it be so nice to have them here?"

Michael shrugged.

"Why the attitude? You can't tell me there's still hard feelings between you and Daniel—over debate? You're the one who dumped him for the pretty girl in your history class!" She caught his eye, gave him a mischievous smile and winked. "If he's over it, I don't see the problem."

"He said something tonight that bothered me." Michael scrubbed the surface of an iron skillet with the rough end of a sponge. "I mentioned my problem with attracting certain clients . . . white clients. He made the statement that, if he joined the firm, he could bring in clients from 'both sides of the Beeline,' I think he said."

Jackie pulled a handful of silverware from the bowl, began rinsing it in the faucet. "And?" she said. "That sounds good, doesn't it?"

Michael was toweling the skillet dry. He didn't say anything for a few moments. "The point is, Jackie, I want those clients to come to me because of *me*. Because I'm the best. How unfair is it that I can dedicate myself fully to this county for years, yet I still can't get certain business, just because of who I am. But someone like Daniel can just plop down out of nowhere, and we just presume he'll be able to get the business that I was never able to? Just because he's white?"

"I think that pan is dry," Jackie said.

He sighed, reached high and hung the skillet on a hook.

"No shit it's not fair, Michael. Nobody said it was fair. But do you want to get the business or not? Do you want to break through that barrier? Or would you rather be able to wallow in your righteousness, content that you never made compromises to get what you were after? This is an opportunity to grow! It's an opportunity to become something bigger. And imagine if he won the election? All of a sudden you're the law firm of the County Commissioner. Imagine how that would affect business!"

"That's the other thing. The presumptiveness that he can just come here, after being away for so long, and expect to be elected County Commissioner! And to presume that I'm going to help him? That is the most obnoxious illustration of white privilege I have ever seen. Of course I've considered running myself! But I would never dream of getting elected, not with these voters! The county went something like seventy-five percent for Trump in the 2020 election! I've got the qualifications, I've got the demonstrated commitment to the county, yet I've got no chance, just because I'm black! And this guy. . ." he trailed off, shook his head, sunk his hands into the water, searching for a dish to dry.

"Do you *want* to run for the seat? Why don't you?"

"I have no desire whatsoever. But that's not the point."

"Isn't it?" She turned to him, put two wet, soapy hands on each side of his face. "If you don't want it, you might as well help him to get it.

"Plus, I really like Amber."

"I know you do," he said. He put his hands on her waist and drew her in.

"You're the one who told that persuasive-ass story about Darby. I think deep down you're excited about all of this."

"You goaded me into that, and you know it," he said.

"Maybe I did," she said and kissed him lightly on his lips.

# 3

TYLER KING sank into the folds of a soft leather armchair, a shallow glass of bourbon in his hand, listening to his boss, Leon Darby, the County Commissioner, a man he despised yet to whom he was beholden.

It depressed him how much he dreaded being in the man's office. Once upon a time, he had felt honored and privileged to be here. Now, every step into the musty lobby, every nod hello to the old receptionist, every knock of permission to enter the man's chamber, seemed like a chore. He dreaded the familiar trod from the lobby into the office, where a visible footpath, worn into the polish of the floor, forked as you entered. The right fork wrapped around Darby's oaken desk to his creaky swivel chair. The left fork led to a sitting area with an oval conversation table, an old leather couch, and two armchairs, in one of which Tyler now slumped. The footpath depressed him every time, the product of years and years of sameness, of unbroken repetition, of a structure and shape that he could never escape. He hated the faded, oddly-dated farm journals on the conversation table, each one selected by Darby because it contained some mention of his farming operation. He hated the wood paneling on the walls, the elaborate molding. He hated the oil paintings, the deer in the meadow, the sunset behind the rotting barn, the gaudy, gold-hued frames that contained them.

Yet here he was, and here he would probably always be. He caught a brief reflection of his face in the glass as he took a sip of drink and lowered it to the table. He was still as handsome as ever, he thought, still young, but with a little age now showing in his face. He didn't look old, he thought, but his wisdom and experience were beginning to show there in the folds under his eyes. He should be out in the world, charming women and juries, not spending his time in this dusty, dark office, listening to this pudgy bastard bitch and moan.

"You lost control of that jury," Darby was saying. He was a slight man who had grown fat, with a round belly and a barrel-like chest that was disproportionate to his thin arms and legs. As he gesticulated with his arms, the rest of his body was still, held fast in the chair by its weight, creating the impression of a cut log with two narrow branches sticking out and wiggling in the wind. "You let that coon lawyer pick a jury of his own kind, and a bunch of dumb crackers who don't understand a goddamn thing about business. And you let that peckerhead from Atlanta give the closing argument. Sounded like a damn Yankee through and through. Jury stopped listening as soon as he started talking!"

Tyler searched for a satisfactory reply. He knew Darby did not expect him to defend himself, but merely to take the beating. He shrugged, mustered a response sufficient to deflect some of the blame, not forceful enough to sound like an argument. "The boy pulled the wool over the judge's eyes," he said. "Kept the most qualified jurors out of the pool. Pulled at the heartstrings of the ones left over."

"Well. How bout some heartstrings for the goddamn defendant. I employ nearly half the goddamn county—I can't get a jury that appreciates that? Can't get a jury with respect for the goddamn office of Commissioner?"

Tyler nodded.

"What would that girl do with twelve million goddamn dollars anyway? Makes me sick to think about it."

An opportunity for humor, Tyler thought. "With that kind of money, she could buy the whole watermelon patch!"

Darby gave a single, short grunt-laugh, one corner of his mouth rising briefly into the beginnings of a smile, then settling back down into a grimace. "How's the appeal coming?" he said.

"We'll get it filed this week."

"We gon' win?"

"We're going to try. The guys in Atlanta say it's a long shot, but. .."

"How come every time I ask you about this case, you start talking about *the guys in Atlanta?*" Darby shifted his shoulders, shook his hands in front of him. "Didn't you go to law school, too? Maybe I should bring one of *the guys from Atlanta* down, see if they're interested in being County Attorney?"

Tyler could not resist the impulse to defend himself. "Those guys know more about appeals is all," he said. "They're familiar with the procedure. When it comes to dealing with local issues, there's nobody better than me."

Darby raised his eyebrows. "Well," he said. "Kindly get me another glass of Four Roses, will you?" He tipped his glass back, crunched down upon a piece of ice, causing tiny shards to fly from his mouth and splash onto Tyler's face. Darby held the glass out to Tyler. Tyler took it, stood, walked over to the liquor cabinet, wiped his face. He poured a glass for Darby, with plenty of ice, and a generous glass for himself, neat. He turned and handed Darby his drink.

"Sit back down, Tyler."

"I was just about to," he said. He had actually been hoping to stay standing, as a segue to leaving. He took his place in the armchair, took a sip from his glass, settled in for some additional scolding.

"If your father had not been so worried about his own reputation, you wouldn't be sitting here today. You know that, don't you? I can still remember the day he decided to send you to law school. I think it was your sixth year at Valdosta State, isn't that right?"

Tyler gave a nervous, shallow chuckle. "It did take me a while," he said. "But. . ."

"He was so torn up about it. That man worked for every dime he has, and he couldn't believe he had ruined you the way he had. Gave you everything you wanted as a child, never made you get a job. Paid for your college when you were failing, bailed you out every time you got in trouble. And there you were, finally about to graduate, with no prospects to do much of anything. He was so embarrassed at the thought of you coming home with nothing to do but cavort around the county and spend his money. I remember when he got you into that law school. What was it called?"

"Gulf Coast Law School . . ."

"Gulf Coast Law School!

"And Tyler, I'll tell you, I was happy to have you as the County Attorney. Your father was my most important business partner, and it was a small favor to give. I needed someone who would do what I asked. And you have, and I appreciate that. I don't want you to get the wrong idea. But this situation with the Everett trial makes me wonder if I need to rethink this arrangement."

"Well, Leon, I was really only at the Everett trial in a support role, you know. The County Attorney's job really is limited to government affairs. That was your private business. . ."

"Don't give me that shit, Tyler. You know it's all one and the same. The County Attorney has got to be my right-hand man, my defender and protector, no matter the situation. I'm beginning to think I might need someone a little more. . . sophisticated for this job. Or at least more aggressive. I don't *want* to have to find someone else. It would kill your daddy. But I've got to think about it."

Tyler took his eyes away from Darby's, looked blankly down at the magazines on the table. He'd been County Attorney for over a decade now, and it really was all he knew. Darby was right, this job was the whole reason he went to law school. And yes, his daddy had arranged it all. Still, though. He knew he wasn't the most brilliant legal scholar, but he *had* been quite aggressive—to use Darby's expression—in his work. He had lied and obfuscated and intimidated and bullied and finessed Darby through many a legal dispute, through many a controversial transaction. He had embraced the opportunity his father had created for him, and he had made this job his life. He had stayed with it even through moments like this.

"Leon. Mr. Darby. I won't let something like this happen again. I've learned from it."

Darby nodded. "We'll see," he said.

"You will," said Tyler. He took another long pull of his drink. "I won't let you down." There was some awkward silence.

"Mm hm. Well. We need to talk about tobacco contracts. Hammond farm has a second renewal coming up. Cyrus family, too. George farm, too. I need you to get in their ears about it. The market's about to get bumpy for a little while, I'm afraid. We need to adjust the rate."

"Adjust it down, I assume?"

"Try to. If they squeal too much, just agree to keep it where it is. That's the same as moving it down. No adjustment for inflation. Most of 'em too dumb to realize that."

"Copy that," Tyler said and drained his glass.

"Anything else?"

"You in a hurry to leave or something?"

"No sir. Just trying to be respectful of your time."

"Mm hm. Nah, I guess that's it." Darby drained his glass, got up from the couch and waddled over to his desk, where he sat and began looking down at some work. He did not look back up at Tyler.

Moments later, Tyler was gripping the steering wheel of his Buick Regal, twisting the leather wrap until it would not twist anymore, pressing the gas pedal down to the floorboard. He gritted his teeth and roared down the Beeline through the dark of night.

In his rage, he wished he had been a better college student. He wished he had drank less and focused less on the rotating cast of freshman sorority pledges. Those had been glorious, wonderful years—the best of his life—but if he had focused more on his studies, maybe he would not have had to rely so much on his father. Maybe there'd be something for him to do other than be Darby's lap dog.

It wasn't all bad, of course. The money was very good, and there was always access to more. County Attorney was basically the perfect position for a small town lawyer. He got a county salary, he was cloaked in the authority of the state, yet still free to maintain a private practice. He could legally work for Darby's private business, as well as anyone else who wanted to retain him for the reputation and influence his official title afforded. He had a beach house down in St. Augustine. Everyone in the county pretended to like him. And he could get away with things. He was never particularly worried about being arrested for DUI; he had received more "informal warnings" than he could remember. He had screwed a lot of women, too, some of them his fellow parishioners at the First Baptist Church, and none of them had told. Even his wife kept her suspicions quiet.

How he wished Darby would just die and give one of his brain-dead sons the opportunity to succeed him. That way, *Tyler* would be the one in control.

He tore west through farm country, through old downtown, crossed over the interstate, kept driving. Several miles outside Goshen County, he pulled the Regal off the Beeline, onto a Treutlen County road. Half a mile down the county road, he turned into a quiet little subdivision, maneuvered the vehicle in front of a small ranch home. He saw a light on inside. He cut the engine and got out.

In her doorframe, Melanie Stewart looked tired, annoyed, and partly scared. Tyler thought for a moment about begging her pardon and turning around and going home, but that thought drifted away and he helped himself inside.

She stepped aside and let him pass. "I wasn't expecting you," she said.

"Oh, I know," he said. "Just stopping by to check on you."

"Uh huh. It's late. You're lucky I don't have the kids tonight."

"Well, I knew you didn't. This is Tommy's week, isn't it?"

"That's right."

He walked through the living room and meandered slowly toward the kitchen, his back to her as he spoke. "Not a bad little arrangement I worked out, was it? You enjoying it, the weekly trade-off? One week of responsibility, one week off. Can't say I'm not a little envious."

She spoke to his back. "It's fine, Tyler. I appreciate it. I appreciate all you did, I told you that."

He opened cabinets in the kitchen, looked around inside. "Good, good. It was my pleasure. Everything else going according to plan? No issues with the child support payments?"

"Everything's fine, Tyler."

"You got anything to drink around here?"

"Tyler, listen, I appreciate everything, I really do. But I'm tired, I . . ."

He turned, held up his palm. "Just stopping by to check on you, Melanie, and maybe have a drink. I thought we had developed a friendship. Something beyond attorney-client."

"I know, Tyler, I know. I've enjoyed your company, I really have. I just wasn't expecting you tonight. I'm really not feeling very well."

He rummaged through the refrigerator, found himself a beer. He hobbled back into the living room, slumped onto the couch, loosened his tie, took in a deep breath, released it, let his head hang back on his neck. "I'm not feeling too well myself, Melanie."

She sighed, walked to the kitchen, came back in with her own can of beer. She sat down in an armchair at an angle to the couch. She wore a resigned expression.

"You getting along alright at the clerk's office?" he said.

"I am. Everybody there is really nice. It's a good job. I appreciate that, too."

"It's my pleasure." There was a silence. He sat there drinking the beer, doing his best to appear morose, to signal that something was bothering him. She did not react, so eventually he said, "Aren't you going to ask how I'm doing?"

"Sure," she said. "Sorry. Honestly, I didn't think you were here to talk. But yes, Tyler, how are you?"

He gave a sad smile, doing his best impression of a man tortured by the burdens of his responsibility. "I'm just ok. Being County Attorney isn't as glamorous as it sounds, you know? Lot resting on my shoulders. Lot of people relying on me."

She nodded shallowly and pursed her lips. It wasn't the kind of sympathetic, admiring response he had hoped for, but it was better than nothing.

"What you been up to tonight?" he said.

"Just watching TV."

"What you been watching?"

"Weather Channel."

He raised his eyebrow.

"It soothes me."

"Maybe I should give it a try. I could use a little bit of soothing."

She didn't move much, just sat there drinking her beer, quiet. He was beginning to lose his patience.

"You know, Melanie, I was just at the Commissioner's office. It reminded me of how big a risk I took in taking on your divorce case. The Commissioner was not too pleased about it. He wants me focused on county business, and he let me know it. But I'm glad I stuck with it. I felt bad for you. I'm glad I got you the deal I did."

She looked at him blankly.

He kept on. "Just tonight, the Commissioner was asking me what I charged you." He was lying. Darby knew nothing and cared nothing about his work for Melanie. "I told him about the bill. All the work I did fighting with Tommy's lawyer. Darby couldn't believe I never tried to collect. He scolded me for it. I guess he just doesn't understand our relationship."

He watched her, detected the anxiety on her face when he mentioned the bill. It was a nice little thing to be able to hold over someone.

"Why don't you come over here and sit next to me?" he said.

She took another drink of her beer, got up, and sat next to him.

"You sure look pretty tonight."

"Thanks," she said. "I'll be right back, I need another beer. You want one?"

"Sure," he said.

Later, in her bed, as he thrust vigorously away, Tyler felt a powerful catharsis. It cleared his head. Darby's abuse was a small price to pay for the power he gained from his position. In this county, he could do basically whatever he wanted. *This moment is a beautiful illustration of that fact*, he thought, as he looked down at Melanie's rump, her face in the covers.

When he was finished, he stood tall, put his arms in the air, arched his back and stretched his entire body, released a grunt of satisfaction. He turned his neck from side to side, relished the cracking sound and the relaxing sensation. He slapped her bottom, thanked her for the beer, pulled up his pants, grabbed his keys and went out the front door. He felt so much better.

He drove home. There was a baked potato waiting for him in the microwave. He warmed it up, ate it, then kissed his sleeping wife on the forehead and went to bed.

# 4

AMBER gritted her teeth with suspense, restraining the impulse to laugh. It would have been hilarious, if it wasn't so nerve-wracking, watching Daniel try to back the U-Haul out of the driveway into the road. The townhouse development that until this moment contained their home sat on a fairly busy avenue, and it was now approaching rush hour. They had meant to be gone by noon, but the forces of chaos, always strong when moving, had conspired against them. There had been no room within the driveway to turn around the enormous truck, so Daniel was stuck backing it down a narrow hill with cars coming and going all the while. She was glad Jonathan wasn't with them in this powerful, dangerous machine that neither of them was truly competent to drive—he was already down at the new home, with his grandparents, awaiting his mother and father's (hopefully) safe arrival.

After what seemed like a very long time, Daniel got the truck lined up properly, found an opening, and rolled backward into the street. He put the truck into drive, and it lurched forward, onward toward Goshen County, Georgia.

Daniel's desire to go back home, his drive to seek office there, had turned out to be more than a fleeting impulse. He had persisted, and Amber had relented. They'd had to make a quick decision. The election would be next November, and Daniel would have to be a resident for at least one full year before Election Day to qualify. Now, it was October. Less than two full months had passed since he proposed the idea.

The previous weeks had been an insane flurry of activity, everything moving so quickly that she'd hardly had time to think about what they were doing. There had been meetings with real estate agents, both the one here in Rosewood and the one down in

Goshen County. There had been the massive effort to clean and pack up their home, the sorting away of things they didn't really need, the trips to thrift stores for drop-offs, the awkward craigslist meetings to sell things too valuable to give away but too useless to keep, the weepy coffees with her friends to tell them the news, the answering of many, many questions from Johnny, the emails to teachers, the emails to her design clients, the emails and phone calls to pediatricians and dentists and optometrists and OB/GYNs and family doctors to transfer records, the many, many phone calls to every medical practice within a 100 mile radius of Goshen County to *find* a decent OB/GYN to take her records. It was the most upheaval, in the shortest period of time, that either of them had ever experienced.

They listened to music on the rental truck's tinny speakers, neither of them talking much during the first hour or so of the drive, grateful finally for a few moments of calm. Amber became lost in her thoughts, lost in the music, not paying attention to the road signs or the mile markers, not keeping any sense of distance in mind. But when her favorite station, V-103, crackled away to the point that it was unlistenable, she knew they were truly leaving metropolitan Atlanta. She would miss this station. She would miss Frank and Wanda in the morning, their mix of poignant commentary and ribald, silly humor. She would miss DJ Nabs in the Lab, would miss hearing fresh-off-the-press, locally-made Atlanta hip-hop weeks before it hit any other city, would miss the homemade-sounding tracks Nabs sometimes played, the ones that might never find play anywhere else. There was decent hip-hop radio coming out of Macon, which was the best they'd get in Goshen County, but it wasn't the same as V-103, Streets 94.5, Hot 107.9, or the numerous other low-budget, DIY hip-hop stations that came and went lower on the dial.

Once V-103 was gone for good, she turned the dial and landed on 89.7, Macon's Georgia Public Broadcasting station. She had great affection for this one as well. As a teenager, it had been an unexpected source of music, arts, culture, and commentary, with its shared broadcasts from Chicago and New York Public Radio. Now, they were broadcasting "Political Pause." It was never her favorite program, but she did love Will Tegan's voice, grandfatherly and friendly, almost cartoon-like, stern and authoritative all at once. It was familiar and soothing.

Will and his guests were talking about the marijuana legislation. It was all anyone in Georgia had been talking about for weeks now since, shortly after their dinner with the Drummonds, the General Assembly had announced the special session to vote on the bill.

Will Tegan: Well, of course we have to talk about the marijuana bill. It was truly a shock to many political observers, myself included. But with the governor's signature, this is going to be the law, with tremendous implications, I believe, for state, local, and even national politics going forward. I have with me today Cynthia Grassley—I'm sure the name is a coincidence—of the National Organization for the Reformation of Marijuana Laws. Welcome, Cynthia.

Cynthia Grassley: Thank you, Bill. And yes, the name is a coincidence.

Will Tegan: Heh heh heh. Alright. And then we also have Blake Coleman, of the Georgia Fruit and Vegetable Growers Association. Welcome, Blake.

Blake Coleman: Happy to be here, Will.

Will Tegan: Well, just to get us started, let me say, what a wild and unexpected ride this has been. Not just from a state perspective, but nationally. I can remember when the idea of marijuana legalization seemed like something from the radical fringe. It was so strictly illegal, for such a long period of time, that there really was no mainstream politician, from the right or the left, who was truly advocating for full legalization. And even when California legalized medical marijuana, and you had a few states follow suit, it seemed like sort of a novelty unique to those places. And of course there was always the fear that the federal government would eventually crack down. But then, very quickly, the dominoes seemed to fall. And, I might venture to say, with legalization in Georgia, this might be the most significant domino of all. For a Southern, traditionally conservative, traditionally religious state, to legalize. It's hard to imagine there won't be full national legalization sometime in the very near future.

Blake Coleman: Well, Will, I agree, except I would say that, from the perspective of our members, whether Georgia legalized or not, the days of national prohibition are shortly numbered. Those of us in the agriculture business, when we saw what happened in Colorado back in 2012, and then what followed in the aftermath of that state's decision, realized that this was a genie that nobody was going to put back into the bottle. The industry was just booming there, and over time has became highly professional and well-organized. And we also saw how little interest the federal government showed in trying to crack down. Through both the Obama and the Trump presidencies, the industries grew and expanded. So, we knew it was only a matter of time, and we did not want Georgia farmers to get beat to the punch, so to speak, by one of our neighboring agricultural states.

Will Tegan: Cynthia, what's next for NORML? Do you pack up shop, declare mission accomplished, find some other cause to focus on?

Cynthia Grassley: One day, I sure hope so. But there's progress still to be made, both here in Georgia and across the nation. National legalization is not a foregone conclusion. And we expect there will remain resistance in Georgia's sister states, despite the great economic opportunity that cannabis provides. In Mississippi and Louisiana, for example, the private prison industry has lobbied heavily against ballot initiatives that would have relaxed marijuana laws there. The Mormon church has quite effectively defeated any legalization effort in Utah. And there are numerous examples of similar things throughout the states. Here in Georgia—and this is what many people don't realize—there are only a handful of pre-selected businesses that will be permitted to retail it. These are businesses run by politically connected individuals and corporations. Your average Joe will not be permitted to set up shop and start selling cannabis in his community. He could be penalized for that. The primary purpose of the bill is to allow cannabis *agriculture*, and to allow a few prominent businesses to sell.

Will Tegan: Sure, but how do you enforce the restrictions on retail sales? If its no longer illegal to possess?

Cynthia Grassley: That's the problem. Enforcement will be selective. Depending on the county you're in. Depending, we fear, on what color your skin is.

Blake Coleman: Oh, that's ridiculous.

Cynthia Grassley: I don't think so, Blake. Historically, these are laws that have been selectively enforced against minorities. The new law itself smacks of selective enforcement. Large farms and established businesses, primarily owned and operated by white folks like you and I, are fully empowered to make money off marijuana, while upstarts, or individual businesspeople, who might distribute it in urban areas—and we're talking potentially about black and brown people—are prohibited from benefiting. That's something that has got to change.

Will Tegan: The new law does afford county commissions a great deal of authority, doesn't it? I expect we will see intense debates within many commissions in the coming months over whether a county will remain dry?

Cynthia Grassley: And let's not forget, Will, that in Georgia, we still have a number of counties governed by a sole Commissioner. I believe there are currently nine. So, in these counties, there is one individual who holds all executive and legislative powers of county government, and that person will have complete and final say as to whether cannabis will be legal there.

Will Tegan: The other big compromise in the legislation was one of timing. Tell us about that, Blake.

Blake Coleman: Well, as farmers, we like predictability, and we like to plan in advance as much as possible. So the law will not go into effect right away. We want to give our members time to carry out plans already laid for the planting of current, mainstream products, and to learn about this new product and make decisions whether to produce it. We also want to give county governments time to decide how they are going to treat it. So there's a roughly fifteen-month window that is built into the law. It passed in September of this year, of course, but it will not be legal to purchase seeds or grow any product until January of—not next year—but the following year.

Will Tegan: I see. To turn to a less substantive issue, Blake. There's been some chuckling over the name of the new law, which I understand your organization played some part in? Can you shed any light on that for us?

Blake Coleman: Well Will, when we thought of the "Cultivation of Commercial Cannabis" Act, we of course were thinking "CCC," which was catchy and easy to remember.

Will Tegan: But there's the "O" in there, for "of."

Blake Coleman: Right, there's the O.

"That can't be serious, can it?" Amber muttered to herself. She thought on this for a while, smiling to herself. She listened to the radio and the sound of the road and looked out the window at the trees rushing by, studied each billboard they passed—innumerable ads for personal injury lawyers, truck stops, farmer's markets, "Asian massage," and a mixture with messages like "Abortion Stops a Beating Heart," "There Is Evidence for God!" and "Secede!" scattered among them.

In a single moment, the absurdity of what they were doing hit her, perhaps for the first time. Out of nowhere, her heart began to race, and she hyperventilated. She gulped desperate, quick breaths, and felt like she was drowning.

"Are you ok?" Daniel said.

She held out her palm to him. She couldn't speak. She felt lightheaded. She saw stars. He slowed the truck down, pulled it over on the side of the road. She opened the door, stepped down from the cab, walked a few paces into some tall grass, leaned over and vomited. The contents of her stomach expelled, she stood there, leaned over, hands on her knees, looking into the grass, gradually regaining control of her breathing. She listened to the sound of cars zooming past on the interstate, the occasional sound of a diesel engine's growl.

Daniel approached her from behind. "Are you ok?" he said, again.

She ignored him, focused on her breathing, focused on calming the nausea. "Just give me a minute," she said after a little while. He stayed standing there. She wished he would go back to the truck.

Finally, she felt ok. She straightened up, took a long, deep breath, exhaled slowly, and said, "I'm fine. Let's go."

It was dark when they finally pulled into the drive of their new home, a spacious prairie-style house in a newly-developed neighborhood near the commercial district. Amber could see into the wide bay window next to the front door, into the living room, where Margaret and Jacob Riley, Daniel's mother and father, were kneeling on the floor, Johnny running back and forth between them. Even from this distance, she could see how happy the three of them were.

She saw something else. In the open garage, she saw the outlines of what looked to be a hefty four-wheeler. As Daniel pulled closer, and the headlights shined inside, she could see it clearly. It looked brand-new, its red paint shiny, its wheels black and sleek and clean. She looked over at Daniel, a question in her eyes. He looked back at her, smiled enormously.

Her jaw slack, she looked back at it, started to say something. Before she could, Johnny's little hands appeared at the bottom of her window, and he banged on the door. She opened the door, picked Johnny up, walked into the garage, put her hands on the smooth, soft surface of the seat. She set Johnny down on the heavy, thick steel of the rear cargo rack. She climbed onto the vehicle, straddled the seat, slid her foot under the gear-shift. The machine sank and rose smoothly on its shocks as she stood and then sat back down again, testing it. She looked up at Daniel, who was standing there with his hands on his hips, looking greatly pleased with himself.

"I love it," she said. She dismounted the vehicle and approached him and gave him a deep, warm hug.

Johnny was back at her ankles again. She picked him up and left the garage and followed the little walkway up to the front door and into the large front room of the home. It was empty save for the new couch she had convinced Daniel to have delivered to the place and a little card table that Daniel's mother and father had brought in. She put the boy down, walked slowly through the house, surveyed every room, each of them a blank canvas for her to fill.

# 5

IN the weeks and months that followed, Daniel Riley cut his teeth as a small-town lawyer. Despite Michael's earlier insistence that he didn't have enough work to spread around, it turned out he actually had plenty he was willing to share. In fact, he had seemed relieved to hand off certain matters. Namely, a pair of never-ending domestic cases, each of them a perpetual argument over alimony; a protracted criminal matter involving the operator of a personal care home for disabled adults accused of defrauding the state Medicaid fund; and a long, drawn-out worker's compensation claim by a Darby Tobacco employee with lung damage due to chemical exposure. Each of these cases represented a reliable source of income, but they had become a drag on Michael's time. None of them was any fun at all. But Daniel was glad to have something to work on, something to get him into court, something to allow him to earn his keep. It felt good to shake hands with his new clients, to present himself as a practicing local lawyer, to announce himself in court here in his hometown, to argue his points to the local judiciary.

As he was settling into his practice, he was also settling into his new life. Moving here had once been a crazy idea, but more and more each day it was becoming simply life, normal and natural. He felt a comfortable satisfaction about it all, about the fact that he was starting to weave himself back into the fabric of the place, and it was not proving as difficult as he might have imagined. Goshen County was his original, natural habitat. He had started once again to speak in the fluid, melodic drawl he'd grown up speaking, and it felt like his lungs were expanding after years of constriction. He realized the extent to which he had been adjusting his accent in Atlanta, the care he had been taking to articulate each syllable out of fear that he wouldn't be understood otherwise, that he wouldn't be taken seriously.

Amber seemed happy, too. She had turned a spare bedroom into an art studio and filled it with paints and canvases and various textile materials that she gathered from who-knows-where. They had decent internet service, thankfully, and she had her computer set up in the studio and maintained some of her original graphic design clients. She was spending time with her mother while Jonathan was at school. She was spending time with Jackie, and the two of them would drive into Macon some weekends to shop and eat and get pedicures. And each evening when he came home, Daniel saw the four-wheeler in a different place in the yard, its undercarriage caked with a new layer of mud, its once-pristine seat cushion showing new cracks from wear. Amber often had a tale of some old trail she had rediscovered, the wreckage of some childhood fort she had stumbled upon, some encounter with wildlife, some act of daring on a narrow path or a ramp of red clay.

And so time had passed in a startlingly easy, uneventful way.

Today, on this morning in February, on the second floor of the old Bank & Trust building, now the headquarters of the Drummond & Riley law firm, Daniel leaned forward upon a squeaky swivel chair, looked out the window over Goshen County's historic downtown. He rested his elbows on the sill and listened to the gentle cracking of the many layers of ancient paint underneath. He could see into the Humble Pie restaurant, where there was an old man sitting alone stirring his spoon into a cup of coffee. He saw the boll weevil monument, weird and crooked as ever, rising amongst the weeds in the little median that briefly split the Beeline in two.

An important day lay ahead. Edgar C. Gardner, III, Goshen County's representative in the Georgia House of Representatives and one of the county's most successful businessmen, was coming to the office for a consultation. Daniel's father did business with Ed, and he had suggested the meeting over coffee one morning after Ed had mentioned a minor legal dispute he was facing. Daniel felt somewhat embarrassed to have gotten the referral in this way, but he could not afford to scoff at it. It would be a fleeting opportunity to impress a valuable client and an even more valuable political connection.

He heard a knock on his door. He swiveled around to see Michael standing in the frame. "Have a seat!" he said.

Michael pulled out a metal folding chair, the kind you'd sit in at a church talent show or a graduation ceremony. Its metal legs banged and rattled as they dragged on the floor. "Are you kidding me with these chairs? You've got to get some decent seating in here. Surely you're not intending to meet with Representative Gardner in here?"

"Cut me some slack. I'm still getting settled in. Weren't you supposed to provide me with some fine accommodations upon my arrival? Where is my mahogany furniture? Where is my fine leather seating? I'm still waiting for it!" He slapped his knee and laughed at his own joke.

Michael twisted his mouth into a weak smile. "You've had enough time to get your office into order by now, I would think. But seriously, where are you planning to hold your meeting today?"

"Let's do it in your office. It's got that worn-in look to it. Papers everywhere. Files stacked up in the corners. Charts and lists. Like it's the workspace of an actual practicing lawyer. And not like. . ." he held up his arms, gestured around the room, "the summer intern's space. And besides, Ed Gardner needs to know whose law firm this is," he said, tilting his head toward his friend, turning his eyes up at him.

Michael smiled openly. "I appreciate that," he said. "But I've got a better idea. There's a reason I set up shop right across from the Humble Pie."

The Humble Pie had once been a popular and successful restaurant, the centerpiece of social commerce, a favorite place for families to enjoy a night away from home, a place where farmers and farm businessmen took their daily lunch, a place where men gathered daily to drink coffee and smoke cigarettes and conduct business. Indoor smoking was no longer allowed, but the old checkered tablecloths, the vinyl of the booths, still smelled vaguely of cigarettes.

Today, the restaurant stayed mostly empty on all days except Sunday, when roughly half the tables would fill with customers in the two hours following church services. During the week, the restaurant was sparsely patronized. Commerce had moved east and left old downtown behind. The brightly-adorned chain restaurants, lit up to be seen from the new interstate exit, drew customers in like bugs to a lamp, leaving Humble Pie empty and alone, a ghost in a ghost town. Nonetheless, a full breakfast buffet was prepared each morning, a lunch buffet every day at 11:30. And there was one man who still took his every meal there. His name was Will King, and it was widely accepted that he singlehandedly kept Humble Pie alive.

As a child, Will King had been a bookworm and a science nerd, obsessed with chemistry since he got his first set of beakers from the back of a *Boys Life* magazine. He'd gotten in to Georgia Tech, where he developed the preservative that would one day make him rich. In his university's own chemistry lab, he concocted a liquid that would allow a freshly cut tobacco leaf to maintain its harvest-time smell and moisture for 90 days, even in the open air. He founded a small chemical plant and for years sold his product in small batches to a distributor in Winston-Salem.

Leon Darby knew of Will King's brew, and he bought a batch of it one year. It had been astounding. The concoction allowed him to keep his tobacco leaves in storage far longer than usual, allowing him to hold out in negotiations for price. Plus, the fact that the tobacco was pre-treated made it more valuable. King's was a very good preservative, better than what the resellers had. So, for seasons thereafter, Darby bought more and more of the brew. And then, one year, he made Will King an irresistible offer. He bought Will's formula and his facilities for an attractive lump sum, plus offered Will a stake in the tobacco business and an annual salary to run the chemical operation. King Chemical became an indispensable part of Darby Tobacco, and both men's fortunes grew. To this day, Darby would claim that the worst price he had to pay for Will's business was keeping his no-good son on as County Attorney.

Getting back to the original point: Will King loved Humble Pie. Ingrained into his being was the childhood memory of slowly moving along the buffet at lunch, gazing down at the food below, the warmth of the heat lamps rising onto his forehead, the scent of the cooking oil flowing into his nostrils. He relished the ritual of scanning then selecting the perfect leg of chicken, scooping crispy okra onto a warm ceramic plate. He *needed* the cornbread, moist and naturally sweet, little flecks of hull in its texture. There was no other place to obtain tea this sweet, this cold, with this many lemons. The flavors, the smells, the very geography of the place, were parts of him that he valued as much as any other thing in his life.

An observant businessman, Will noticed as the restaurant's business dwindled along with the rest of downtown. Over the years, he had watched with sadness as the downtown department store, the grocery, the various professional offices, and finally the Goshen Bank & Trust, closed their doors and moved east. And so, as the rumor goes, one day, as Will sat enjoying his lunch in the hollow echo of the restaurant, he caught the owner's eye—old Catherine Humboldt—and gestured for her to come and sit down with him for a minute. Nobody knows exactly what he said, but since that day, there had never been any risk that Humble Pie would close, and there had never been any real question whether it would maintain the exact buffet repertoire as it had when Will King was a boy. Humble Pie stayed open because Will King wanted it there, and he had the money to keep it there, and by God, nobody would deny him the right to do it.

Other than Will himself, Humble Pie's most reliable customers were the old elites of Goshen County, those whose families had been in the county for generations, those who remembered and cherished its old days. Precisely because it was so unknown to newcomers, and also because it was so lightly attended and therefore basically private, the restaurant had become a place where old money conducted business and shared confidences. Michael knew this, and he had made himself a fixture of the place over the years in the hopes of being accepted into this circle. He was treated politely, and people like Will King would smile and nod at him, but the inclusion he sought had never materialized.

"Today," he told Daniel, "we will have a private business meeting, with a powerful figure, at the Humble Pie. And we will be seen doing it. This is a more important occasion than perhaps you realize."

This caused a knot in Daniel's gut, excitement mixed with fear.

\* \* \*

Michael walked in first and held open the heavy glass door. Daniel pressed the door with his hand as he entered and felt the chill of the February air on its surface. As the door closed behind him, the warmth of the dining room, the smell of bacon and butter and coffee, a comforting cloud of nostalgia, washed over him. He scanned the place, the old faded wood paneling of the cash register stand, the frilly curtains on the windows, the big empty dining space with far too many set tables, the double-doors leading back to the kitchen, the black and white photos on the walls of people he did not recognize, the majestic, steaming buffet in the center of the room. He looked over at the man he had earlier observed from the window in his office, the old man stirring his coffee, and realized it was Will King himself, the powerful, quiet chemical businessman. Will looked up from his newspaper, met Michael's eyes and issued a polite, knowing nod. He glanced at Daniel, issued a similar, but shallower greeting, which Daniel returned with a smile and a little wave, about which he immediately felt very stupid.

The place was quiet. Daniel followed Michael to the buffet and picked up a warm plate. He walked along the buffet table and scanned the food below with a certain degree of reverence. The clang of the serving tongs on the metal heating trays were loud in the strange silence of the place. He took some eggs, some bacon, a scoop of grits, a biscuit. He and Michael moved to a table in a corner of the room and sat down.

A little tinkling bell sounded from the direction of the front door. There was Ed Gardner. Ed was a portly man, his head shiny and bald. He wore rumpled khaki pants that were held onto his body by a pair of grey suspenders. The suspenders stretched tightly up and down a thin polo shirt that covered his chest and his protruding belly. He wore an unzipped, brand-new looking brown jacket with the emblem of Gardner Granaries emblazoned in white on one breast. He smiled widely and spoke loudly and greeted Will King, shook his hand and asked him how his morning was going, to which Will issued a quiet "just fine." Ed sauntered over to Daniel and Michael's table, and the two younger men stood. Ed held out his hand first to Daniel. "Young man," he said, "your father informs me you're a pretty good lawyer. If you've got half the sense he does, I'm sure he's right."

Daniel laughed nervously. "I hope so," he said and shook Ed's hand. "Representative Gardner, I'd like you to meet my law partner, Michael Drummond."

"Oh, I know all about Mr. Drummond," Ed said, turning to Michael. "No offense, Daniel, but the fact that you partnered up with this one is what led me to believe you might be as smart as your daddy claims!" Ed winked at Daniel as he turned to Michael to shake his hand. "Nice to meet you, too, young man. Now let me get something to eat and then we can talk about my little legal issue."

Sopping pieces of biscuit in gravy as he spoke, Ed explained his legal plight in a jovial, casual manner. Listening to him talk, you could understand why he was so successful. There was a certain magnetic glee to him.

"Well now, boys," he began, lowering his voice. "I got a brother-in-law—I don't know if y'all know him, his name is Breck Stoddard. Real dumbass. He got himself hooked on pills from this so-called pain management clinic over in Vidalia. Messed him up real good. Supposedly, he's doing better now, but . . .

"Anyway, ol' Breck's got a little farm, grows feed corn and soybeans mostly. Well, this last summer, he stored several acres' worth of corn in one of my bins. We had some heavy rain, and there was a leak in the bin, and his corn spoiled. Bacteria got in there.

"Normally, this is the type of loss that would be covered by insurance. But ol' Breck, bless his heart, was not exactly cognizant of the world around him at the time, and he had not paid his premiums. He lost his corn, he had no insurance to cover the loss, so now, of course, he's suing me."

"I bet that made for some awkward conversation around Thanksgiving," Daniel said.

Ed looked at him blankly for a moment, then suddenly exploded into laughter. "The hell you say! I imagine it would." He took a long sip from his cup of coffee. "But I've got a big family, and there's always someone fighting about something, so it's nothing new. Breck and that particular sister did not attend Thanksgiving dinner at the Gardner home last year, unfortunately. Maybe we can work this out and we'll invite 'em back this year."

"Did you and Breck have a contract? Anything in writing?" Daniel asked.

"I believe we did sign something, but that would have been many years ago. He's stored his corn with me for a long time. If there is a contract, I don't know if it's still any good. I'm not even 100% sure where the thing is."

"Would you mind if I came over to your office to look?"

"Of course not," Ed said. "I'd be glad for you to. Cathy!" he shouted toward the kitchen. "Could you bring me another cup of coffee? I've been talking so much I let this one get cold!"

Daniel travelled to Ed's office the next morning. The office was really just a trailer, which sat atop an exposed metal frame, elevated by stacks of cinder blocks. There was a bed of gravel in front for parking. Behind the office, two enormous aluminum cylinders rose into the sky like fat rocketships. These were the largest of Ed's many grain bins. They were quite possibly the tallest structures in the county. Several yards behind them were rows and rows of smaller bins. Daniel wondered which one had the leak. He parked his Explorer in the gravel, climbed a narrow set of wooden steps onto a small porch, and knocked on the vinyl door of the trailer. Ed opened it and said, "Come on in, boy!"

Ed showed Daniel to a dark and musty side room filled with rusty old file cabinets, cardboard boxes, and stacks of loose paper. "I'm not much of a record keeper," he said. "But you might check in those filing cabinets or these boxes in the corner. All kinds of stuff in there. I feel pretty sure Breck signed some kind of contract, and if he did, it should be in here."

Daniel looked at Ed with polite exasperation.

"Hell, you're billing for it, ain'tcha?" Ed said with a smile.

Daniel chuckled. "That's true," he said. "You mind if I poke around?"

"Not at all. I'll be here in the office or wandering around the bins. Just holler if you need me."

Daniel dug through rusty cabinet drawers and falling-apart, haphazardly stacked boxes. Dust rose up from the boxes and papers and caused him to sneeze. After awhile, his eyes began to itch, and his hands became dry and grainy. He found many tiny, tan-colored spiders, their little webs built into the corners of paper-filled boxes, living off dust mites and whatever other microscopic bugs must exist there.

He opened one box to find a stack of faded "Juggs" magazines. The issue at the top of the stack was dated 1986. He walked over to the door of the room and peeked out. Ed was gone, so he sat back down on a banker's box and opened up one of the magazines. He flipped curiously through the faded pages, admiring the enormous breasts. The models' faces were all covered with bright pink blush; they all had large, blown-out, hair-sprayed hairstyles. He looked at the unkempt bushes of pubic hair and wondered to himself precisely when in time that had gone out of fashion.

Daniel was musing about this important historical development when he heard the trailer door bang shut. He began to lower the stack of "Juggs" back into the box. As he did, he noticed a stack of papers, held together by a large rubber band, that had been left beneath the magazines. He brushed the dust off the stack and read the letters at the top of the first page. There it was, "CONTRACT," written in large type in the center of the page. Had it not been for the allure of those ancient mammaries, he would have seen this thirty minutes ago.

He was holding the stack of contracts on his lap, flipping through them, when Ed poked his head through the door. "Find anything?" Ed asked.

Daniel held up the contracts proudly. "I think so!" he said. He felt his face blushing, ever so slightly. He still had a slight erection. Ed walked into the room, and Daniel's anxiety grew. He hoped he could avoid standing up.

"Oh yeah," Ed said. "Those look familiar."

"I still haven't found the one for Breck. But I found these literally right before you walked in. I was just about to start reading them."

Ed's eyes scanned the materials that surrounded Daniel on the floor. "Ah," he said. "My old 'Juggs' collection! They don't make 'em like that anymore. You didn't get into those, did you?" His eyes were wide and he had a mischievous, teasing grin on his face.

Daniel laughed nervously. "Oh," he said, and looked down at the magazines, as if he hadn't even noticed them until now. "Of course not," he said.

"Heh heh, alright, I'll take your word for it. Well, I'll let you get back to it."

Ed left. Daniel sighed with relief and took the rubber band off the stack of contracts. They were documents that had been executed many years ago and then forgotten amidst the friendly informality with which business was conducted here. Half-way through the stack, he found the contract between Breck Stoddard and Gardner Granaries, LLC.

He studied the document carefully. "Jesus Christ," he said to himself. "This is a pretty terrible deal for the farmer." He walked out of the dusty back room and held the contract up for Ed to see. "You remember this?" he asked.

Ed walked over to Daniel and took the document from his hand. He issued a satisfied smiled. "Heh-heh. I had forgotten all about that. I remember it now."

"You mind if I take this back to the office and make a copy?"

"Of course not," Ed said. "Take whatever you need."

"Alrighty," Daniel said. "Let me take a closer look at this, and I'll give you a call as soon as I can. We'll figure out our strategy."

"Sounds good," Ed said. "Give 'em hell!"

Daniel sat at his desk, pouring over the contract. It wasn't very long, but it was dense and legalistic. It placed the full burden on Breck to insure against losses sustained due to unknown defects in the bin, including leaks. It stated that Gardner Granaries was not liable for losses arising from Acts of God, which included excessive rain. It provided that Breck was permitted to perform his own physical inspection of the bins prior to storing his corn there and, in the event he did not, he assumed the risk of losses caused by defects in the structure.

*A pretty shitty deal for Breck*, Daniel thought. But he was as thankful as he could be, because with this contract, he might just get this case dismissed. He turned to his computer screen and began to type.

Tyler scoffed aloud when he received the envelope bearing the name of Drummond & Riley and containing the response to Breck's lawsuit. "Let's see what kind of chicken scratch we got here," he announced to no one in particular and leaned back in his squeaky leather chair and propped his feet upon his desk. He began to scan the document.

As Tyler looked over the pleading, he grew concerned. He swallowed hard. It was not the typical Goshen County response. For many years, the same small group of lawyers had litigated these farm disputes so many times that pleadings had taken on the appearance of form. The typical Goshen County pleading was filled with generalized allegations followed by generalized denials and defenses. But Daniel's response was something different. Along with the Answer, he had filed a Motion to Dismiss, with a succinct, but well-researched brief in support. Attached to the Motion was a copy of the contract between Breck Stoddard and Gardner Granaries.

As Tyler read through the Motion, he grew nauseous. His head began to ache. He had not seen this contract before. He picked up the telephone and dialed the offices of Drummond & Riley.

"Mr. Riley, how are you? This is Tyler King. I'm calling you about this case with the granary." Tyler was doing his best to sound friendly and professional, to hide his bitter annoyance, though it certainly shone through.

"Mr. King, good to hear from you. How are you?"

"Aw, I'm just fine, Dan. Do you go by Dan?"

"It's Daniel, actually."

"Well alright then. Of course, you just call me Tyler. No misters around here." What a generous concession, Tyler thought to himself. "Anyway, Daniel, I got this motion y'all filed here and, let me just be perfectly honest, I don't think much of it. I don't know how long you've been practicing, but this prob'ly ain't gon' fly with Judge Roundtree. This contract is unconscionable. It's outrageous. I can't imagine where Ed Gardner ever got such a thing. Lawyer to lawyer, I'd like to try and spare you some embarrassment. I'm asking you to withdraw this motion to dismiss."

Daniel laughed. That annoyed Tyler immensely. "Well sir, I appreciate the call. But the contract is good. I don't know if you've had a chance to look at our brief, but there is some precedent for this sort of thing."

"Now listen, Riley—eh, Daniel—I looked at the brief. It's a very well-written thing, it really is, but . . . how should I say this? I understand you've been living in Atlanta for several years, and that's just fine. I'm sure you got yourself a lot of experience up there. But we do things a little differently around here."

"Well, Mr. King," Daniel said, "it looks like we're going to disagree on this one. I've done some research—the cases are cited there in the motion—and these terms are enforceable. I hear what you're saying: it's a tough deal for the farmer. But it's all valid and enforceable. I don't think your guy's got a leg to stand on."

"Well," Tyler croaked through the phone, and then paused. "I guess we'll just have to take this one up with the judge."

"I guess we will."

There was a long pause. Tyler detected he wasn't getting anywhere with his charm offensive. So he returned to his default position: nasty. "Tell me, Daniel, what exactly do you think you're doing, getting involved with that black lawyer, that Drummond boy? I know your family. Your daddy's a good man. I just wonder what he thinks of all this?"

"We'll see you in court," Daniel said, and he hung up the phone.

Daniel had filed a request for a hearing on the motion to dismiss, and Judge Roundtree's clerk had scheduled it promptly.

By that time, Daniel was no stranger to Judge Roundtree's courtroom. He had appeared before him several times now and had grown to understand the judge's strict, business-like style. He'd come to understand that Judge Roundtree demanded neat appearances—suits and ties on lawyers appearing before him—and formal manners. He knew that the judge expected everyone to stand silently and attentively when he entered, and sit only when the bailiff said sit. He wanted attorneys to stand when addressing the bench and address him as "your Honor" at all times. This was not because the judge was self-important or arrogant. He was nothing of the kind. But he had been a judge for many years now, and he valued order and structure.

The judge was also known for his fairness. Evan Roundtree, Jr. had been the superior court judge for Goshen County for as long as most could remember. This was, in fact, his 19th year on the bench. He'd grown up here in Goshen. His father before him (that would be Evan Roundtree, Sr.) was born in the county as well and for many years was one of only two lawyers in the region. In his father's day, Goshen County did not even have its own judge; instead, it was part of a circuit of rural counties, with a single judge who would dedicate approximately two months out of each year to each county's legal business.

Judge Roundtree was seen by most in the community as incorruptible and good. This was a rare instance in which that impression was accurate. He didn't owe anything to anybody. His father had died wealthy and left the Judge and his sisters his land and his money. Roundtree had run his own successful law practice for many years before taking the bench and had amassed a substantial savings. He continued to manage his family's farm business, mostly leasing the substantial acreage to other farmers. And, although he had to run for re-election every four years, there was never anyone to challenge him, and nobody ever would, because he was so universally respected.

On the day of argument, Daniel felt good. He'd had plenty of time to prepare, and he had slept soundly the night before. He'd had a good breakfast that morning and just enough coffee to give him an extra kick of alertness. He stood behind counsel's table, chatted quietly with Ed, waiting for the judge to appear.

He detected the door to the courtroom gallery opening, and he turned to see Tyler King enter, followed by a disheveled, downtrodden looking man who must be Breck Stoddard. It had been a long time since Daniel had seen Tyler face to face. Daniel wondered if Tyler remembered him from high school. To Daniel's recollection, Tyler had been a senior in high school when Daniel was a freshman. Through the lens of Daniel's teenage eye, Tyler had been a larger than life figure, the wealthiest, best-looking, most popular kid in school. Not a star athlete, but certainly *on* the football team, and a central presence at pep rallies and homecoming parades. Rowdy and fun-loving and drunk at bonfire parties, surrounded by the prettiest girls. In those days, he was the type of person who Daniel dared never approach, someone who dwelled on another plane of existence.

As Tyler approached him and offered his hand to shake, Daniel could see that the man still regarded himself the same way. That same calm, dismissive confidence, that sense of ownership over his surroundings. But as Daniel took the man's hand and looked at his face, the intimidation he once felt melted away. Tyler was still basically handsome, but his cheeks now sagged considerably, the weight of fatty deposits pulling them down into folds. The skin between his chin and his throat bulged forward, pushed out by his too-tight collar and tie. His hair was thin, and he had obviously combed over his baldest spot. But the most striking thing was his smell, which was a strange combination of putrid and enticing, as if he had put on a great deal of expensive cologne, yet forgotten to wipe his ass.

It was a moment of realization. If Tyler King represented the competition, both here in the courtroom and later in the election, these were contests Daniel could win.

"Nice to see you," Daniel said, consciously choosing "see," instead of "meet," to see if Tyler remembered him.

"You as well," Tyler responded, made brief eye contact, then turned to his table.

Daniel shrugged to himself and headed to his own table.

Judge Roundtree called the case. He wore narrow bifocals that rested on the tip of his nose. His thin grey hair was parted neatly and combed to one side in thick, discernable lines. He was a thin man, and the smallness of his face hid his age—there was simply less flesh to wrinkle and fold than one might expect of a larger man. Yet, as he looked down at the parties and issued his polite smile of greeting, the lines at the corners of his mouth and eyes, the creases in his forehead, showed his experience.

Daniel stood, as did Tyler. "Good morning, gentlemen," the judge said.

Daniel nodded, "Good morning, your Honor."

Tyler displayed an enormous grin and announced loudly, "Good morning, your Honor, good to see you today!"

*Boll Weevil*

"Nice to see you, too, Mr. King," the judge said politely.

"I've looked at the briefs," the judge said. "I understand the issues here, though I do have a few questions.

"Mr. Riley." He looked at Daniel. "Let me hear from you on a couple of things."

"Yes, your Honor." Daniel stood. "Daniel Riley, for the defendant, your Honor. I'm here with my client, Ed Gardner." Daniel gestured toward Ed, who rose and greeted the Judge.

"Good morning, your Honor," Ed said.

"Representative," the judge said.

*That's a good sign*, thought Daniel. It couldn't hurt that the judge recognized the official status of his client.

"Mr. Riley, I am somewhat troubled by this contract. In particular, the notion that it deprives the granary of any responsibility whatsoever for losses. My question is, what incentive does the granary have to take care of its bins? To guard against its customers' losses? What recourse is there for the farmer if something goes wrong?"

Tyler was nodding his head vigorously. "Good point, judge," he muttered. Breck was nodding gravely in the seat beside him.

"Your Honor," Daniel said. "I would direct the court's attention to the case of *Slack v. Percy*. It stands for the premise that the court should not interfere with a contract negotiated at arm's length between two competent adults, even when it leads to a harsh result. Under the law, the contract is a sacred thing that ought not be disturbed."

Judge Roundtree nodded. "Well," he said. "I do agree that it is a harsh result. But it would appear that I am bound by the *Slack* case, at least in law. I'll hear from you, Mr. King."

"Good morning, Judge. And thank you for hearing us today. The law cannot allow for a hard-working farmer to be taken

101

advantage of like this. Mr. Gardner's grain-bin wasn't fit to store anything. Water just poured right in, ruined my client's entire harvest. The sealant was several years old, should have been replaced long before last summer. To enforce this contract by its strict terms would be inequitable, your Honor."

Judge Roundtree looked down at some papers, studied them. He looked back up at Tyler. "Mr. King," he said. "What your client did was foolish and irresponsible. My family has been in the farm business for years, and insurance is a number one priority. You don't pay that, and you're playing with fire. I have to be honest with you, the contract does seem harsh, but I've seen them like this before. It's not unheard of to require parties to insure against their own losses. It adds predictability to the business, and that's an important thing, wouldn't you agree?"

"I would, your Honor, but . . ." Tyler stammered. "I'll be honest with you, this just ain't the way we usually do things. This motion, this contract. It's very unusual, your Honor."

"I do understand what you're saying, Mr. King. But this is a court of law, and I believe Mr. Riley is correct about the *Slack* case."

Daniel resisted the urge to smile. He felt excitement and happiness in his heart as he anticipated the judge's announcement that the case would be dismissed. His political career was about to get the boost he so very badly wanted.

"Mr. Riley," the judge said, and Daniel stood.

"I agree with your legal analysis. But as you know, a Georgia superior court has powers in equity as well as in law. There is also the concept of unconscionability, which could certainly be argued to defeat this contract.

"I'd not be inclined to award any kind of extraordinary damages were this case to go forward, because I do think the law goes in your favor, Mr. Riley. But I do foresee there being equitable remedies at my disposal that could bring a little justice to this situation. I could reform the contract. I could find that the granary has been unjustly enriched and order a refund of fees paid. Each of these could expose the defendant to liability."

*Damned equity*, Daniel thought.

The judge paused, looked off into space for a moment.

"I'll tell you what," said the judge. "Gentlemen, I'm going to deny this motion to dismiss. But Mr. Riley, Mr. King, these are issues I might revisit on a motion for summary judgment. So why don't you all see if you can get together and settle this. If you can't, let my clerk know. We'll get you a written order, and we'll get the discovery process going. Understand?"

"Yes, your Honor," Daniel and Tyler said in tandem.

"Anything else?"

"No, your Honor. Thank you," Daniel said, his heart sinking, a feeling of defeat creeping in to overtake the sense of impending victory that had been steadily building in the moments before.

As he and Ed walked out of the courthouse together, Daniel did his best to prevent the disappointment in his heart from showing on his face. He turned to Ed. "Well," he said. "This is not the result we were hoping for, but I think we made some dents in their armor."

Ed gave Daniel a gentle, grandfatherly look. "Young man, you did a good job. I always knew I'd have to settle this case. I never thought Ol' Judge Roundtree'd let me get away with paying Breck nothing at all. 'Equity' is the judge's favorite word. That's the way we make things right here in the country when the law don't exactly do the job. But what you showed 'em today is that equity is all they're gonna get; not to expect any big windfall from this.

"Now, don't go making any commitment without running it by me first, but I'd like you to get Tyler on the phone in the next couple of days and see about getting this resolved. Drive a hard bargain, now, you hear?"

"Yes, sir," Daniel said. He felt embarrassed. He had gone into court this morning feeling like the top man in the room. He had imagined Ed Gardner hanging onto his every word. He had imagined the judge and the opposing counsel being awestruck by his oratory, by his command of legal principals. Instead, he realized now, he was a kid lawyer in a jurisdiction to which he was still an outsider. Worse yet, Ed Gardner seemed to have known that all the time. His important new client did not view him as a great lawyer who would crush his opponents, he viewed him as a nice kid he could use to shepherd through a settlement.

He couldn't let any of this show, though, of course. "I'll get it done," he said, and offered Ed Gardner his hand to shake.

"I know you will, Daniel," Ed said and shook back, that same disconcertingly paternal look on his face.

Daniel settled the case for a fair amount, and one with which Ed was satisfied, roughly 25% of what the lawsuit had demanded. He sat at his desk one morning in March putting the final touches on the settlement paperwork. Satisfied with it, he closed the document on his computer and emailed it over to Tyler for Breck Stoddard to sign.

Then, he turned his attention to some paperwork that had been sitting on his desk for weeks now, the sight of which now made his stomach churn.

"Affidavit of Qualification," said the heading on the top sheet. He read aloud the words that followed. "'I have been a resident of Goshen County for __ one __ consecutive *years*'. . . That sounds awkward. Especially since I haven't been here a full six months yet."

He had done the research, though, and had called the Secretary of State's office, and he knew that the statute required residency for twelve months prior to the *election*, not qualification.

He drew his pen to the paper and signed the document. He flipped through the remaining forms, which Michael had helped him to compile, all of which had to be filed to make his candidacy for Commissioner a reality. He glared down at the check he had written to the county coffers for the qualification fee—not an enormous sum, but not insignificant either. A terrible feeling swept over him. The feeling that maybe he shouldn't do this after all. That day in court with Ed Gardner had made him realize just how out of his league he was here, how unfamiliar he was with the business and legal culture of the place. The way Ed had looked at him, like a good kid, but certainly not like a great lawyer, had dashed his hopes that the representative would look to him as a political ally.

But this is why he had come here. And the qualification deadline was today. He had no more time to think about it. He stacked the papers together, pushed out his chair, grabbed his keys, and headed out of his office en route to the courthouse. After today, he would be a candidate.

Tyler sat at his desk, picking his nose. His cell phone began to buzz in his pocket. He had a booger on the index finger of his right hand, so he struggled with his left to dig the phone out of his pocket. He finally got it out, dropped it on his desk, and pushed the speaker button.

"Hello, Melanie, what can I do ya' for?" He flicked the booger into the air and watched it land in a corner on the wall.

"Hey there Tyler. We just got something down here at the clerk's office you probably want to know about."

"Let's hear it."

"It looks like someone's going to run against Mr. Darby for Commissioner. He brought in the paperwork a little while ago. The candidate has only been living here for about six months, and we argued with him back and forth about it, but he showed us this order from the Secretary of State's office, says as long as you're a resident twelve months before the election, you're qualified. So, we accepted it."

"Oh yeah? Who's the candidate?"

"Daniel Riley?"

Tyler was silent for quite a while.

"Tyler?"

He chuckled. "You gotta' be fuckin kidding me."

# 6

WHEN LEON DARBY heard about the Riley boy's qualification for office, he did not feel angry, certainly not worried. But he did feel rather annoyed. In all his years as Commissioner, he had never been challenged. Election season came and went without requiring any change to his daily routine. He'd barely known that elections were happening, to be honest. Having an opponent would probably require him to acknowledge that there was an election and, worse yet, that someone was challenging him. He couldn't imagine that this young man posed any real threat to his seat. The kid had made no public announcement and, so far as Darby knew, no one in town even knew he was running.

Then again, truth told, the timing of it did make him uneasy. The cannabis law would go into effect next year, and he knew there were some in the community who contemplated growing the damn stuff. He would have to make a decision soon about whether to exercise his right as County Commissioner to keep the county dry. He knew he would be pissing someone off with either decision that he made. Those who wanted to grow would grumble if he used his veto. The moral conservatives in the county—and there were plenty of them—would seethe if he didn't. And of course, neither he nor his business associates were eager to see a new crop come in, one that might supplant some of Darby Tobacco's control of the economy.

Frankly, he had no intention of letting in the weed.

Yes, there was certain to be plenty of bitching and moaning to come, and it annoyed him greatly that this would coincide with the election. He decided he needed to make his position clear on the marijuana question sooner rather than later, so the grumbling could rise and then subside before voting time came. The bi-weekly meeting of the Goshen Gophers would make the perfect forum.

The Gophers had been an important force in county business and politics for decades, though its membership had dwindled, and its influence was waning. Goshen's young people—themselves a shrinking contingent—simply were not interested in the Gophers' musty old lodge, its smell of mothballs and aftershave. The Gopher lodge existed in a sort of time-freeze, a relic of a dying tradition hanging on to its final clutches of life. Old friends—mostly aging, all white—drank coffee in the evening, talked about farm business, and retold old stories. It seemed to Darby an appropriate place to reassert his authority. He asked the Chief Gopher if he could give an address to open the meeting, and of course, the Chief Gopher said yes.

Ed Gardner was a proud Gopher. He had learned through the grapevine that the Commissioner planned a rare address for the upcoming meeting, and it piqued his curiosity. Being closely connected to the business of county government, he was one of the few in the county who, like Darby, knew that Daniel had qualified. Always happy to see a political contest, he hoped that this was the reason for Darby's address tonight. He wondered what he would say, and he licked his chops at the possibility of an entertaining fight.

Ed wandered into the lodge with his best friend Jeff Jessup, a slight, short, quiet tobacco farmer who stood in almost perfect physical contrast to Ed. The men meandered about the lodge, greeting their compatriots, exchanging niceties, and speculating about what the Commissioner might have to say. There were notably more people here tonight than usual. Ed felt a certain excitement in the room, something increasingly unusual at the

Gopher lodge. He could see he wasn't the only one anxious for the possibility of a controversy.

Ed was chatting about the peanut business with a fellow Gopher when the murmur in the room began to subside. Ed looked up to see that Darby had taken to the podium. Many of his associates took their seats around the various tables, but still others stood gathered in front of the raised platform from which Darby would speak.

"Gentlemen," Darby began. "These are morally challenging times for us here in Goshen County. The world around us is changing. Our institutions are under attack. Y'all know what I'm talking about." Several men nodded. A few said, "mm hmm."

"Everywhere you turn, you hear about one thing or another: abortion on demand, homosexual marriage, boys who think they're girls, threats to our Second Amendment. . ." He paused for effect. "And now, legal marijuana." He surveyed the room, cast stern, authoritative looks into the eyes of his audience.

"Marijuana," he repeated. "Dope. Drugs. If you're anything like me, you remember the 1960s, when the draft dodgers, the hippies, the free-love lobby, were pushing this stuff. Saying we all ought to have ourselves a smoke of it, so we could be more like them." Several men chuckled. "Well, I don't know about you, but I don't want to be like them. What was it that Ronald Reagan said? Out in California, he'd seen a man who looked like Tarzan, walked like Jane, and smelled like Cheetah the chimpanzee!" Several men laughed at the reference. "All because of this dope. I don't want it in our county, as I'm sure all of you don't. I can't imagine what in the hell is going on with our General Assembly, I really can't. The devil finds the most unexpected of places to work his influence.

"Now, I've heard tell of a young boy who plans to challenge me for County Commissioner. If he's got in mind that he wants to bring in the weed, that he wants to change our way of life, well. . . he's got another thing coming. I want to assure you that I will guard our moral foundation. I will not allow it to be undermined. And as long as I am the County Commissioner, we will not grow marijuana in Goshen County."

There was a hesitation. Then, a polite round of applause rose from the audience.

*As long as I am the County Commissioner, we will not grow marijuana in Goshen County.* Ed pondered this. This was something Darby ought not to have said out loud, he thought. It was something he would regret. Ed knew there was real desire among the farming community to try this new crop, to at least explore the possibility. Darby was severely underestimating this desire, Ed decided. He had grown complacent in the comfort of his monopoly. Now, he was taking a firm, immovable position, drawing a line in the sand. Anyone who had contemplated this opportunity now faced a leader who had vowed unequivocally to block it.

Ed could feel the ambivalence in the room. Though there had been some applause and heads nodding here and there, there was nothing like unanimity, nothing like enthusiasm. There had been no impassioned *hell yeahs*, no *amens*. Most of the men in the room did agree, in a general sense, that marijuana was something vaguely immoral. They would never condone their own children smoking it, and they were not altogether comfortable with the idea of it being produced in their fields. But even among those, there were some whose attitude was that if the law said they could grow it, this was a free country, and by God, they should be allowed to grow it.

Nobody brought up these points that evening. They kept their mouths shut. But, Ed thought, they must be thinking it.

\* \* \*

Early the next morning, Daniel heard his phone buzzing on his desk. He looked down at the screen. "Gardner, Edgar," the screen read. Daniel snapped to attention, curious and anxious as to why Ed might be calling. The granary lawsuit had been settled, the monies had been paid, the dismissal filed. *Maybe some other business?* Daniel thought. *Maybe he heard about my qualification,* he allowed himself, though he pushed that aside. No need to get his hopes up.

"Mr. Gardner?"

"Mr. Riley—how are you?

"Fine, sir, just fine."

"Daniel, I'm calling to invite you and your law partner, and your wives of course, to my spring picnic. It's a little something we do with our church each year, and we'd love to have y'all."

Excitement stirred in Daniel's chest. "Yes sir, we would love to come!"

Each April, Ed Gardner hosted a big picnic in the acres-deep yard surrounding his restored Victorian home. The official purpose was to celebrate the arrival of spring, but its actual function was for Ed and his wife Velma to show off their success, to nurture their friendships, and to develop their business relationships. They borrowed many fold-out tables from the Christ Episcopal Church, where Ed was on the finance committee. Velma and her fellow parishioners worked through the week to produce more fried chicken, catfish, coleslaw, hush puppies, potato salad, green beans with ham, baked beans, and banana pudding than you could possibly imagine. Sweet tea and lemonade flowed like rivers to the ocean. The Gardners' friends brought additional foods, like even more fried chicken, macaroni and cheese, hash browns, scalloped potatoes, deviled eggs, a thousand finger sandwiches of various contents, Watergate salad, and lemon cake. It was a feast among feasts. Children ran and played in the yard and spilled out into the cornfields. Those so inclined snuck in and out of Ed's toolshed, where he quietly served bourbon and beer to whoever wanted it.

Ed bellowed Daniel's praises to his friends and fellow Episcopalians. "Woo, boy, you shoulda seen it! This boy whooped ol' Tyler King's ass all up and down that courtroom!" He wrapped his burly arm around Daniel's shoulders and squeezed him to his side. "I never seen nothing like it! Ol' Tyler looked like he ate himself a shit sandwich!"

Ed shook Daniel's narrow frame against his rotund body. Daniel smiled, somewhat embarrassed. He was pleased to see that Ed viewed the case as a victory. Or maybe he was just spinning it as one for his audience. In either case, Daniel was glad he had never let on what a defeat it had felt like to him. His head wobbling on his neck under the power of Ed's grasp, Daniel glanced over at Michael, who wore an amused, proud expression.

"And y'all meet Michael Drummond, his law partner," Ed said. "Daniel's daddy tells me these boys were state debating champions here at Goshen County High, and now here they are practicing law together. What a wonderful thing."

Ed turned to Amber and Jackie, who were standing together. "And look at these beautiful young ladies," he said. "These boys just have it all, don't they?" Everyone turned and smiled at the two, and each of them blushed, unable to resist the charm of being complimented, despite each of them objecting, in principal, in their own minds, to being objectified in this way.

In this moment, perhaps for the first time, Amber saw hope for Daniel's election. Her greatest anxiety had been that he would repeat what he had done in Rosewood, that he would bumble recklessly into a place where he didn't belong, presupposing himself worthy to lead a people who barely knew him. But Ed Gardner was someone at the root of this county. The people here were bedrock. With the support of someone like this, there was hope. And seeing Ed believe in him made her believe in him.

Moreover, she saw the possibility for friendship here, and a social life. Amongst the group to whom Ed was singing Daniel's praises, she saw Donna Pinkerton, the dentist's daughter and someone she had known since girlhood. Donna was sipping a drink, wearing a cute, royal blue, long-sleeve but short-hemmed dress and suede gladiator sandals with straps around her ankles. She also recognized Jessica Coker, who she remembered as the high school floozy, chasing her little boys through the yard and kissing her handsome husband on the cheek, happy and carefree. And there among the children, she saw her own little Jonathan, smiling widely, running and laughing and playing, blissfully unaware and uncomprehending of any social history that might exist among the adults, just glad to be with other kids in a big grassy yard.

Back in Rosewood, her best friends had been the parents of Johnny's playmates. Even if they connected on nothing else, they had in common their love for their children and the many anxieties of parenthood. Children's birthday parties were important social occasions—getting the kids together forced the grown-ups together, and standing with other uncertain moms and dads, everyone watching their children develop social intelligence from raw material, was somehow a bonding experience. Seeing your kid fall into blissful, unconditional friendship with your neighbor's kid tended to break down whatever insecurity or sense of social difference that otherwise would have kept you from forming your own adult friendship. And then there were playdates, where meaningful friendships grew, where you spent one-on-one time with those toward whom you had formed the greatest affections. *Maybe that could happen here, too*, she thought. She saw Jonathan tumble down laughing with one of Jessica's little boys, and she and Jessica met eyes, and Jessica gave her a friendly, inviting smile, and this made Amber so very happy.

Donna and Jessica had never been outright nasty to her during her school days, but they had never been especially warm to her, either. Maybe that had been her fault as much as theirs, she wondered. She had always withdrawn herself into music and art and never made much effort to be a part of their world. Even still, she had always privately wished she had fit in with girls like that, that she could have moved effortlessly through the social strata of the county like they seemed to. While as a girl she had resented them, now, she felt her grudge melting away into irrelevance as she watched the children play. These girls were no longer the popular kids in school; they were mothers like her, doing their best.

Even if she had wanted to hold a grudge, she couldn't afford to. She was here now, and though she loved her riding trails and her studio and her time with Jackie, she missed having a social life. Though she loved the time spent with her mother, she was separated from her by age and by that inequality that always exists between mother and daughter, that desire by the daughter always to present an image of herself as self-sufficient and accomplished, that desire by the mother always to instruct and occasionally to scold.

She missed the numerous, casual friendships she'd known back in Rosewood. She missed happy hours on Friday afternoons. She missed the other thirty-somethings with kids in grade school who got together on the weekends to drink beer and cut up while their kids played in the yard. Here, she saw the possibility for something akin to what she had back in Rosewood, and she wanted it badly.

As the men broke off into an extended dialogue about Ed's legal case, Amber nudged Jackie, muttered to her quietly, "I hear they're serving big girl drinks over in that tool shed."

"Oh, let's go then."

"You mind if we socialize a little bit? I recognize a couple of those girls from high school."

Jackie looked over at the group, scanned them cautiously. "Sure. Just don't leave me alone. They're liable to hand me their trash. Or ask me to bring them a refill." She made a twisted, sardonic smile.

Surprise struck Amber's face, but her expression resigned shortly to one of comprehension. Her would-be friends fit the mold of those who had made Jackie feel so unwelcome in her first years here and who continued to give her sideways looks in town. Amber saw the anxiety in her friend's face, and it gave her a guilty, sinking feeling.

She met Jackie's eyes. "If any of them act like bitches, we'll leave, and that'll be the end of it. Fair?"

Jackie sighed, smiled meekly. "Fair enough," she said. "But I'mma hold you to that."

Meanwhile, Daniel and Michael had seated themselves at a picnic table with a group of older men. They were blabbing about state politics when Ed brought out a watermelon and thumped it down upon the checkered red-and-white tablecloth. He plunged a knife into the melon's center, then pushed the blade down, slicing its sturdy hull. He rocked the blade back and forth until the thing gave way and opened into two halves. He sliced each half into quarters, then those into eighths. "Y'all get you a piece," he said.

The folding table was now bereft of the food that had once covered it. The tray of watermelon slices was passed around, and everyone gladly took one. Sitting next to Ed was Jeff Jessup, whom Daniel knew as a successful tobacco farmer. When Daniel was a boy, Jeff would sometimes come to talk farm business with his father. Jeff was short with a head full of neatly combed grey hair. His skin was leathery from years of outdoor work. He had a reputation as a quiet intellectual, someone who understood the farm business deeply. He was one of the few farmers in Goshen County who had avoided Darby's contracts. He continued to sell his tobacco on the free market and made a profit most years.

"So what do y'all think of this cannabis law?" Ed said, slightly under his breath, looking cautiously over his shoulders, signaling that this was a dangerous topic. Daniel looked around at the others at the table and surmised that these were the people Ed felt the most comfortable around. Daniel began to fidget in his seat; this excited him. Some others at the table fidgeted as well. One fellow gave an audible sigh. One gentleman shook his head, as if he couldn't make up his mind about the issue. One man spit some tobacco into the grass, then allowed himself a cautious, noncommittal smile.

Ed looked around at the group with some sternness in his eyes. He seemed to be hoping for them to take a position on the issue. Jeff beside him looked about the group as well. Daniel returned Ed's glare, though without signaling his opinion. He suppressed his desire to deliver a speech. *Take it easy*, he thought.

"Well," Ed said, finally. "This is what I think, and I ain't scared to say it. The damn stuff ain't no worse than booze. I smoked it quite a bit when I was in Vietnam, I'm not afraid to say. Lot of us boys did. Haven't touched it since, but . . . Honestly, there ain't *that* much to it. And in any case," he said, "I don't care too much how bad it is—if the law says we can grow it, I say we ought to be able to grow it." He scanned his audience. They seemed attentive.

"Ol' Leon's talking about it like it's a damn moral issue," he continued. "You know and I know that if he prevents us from growing here in the county, it will be for one reason, and one reason only: he's looking after his own damn pocketbook. All this moralizing is a bunch of bullshit, and anybody with a brain in his head knows it."

Ed seemed to be expressing the precise sentiment Michael said they'd need to tap to have a chance in the election. It was astounding. Daniel could see pieces of a puzzle beginning to move toward one another. He made brief eye contact with his friend, who waggled his eyebrows. Daniel could barely contain the smile forming on his face.

As Ed spoke, Jeff nodded his head openly and unambiguously. Finally, he spoke. "I'd sure like to grow it," he said. "Tobacco's a losing business. If we don't get in on the cannabis thing now, every county around us is going to, and we're going to be left shit out of luck."

Daniel allowed himself to nod, ever so slightly, almost imperceptibly. He wanted Ed and Jeff to understand he was on their side. But he didn't want to come across as too anxious, too eager. He thought he could detect agreement from the others at the table as well. He wasn't sure. But he certainly saw no objection to Jeff's words.

"Well," Ed said. "I don't know that there's much can be done. As long as Leon Darby's our County Commissioner, we might be just that: shit out of luck. A while back, a group of us had talked about going to the state legislature, trying to get Goshen changed to a three-commissioner system, dilute the man's influence a little bit. But there's just no support for it. Darby makes a lot of money, and he spreads it around the legislature quite effectively. And the folks around here are so afraid of the man, won't nobody step up to challenge him. I personally don't have the energy for it. My political career is entering its twilight, I'm afraid. Without a viable candidate, without someone willing to put it all on the line and give the man hell, I'm afraid we're stuck."

He paused for a long moment. Then he said, "Unless there's somebody already set to challenge him, and we just don't know it yet." He glanced at Daniel, very briefly, perhaps imperceptibly to anyone else, and winked. He then went back to looking down at his hands upon the table, where he was fiddling with a leaf. Daniel knew that, in this moment, he had to communicate something. These few seconds represented a fragile and fleeting opportunity. His nerves vibrated as he stepped delicately toward the precise communicative task before him.

Ed looked up to scan the others at the table, and Daniel looked at Ed with purpose and conspiracy in his eyes. Ed caught Daniel's glare and locked eyes with him. Daniel made his best attempt at telepathy—he pushed from his mind, into his eyes, the notion that *he* was a viable candidate, that he was the man to beat Leon Darby. As he glared, he saw Ed's eyes widen ever so slightly. He saw that Ed perceived the communication. He saw Ed's jaw loosen ever so slightly. Then he saw a minute, almost evil smile form on Ed's mouth. Daniel allowed his own subtle smile.

The message had been delivered and received. Well-received, at that.

Years back, Ed had a fishing pond dug on his property and stocked with catfish, bass, and bream. He enjoyed taking his little rowboat out onto the pond and seeing what he could catch. He seldom kept anything, usually threw the fish back. But every once in a while, he'd catch a big catfish. He'd nail it through the eyes to a wooden beam in his workshop and peel off its slippery skin with a knife, and Velma would cover it in cornmeal and fry it for dinner.

On this evening, after the picnickers had all left and the sun was going down, he sat in his rowboat across from his quiet friend Jeff, drinking Milwaukee's Best from a can. The sunset had turned the sky a silky brilliant orange. The air was cool. Ed enjoyed the weightlessness of floating on the water, loved the way it mixed with a good beer buzz.

Jeff asked, "You think the Riley boy's got a chance?"

"Shit, who knows. He obviously has no idea what he's doing. But he did do one thing that nobody else has: he put his hat in the ring. And that's half the doggone battle."

He thought for a second, took a sip of his brew.

"He ain't perfect, but a candidate never is. Most anybody who runs for office ain't worth a shit, if you think about it. It's very rare that you get someone who's sophisticated and cautious and wise running for office, you know? Most people like that know better. They know it's not worth the toll it takes on your life. The scrutiny, the headache. They're not willing to reduce themselves to the sort of pandering and lying you have to do to win. Heh, most anyone who runs for office is at least a little bit stupid and a little bit reckless. Someone with some kind of delusion that they're destined for greatness, and too stupid to know any better. Lord knows that's how I got my start." He looked at his friend and chuckled. He looked out at the sunset and thought for a moment.

"And every once in a while, they turn out to be pretty good leaders anyway." He took a deep breath of the cool, clean air and sighed. "Darby needs to go. There's no question about that. And the boy is what we got. This marijuana thing presents the kind of opportunity I've never seen before in my political career. It's that rare thing where everybody's interests are aligned. People who are usually at each other's throats. The blacks want it because they're tired of getting put in jail for something so pointless. And the farmers want it, of course. And most anybody in business wants it. The diehards who were against it are all dying out."

Jeff nodded in agreement. He took a pull from his can of Beast.

"I'm going to get behind him," Ed said. "And if Leon Darby doesn't like it, he can kiss my hairy ass."

Jeff chuckled and stomped his feet on the hull of the boat. Ed laughed, too, a vigorous hearty-har-har that echoed through the night.

The following Monday evening, after the work day had ended but before suppertime, Ed and Jeff traveled to the Riley home, unannounced. Both men were brought up in an era where you were not expected to text or email or call before initiating face-to-face contact. In their day, a visit to a neighbor's home was the typical and expected way to start a conversation or check on someone's wellbeing or simply gain some company.

Daniel and Amber had been sitting in their living room, looking at their computer screens, still working on one thing or another, when they heard a knock at the door. Daniel rose from the couch and walked over to the door. He looked through the peephole to see his portly client and his slight friend, their features exaggerated by the curvature of the lens, as if entrapped in a glass bubble,

He opened the door. "Good evening, gentlemen," he said. "Is everything ok?"

"Young man, we'd like to give you some money," Ed said. He pulled out four checks, which he handed to Daniel, like tickets of admission to the house. Daniel looked down at the checks with dumb surprise. Each check was written for $2,500, one from Ed, one from Ed's wife Velma, one from Jeff, and one from Jeff's wife. $10,000, divided into four checks to comply with the maximum per-person contribution limit.

"I don't know what to say," Daniel said. "Come in." He moved aside and gestured for the men to come into his home. Ed waddled through, Jeff hovering in behind him. Amber's eyebrows raised into a question mark. Daniel said, "Amber, Mr. Gardner and Mr. Jessup here just gave us $10,000 for the campaign."

A surprised, grateful smile formed on Amber's face. "Please come in!" she said. She offered a hand to Ed, who came in first, and then to Jeff. "Would y'all like something to drink?"

"Sure!" said Ed.

"A grown up drink?" asked Daniel.

"Ha ha, oh yes."

Daniel appeared to think for a moment. "I have something special," he said.

He went into the kitchen. When he emerged, he was carrying a very old looking brown jar filled with a syrupy brown liquid in one hand, four short glasses of ice pressed together in the other. He sat down at his dining room table, where the men were chatting with Amber. He set the glasses on the table and poured everyone a drink. The two men watched as the liquid caressed the cubes of ice and sank down into the glasses. As Daniel poured the drinks, he spun a tale.

"You may not know this, but my grandfather—my father's father—was born and raised in Kentucky. We still have family there. Well, during the days of Prohibition, *his* father, my great-grandfather, took some of his surplus rye and brewed small batches of whiskey in a cellar below his house. He sold it covertly there in the community.

"Well, he had ten or so barrels that he just let sit there, let the whiskey keep aging. Around 1935, shortly after Prohibition ended, he began bottling 12-year rye. Sold it to a little distributor. Word is, it was quite famous during its time. Now as far as we know, none of those original bottles remain. What we do have, however, is a few of these jars, where he had kept some for personal or family use. This one has never been opened. To tell you the truth, this will be the first time I've allowed myself to finally enjoy some. I've been saving it for a very special occasion. Tonight, my friends, meets that criteria. We are about to try a nearly century-old, 12-year rye. I just pray it will be good," he said.

The two men gazed at Daniel with expressions of great admiration, complete loyalty. "Well, thank you," Ed said. "What an Honor." He raised his glass, and the others raised theirs. They took delicate sips of the mysterious brew. "That is truly fantastic," Ed said.

He continued: "Daniel, if you're going to have any chance, you've got to start fighting hard, and you've got to start *today*. I know a man in Treutlen County—he's in the printing business. He made the signs we just put up on our grain bins. You seen 'em? Two enormous vinyl signs, American flags, and *Gardner Granaries* in big letters below. They're awesome.

"Anyway, he does campaign signs, too. If I were you, I'd call him first thing tomorrow morning. That'll be a start." Ed handed Daniel a business card.

"Thank you," said Daniel, and he took the card.

Daniel and Amber lay in bed that evening, sleepy yet excited. Amber looked to Daniel. "I'm proud of you," she said. "That was a great move, bringing out your great-grandfather's rye. It made quite an impression. I had never heard that story, you know that? I had no idea we even had that here. When did you get it?"

Daniel's eyes grew wide. He fought against the guilty smile that was forming on his face.

"What?" Amber said.

Daniel turned and put his head in his pillow. Amber could hear his muffled laughs rising from the fabric.

"Oh God," she said.

He pulled his head up from the pillows. "That was from an old bottle of Bulleit that's been sitting in the china cabinet since we moved here. Still good whiskey, but not a 12-year, barrel-aged relic. Before I came out, I poured it into an antique jar that I found in my dad's woodshop."

"I can't believe you," she said, a smile creeping through her shocked expression. "Why on earth?"

"God knows. I felt like the moment needed some gravity, I guess. I saw the chance to cook up a good story, and I couldn't resist. You saw how impressed they were though, right?"

"They certainly were," she said, shaking her head, her smile mellowing. "Be careful, though. Just remember that every now and then, someone sees through your bullshit."

"I know, I know. That was a damn good story though, wasn't it?"

# 7

SECURE that Ed Gardner was his ally, Daniel steeled himself for his next task: approach his father.

Jacob Riley was an intelligent and creative businessman who never grew tobacco, not even during the economic bubble that existed in the early days of the Darby contracts. He had, in fact, consciously avoided growing what others grew. He understood supply and demand, and he sought out gaps in the market. He looked for opportunities that others had overlooked. He had a contrarian impulse that he had, in many ways, passed to his son.

His cash crop was sweet corn. Not the industrial feed corn that most farmers grew, not the kind meant to be ground into animal chow and fed to chickens and cows in industrial meat factories. Jacob saw no sense in expending acres and acres of farmland on a corn whose only purpose was to maintain animals who themselves required acres and acres of farmland. He was no vegetarian, but he was highly dissatisfied with the commercial meat industry to whom most growers of corn sold their product, only to see it fed to sad animals with futile lives spent in metal troughs, waiting to be mechanically separated from one another, ground up, mixed with soy, and placed into sandwiches. Instead, he grew fields full of sweet, delicious corn for human consumption. He had found a distributor that specialized in selling organic produce to high-end groceries. Over time, his operation yielded a healthy profit. He was not exorbitantly wealthy, but he was successful, and he felt good about what he was doing.

He also experimented with lesser-grown food crops. He tried blueberry bushes, red peppers, carrots, radishes, new potatoes, arugula. He found that the leaves of the arugula plant couldn't take the heat of the South Georgia summer, but carrots and new potatoes did very well, buried in the dirt, so long as there was plenty of moisture in the ground. He learned that the climate was perfect for blueberries, which he could grow at the edges of his fields, in the rocky slopes near the creek.

His latest experiment was perhaps the most unusual: he maintained seven honeybee hives. He had leased a hive from a guy in Jacksonville one year to help pollinate his blueberries, and he became fascinated by the business. Hives were actually fairly low maintenance and took up little space compared to acreage crops. He did his research and found there was growing demand for leased honeybees among growers of apples, blueberries, cucumbers, cantaloupe, squash, and watermelon. He enjoyed the challenge of doing something new, and he enjoyed driving the beehives around to different farms throughout the Southeast, learning about those businesses and meeting the many interesting people behind them. He enjoyed collecting the honey and jarring it and giving it away to his friends and neighbors.

Most everyone in the county knew of Jacob's success, and they respected him for it. Even though he had a reputation as an outlier, he was known to be generous and fair. He gave 10% to the First Presbyterian Church. He paid a good wage to his laborers. He didn't drink, he didn't curse, and he was honest in business. He was quiet and cordial. As a child, Daniel had seen the way others admired him, and he in turn admired him unqualifiedly.

Despite all this, Daniel's relationship with his father had become a difficult one. Daniel never developed an interest in farming, and though Jacob never said so, Daniel always felt this had disappointed him. Daniel knew his father viewed lawyers and politicians with contempt. He valued a man who worked with his hands and lived off the land; yet Daniel was a man who worked with his words and lived off his wits. His father had expressed no special excitement when Daniel announced his decision to go to law school. He had not protested or discouraged him, but he had been fairly neutral about it, as if it was basically what he expected, but nothing more.

There was also his father's political conservativism. He regarded Ronald Reagan, champion of the free market, as the greatest hero of American history, and William Jefferson Clinton, adulterer, as the vilest of villains. The last time the two spoke about politics was in the aftermath of the 2016 election, when Daniel had asked his father who he had voted for, and Jacob had gone silent and muttered something about the lesser of two evils. Daniel had become indignant and emotional and demanded that his father justify his decision. The 45th president was a liar and a wretch, Daniel said. His father had always insisted that his political choices were based upon his Christian morality. That had always been his objection to Bill Clinton—that he was a liar and philanderer. How could he square that with his support for Donald J. Trump? What was it that really drove his political choices? Jacob had refused to talk about it and had marched off sullenly into his corn fields.

Daniel hated to say that the incident caused him to think less of his father, but it certainly clouded his understanding of the man's principles. Things had been tense between the two of them since then. Never so tense that they stopped talking. There was nothing like hatred there. In fact, Jacob had been genuinely happy, if a little puzzled, when Daniel told him of his family's plan to return to the county. But Daniel had never been able to shake the resentment he felt, just below the surface, at what he saw as his father's part in denigrating the national culture. He could not shake the feeling that he had been lied to all this time when his father told him his political posture arose from some pure moral conviction. What *were* his father's morals, if they were consistent with those of a man like Trump's? Whatever they were, Daniel wanted no part in them, he was certain. He grieved over this—to be so separated and opposed to a man that, as a child, he had idolized.

So the task before him, the request for his father's approval of his candidacy, was one he dreaded.

On a warm Saturday morning in May, Daniel drove out to his family's farm, his purpose to ask for his father's blessing. His father had asked him to help with something, and it presented the perfect opportunity for some uninterrupted one-on-one time.

Father and son were covered from head to toe in white beekeeper suits, their faces blurred by the suits' protective mesh veil. Jacob reached inside a painted-white wooden box and slowly pulled out a rectangular frame crawling with hundreds of fat, yellow and brown, agitated insects. He held it out before him, turned it from side to side. "Plenty of brood on this one, looks like," he said. He shook it, and the bees dispersed from the frame and buzzed chaotically around him in an angry, shape-shifting cloud. "Set this one right there in the middle," he said and handed the frame to Daniel, who walked a couple of steps over to another box and lowered the frame inside. Daniel looked with satisfaction down upon the bee box, then focused his eyes onto the surface of the mesh veil before him, at the details of the bodies of the insects crawling there.

Jacob pulled a little rectangular carton, smaller than a matchbox, from his breast pocket. He brought it over and showed it to Daniel, who saw a single bee, slightly different in appearance from the others, in a little chamber beneath a strip of mesh. "This is the queen cage," Jacob said. "If all goes well, she'll create colony number eight."

Daniel watched his father gently place the cage in the new box. "Let's hope they don't reject her," Jacob said. "Now, help me lift this into the truck and we'll drive these bees to their new home."

The goal was to take the prospective colony as far away as possible from the one from which it derived, to keep the bees from trying to return. The original hive was on the southwest corner of the Riley farm, so now Jacob drove his F-150 in the direction of the farm's northeast point. They arrived at the intended spot, and Jacob cut the ignition. "Let's get our hoods back on," he said.

Daniel drew in a deep breath and said, "Daddy, before we go back out, I'd like to talk to you about something."

Jacob looked at his son for a moment, then took off the hood, which he had just placed back over his head. "Ok," he said. "What's on your mind?" Daniel saw a softness in his father's eyes that he had not expected.

"I've gotten myself into something." He paused and took a deep breath. "I haven't told you this yet, but we came back here for a reason."

"I figured you did," said his father.

Daniel smiled nervously. "I'm planning to run for County Commissioner. Against Leon Darby."

He watched his father, waited for his reaction. Jacob looked away from him, out the windshield. Daniel could see his mind working. Moments of terrible silence passed. Slowly, a small, amused smile formed on Jacob's face. "I was afraid that might be what you were up to," he said. He started to chuckle very lightly under his breath. Daniel felt his throat constricting.

His father looked him in the eyes. "Well," he said. "I sure hope you win."

Daniel's lip began to quiver. "So," he said, his voice shaky, "Do I have your blessing?"

"Of course, son. I will support you every way I can. I've known since you were a boy that you could do anything you put your mind to. I'm proud of you."

A wave of joy and anguish washed over Daniel. It caught him by surprise. He had not realized until this moment how truly frightened he had been to seek his father's approval. He realized it now, all of a sudden, and emotion overcame him. Tears poured from his eyes. He tried to speak, but he gasped for air, overcome by the sobs rising from his chest.

"Son, are you ok?"

He nodded, still unable to speak.

His father put his arm around his shoulder and pulled him close. Daniel cried into his father's shirt, as if he was a little boy. It was something he had not done in a very long time, and it felt good. They held each other like that for a little while, until Daniel finally calmed himself. "Thank you," he said.

"You're welcome, son. Now let's find a good home for these bees."

The next day was Sunday. Daniel dressed in his nicest, most conservative navy suit and a striped black and forest-green tie. He smiled and shook hands with the men who gathered each Sunday morning in the kitchen of the First Presbyterian Church to drink coffee and eat cheese Danish. Unlike Ed's Episcopalians, who celebrated the arrival of Spring with boisterous political conversation and bourbon-spiked lemonade, the Presbyterians were more traditional in their religious gatherings. They were a quiet, reserved set, who observed temperance and avoided vulgar language. Their principal social gatherings were fellowship services held on Sunday and Wednesday evenings, which revolved around song and worship and were often followed by a wonderful potluck meal.

It was not often that Daniel came to church at all, much less this early, well before Sunday School. The men were surprised but pleased to see him. It struck some of the older men as funny to see Daniel in a suit and tie, drinking coffee. They remembered him as a rascally, precocious little boy, running around the churchyard and cutting up during the sermon.

As the men took their seats for Sunday School, Jacob Riley cleared his throat and stated that he'd like to make an announcement. The room grew quiet. The men looked to Jacob. Daniel watched his father anxiously.

"Well," he began, "I believe all of you here know my son, Daniel. He left us for a little while to get his law degree and start his family, but now he's come back home, and we couldn't be happier. Many of you probably remember when Daniel was a little boy. You probably remember that time he fell out of the dogwood tree over beside the fellowship hall, and the ambulance had to come and pick him up."

The men laughed. Daniel did, too, and bowed his head in embarrassment.

Jacob smiled, then swallowed hard. "Well," he said. "Daniel has decided that he'd like to throw his hat in the ring for County Commissioner. He'll be on the ballot in November. I hope you'll give him a chance and that you might consider voting for him."

You could have sucked the air out of the room. For a few moments, there was complete stillness. The surprise, the sense of uncertainty, was palpable.

Jacob began to sit down and then, as if he forgot something, he stood back up. "I'll be voting for him," he said and laughed ever so slightly.

This touch of humor broke the tension in the room, and the men chuckled. Several nodded in smiling approval. One man clapped his hands a couple of times, then remembered that you're not supposed to clap at church so crossed his arms and gave big, vigorous nods. A few men nodded in simple comprehension, faces without expression. One man frowned and folded his arms. The group looked to Daniel, expecting him to say something. Daniel saw this and stood.

He seemed apprehensive, almost shy, certainly humble. He stood and said, "Thank you, Dad. Thank y'all for hearing us out. I don't want to disrupt Sunday School, so I won't give a speech. But I sure would be appreciative if you'd come up and talk to me after church. I love this county and I want to help. I'm so glad to be home. So I hope you'll consider voting for me." He spoke quietly and with a measured humility that he knew would be necessary to have a chance with the conservative, religious men before him.

His mother made the same announcement in the ladies' Sunday School class while Amber looked around the room and smiled. Amber gave soft handshakes and hugs at the end of the lesson and said "oh, we appreciate y'all so much." Of course, she was acting a bit. The role of supportive church wife did not come especially natural to her. But more and more, she was coming to accept that, if she was to find a place for herself and her family here, there were certain cultural traditions, a certain etiquette, that she would need to display at times, depending on the audience. It required very little learning on her part—after all, she had been raised here and was familiar with the rhythms and manners of the place. But it did require some theatre. She didn't especially enjoy this role, but she was willing to fake it now and then for the sake of her family's social standing and, relatedly, this election.

Besides, she had come to realize, as she observed the mannerisms of other local women her age, like the ones from Ed's picnic, that everyone was faking it a little bit. She saw the way they switched to soft, submissive tones, the way they repeated *sir* and *ma'am* and nearly curtsied when they spoke to Representative Gardner and his wife and the other pillars of the county, the way they switched back to their natural, worldly tone when speaking amongst their peers. The Southern belle vibe was useful, and employed strategically, especially when interacting with older people, people whose influence was rare and valuable, and it could be cast off when it wasn't needed.

Amber had made the decision to invest herself in this county, and she was willing to put on this mask occasionally if it helped her family to cement their place here, if it helped to avoid a defeat like the one they had experienced in Rosewood.

By Sunday evening, most everyone in the county had heard the enticing, almost scandalous news that young Daniel Riley would challenge Leon Darby for the office of County Commissioner. The news struck most people as somewhat unbelievable, somewhat incredulous. Many liked the *idea* of challenging Commissioner Darby. He was, after all, a greedy, awful man who held their livelihoods under his thumb. But the man was powerful, economically and politically, and it struck many as foolhardy to believe that this young man, who had not lived here for many years, could beat him. Even among those who understood Darby's vulnerability and supported the idea of opposing him, there was deep skepticism over whether Daniel Riley was the man to do it.

# 8

IN THE SUMMER that followed, Daniel spent each morning before the workday began traveling to the home of anyone who would agree to meet with him. It was a small constituency at first, mostly his family's friends and their fellow Presbyterians, along with Ed's Episcopalians and others to whom the representative introduced him. He shook hands, talked just a little bit about his family's farm business and his law practice, then asked the same question each time: *what's on y'all's minds?* It was a brilliantly vague question that took the focus off of him and invited his potential constituents to share anything they were thinking about, personal or political. Ed had told him to do this, and it had been great advice. He listened more than he talked, and he learned what people cared about. This helped him to become more and more fluent in local affairs as the days went by, and it strengthened his ability to speak competently on the issues that mattered to people. When the issue of marijuana came up, he had a default response, which he stuck to religiously: "I just want us to have the same opportunities as our neighbors." That was what Ed had told him to say, and it worked. He took no stance on any moral question surrounding the issue. He just didn't want his county to be deprived of something all the other counties had, and this satisfied most everybody.

He also drafted a press release announcing his candidacy, and sent it to outlets that covered South Georgia politics. This had been Michael's idea. Daniel could tell Michael enjoyed the press, appreciated the attention it brought to the firm. In the release, Daniel was described as "a partner in the law firm of Drummond & Riley," which was just fine. He did a couple of interviews with local papers, including the *Macon Telegraph*, the *Tifton Gazette*, and the *Valdosta Daily Times*. He even spoke to a couple of bloggers who specialized in Georgia politics. The cannabis law was the big story—Goshen being the one county where the commission had already vowed the block the crop—and Daniel always gave the same statement to the papers that he'd given his constituents. In this way, interest in the election spread. To many, it was a bellwether contest, a microcosm of the demographic and political changes encroaching upon the state.

Now, as summer came to an end, and fall—the true election season—approached, there was a sense that something significant was going on here. There was excitement in the air. This bone-headed idea, hatched just over one year ago, was starting to look not so bone-headed after all. It was starting to seem that the Rileys were doing something significant, something important.

Despite all his home visits and shaking of hands, and despite the attention from outside the county, Daniel had done very few public events. Ed had hosted a few "meet and greets" at his home, attended mostly by his fellow Episcopalians, and the elder Rileys had invited friends and fellow Presbyterians to their home, where Daniel and Amber had the opportunity to smile and show themselves off in a comfortable environment. These had been important to building a core of support, but the campaign lacked a watershed moment, an event to turn the buzz into something tangible, something real, something that the citizenry at large could become a part of.

The Agriculture Fair, held each year in September at the Jessup Loose Floor, presented perhaps the greatest opportunity for such a moment. Jeff had invited Daniel to speak, and of course he had accepted. Word of the address had spread, and, it was rumored, this would be the most packed Ag Fair in years.

\* \* \*

Amber walked beside Daniel through the wide, expansive opening of the Jessup Loose Floor. The Loose Floor was a significant warehouse owned by Jeff Jessup and his family. The Jessups stored their own tobacco here and leased space to others in the community for storage of post-harvest produce or anything else that needed a dry place to sit for a little while. Amber scanned the expanse of smooth grey floor. She gazed up at the wooden beams beneath the aluminum ceiling, at the fluorescent light fixtures hanging there, giving the place a light, pleasant illumination. She smelled the smell of fresh tobacco, the undercurrent of gasoline and motor oil; it was a familiar, homey smell, and it pinched her heart with nostalgia. She saw the rows of booths set up by various seed companies, equipment manufacturers, pesticide dealers. She saw people milling about the vast space, inspecting the wares, occasionally gathering in clusters to chat.

She squeezed Daniel's hand. There was sweat on his palm. He looked at her, and she could see fear but determination in his eyes.

She slackened her grip with relief when Jeff Jessup approached them. He smiled a broad smile that caused the eyes upon his small face to squint almost to closure. He reached out his hand and shook Daniel's, then Amber's. "Thank y'all so much for coming," he said, quietly. "Y'all want to come into the office?"

The couple followed Jeff to the right and through a small vinyl door. They went inside to a brightly-lit alcove, where many others were gathered around the edges drinking iced tea or cider and chatting. There was Ed and Velma. There were many of the Episcopalians from Ed's picnic.

Donna Pinkerton and Jessica Coker and their families were there. Amber was glad to see them. Jessica had a couple of little boys around Jonathan's age, and Amber had made the effort over the summer to get the kids together to play, and the kids had taken to one another. Amber liked Jessica. It turned out that her bad reputation in high school had arisen entirely from what was, in retrospect, a perfectly healthy, if somewhat above-average, sexual appetite and, more to the point, her decision not to suppress it. It was something that struck many of her classmates, and several indiscrete adults in the know, as scandalous and nasty. But if she had been scarred by any of this, it didn't show. She was confident and attractive and continued to wear her sexuality on her sleeve, letting her voluptuous, womanly shape show through behind well-fitting dresses or tight blue jeans. She was loyal to her husband, who was attractive himself, a sort of modern country-singer look, always with a baseball cap and a well-trimmed beard, and he seemed to appreciate her for who she was.

Donna had daughters who were a little older than Jonathan and weren't especially interested in playing with him, but she came attached to Jessica, and Amber had developed a friendship with her as well. Donna was very much into guns, something she had inherited from her father, the regional dentist and a wealthy man who went on jaunts out west and overseas to hunt exotic game. It was a happy day indeed when Donna invited her and Daniel to go skeet shooting with her and Jessica and her husband, and the five of them had ridden out to a piece of her family property and drank beer and shot box after box of clay pigeons. They'd laughed and shared embarrassing stories from high school, traded gossip on the terrible fates that had become some of their classmates. Donna was divorced and, Amber thought, a little sweet on Daniel, a suspicion she shared with him despite the obvious, unneeded boost it gave to his ego. It was harmless, and she found it flattering, in a transitive sort of way.

If she regretted anything about these new friendships, it was that they seemed to come at the expense of her original one, with Jackie. She had actually asked Donna if she could invite the Drummonds along shooting, and Donna had of course said yes, but Jackie had declined the invitation. She didn't like guns, not at all, she had said, which was understandable. But there was more to it than that, Amber felt sure. Back at the Gardner picnic, she could tell that Jackie never grew comfortable with this group. Everyone was cordial to her, if not curious, asking her loads of questions about her family, where she was from, how she and Michael had met. At first, it struck Amber as typical conversation. But in retrospect, maybe the questioning was more probing, more invasive, than she had appreciated. Maybe it had been tinged with suspicion, something that Amber did not at first detect or appreciate. Maybe they were implying that she was somehow out of place, that her presence required some explanation. Whether they meant that or not, maybe that's what Jackie heard, and who was Amber to argue.

She and Jackie still spent time together, and Amber felt sure that Jackie's affection for her had not diminished, but she also felt that they were growing apart as she invested herself more deeply in these new relationships. She sighed and, as it always did when she thought about this, guilt rose in her chest.

Still, she was glad to be here, the center of attention among a group that she liked and respected and felt comfortable around. She was finally beginning to feel like she belonged somewhere. At the same time, under the surface, she felt great anxiety. Today would be Daniel's first major address. When he ran for office in Rosewood, his first big speech had also been his downfall. It had been the beginning of the end of the life she had built there. Surely he had learned from that. Surely he wouldn't repeat his mistake. But she wouldn't know for sure until he opened his mouth and started speaking.

Donna approached the couple. She gave Amber a big hug, looked to Daniel and said, "You got your speech ready?"

Daniel gave her a puzzled, surprised expression. "What speech?" he said.

"You crazy thing. Here, let me fix your tie." She leaned in close, pulled the collar down around the edges of the tie on his neck, tightened the knot a little in the front. "You'll do just fine," she said. "Just picture the audience naked—isn't that what they say?" She looked at Amber and winked and walked back toward the edge of the room, joining her family.

Amber turned her head in Daniel's direction, looked back toward the door, feigning an interest in something going on behind him. "She's flirty," she said, quietly into his ear, a smile in her voice.

A little while later, Amber and Daniel, in a group with Donna and Jessica and her husband, left the office and moved back onto the main warehouse floor. Amber had been chatting lightly with her friends when the sight of the substantial crowd forming around the raised platform near the entrance caused her to grow silent. It was a lot of people. She gulped, looked at Daniel. She looked back out and, near the edge of the crowd, she saw Michael and Jackie. She met eyes with Jackie, gave a timid smile, and waved, and Jackie returned the same expression and waved back. Amber turned to her friends. "Y'all, there's Jackie Drummond, I'm going to go over and say hey." She broke away and worked through the crowd and met Jackie and gave her a deep hug.

Daniel's heart pounded as he stepped onto a flimsy wooden crate, and from there onto the raised platform. Jeff had just finished introducing him to the substantial crowd that was gathered there.

Daniel shook Jeff's hand and mouthed "thank you" in an exaggerated fashion, so that the audience could see what he was saying. He smiled broadly, making a big display of how happy, confident and carefree he was, though in fact he was filled with terror. He walked to the center of the riser, took the microphone that was still mounted there in the metal stand. A burst of feedback emitted from the speakers behind him, and he lurched backward. He looked down at the microphone, said "testing," and smiled nervously. He looked out at the people standing before him. The crowd looked even larger from this vantage point, and everyone was watching him intently. He scanned the crowd. He saw Amber near the back. She was giving him an encouraging, confident face. He saw his mother and father, more toward the front. There were Michael and Jackie. Michael gave him a subtle thumbs-up. He saw many other faces, some familiar, some not. He took a deep breath and began to speak.

"Good afternoon. My name is Daniel Riley, and as you might have heard, I'm running for County Commissioner. Thank you all so much for coming here, and for being willing to listen to what I have to say. I really don't deserve your attention, I realize that. I spent my childhood here, learned everything I know from this county, but I haven't been here in a while. I've been gone—seeing the world, as they say—and I've only recently come back home. So some of y'all might think that I don't have much business running for office, and I can understand that. I'd only ask that you give me a chance. Get to know me. See what I have to say. See if we have the same perspective. And keep an open mind.

"When I was a boy, one of my favorite things to do was go out to lunch at the Humble Pie restaurant after church on Sundays. I grew up on the fried chicken there. To tell you the truth, whenever I sit in church nowadays, no matter where I am, when it gets close to the end of the service—say, 11:45 or so—I start to taste that chicken."

A wave of light laughter came from the crowd.

"It was the one thing I looked most forward to all week. And every Sunday, after lunch, my daddy would let me play outside on the square with the other kids. And we'd gravitate toward that boll weevil statue there in the middle of the square. We'd climb onto it; we'd walk around the little marble ledge there near the ground. We'd jump up and try to reach the bug there at the top.

"I never understood what that structure was all about until I grew a little older, and I asked my father, I said, 'Daddy, why *is* there that statue of a funny little bug?' And he told me the story, and it's something that has stuck with me ever since. I know y'all know the story, but it's one worth retelling, because it forms the fabric of who we are here in Goshen County.

"For a very long time, this county's economy depended on cotton. So, the boll weevil was a frightening thing. It was a terrible, destructive cotton pest that ruined harvests wherever it went. The USDA tried desperately to stop the migration of the bug, and everyone hoped that it might be eradicated before it made it to Georgia. But those efforts failed, and by around 1918, the boll weevil had made its way all the way up from Central America, through Texas, across Arkansas, Mississippi, Alabama, to South Georgia, and right here to Goshen County. And sure enough, our cotton harvests were ruined, for several years in a row. People went broke, and they went hungry. Our farmers believed they had met their doom. Our way of life, our very existence, was threatened.

"Out of sheer desperation, a number of farmers switched to an experimental new crop." He paused for effect. "Peanuts. Now, maybe it was fate, maybe it was coincidence, maybe it was Booker T. Washington, but around that same time, demand for peanut products began to boom. Peanut butter, peanut oil, salted peanuts, all became huge economic commodities. This county's soil, its climate, its farming infrastructure, turned out to be perfect for the new crop. Farmers began once again to see healthy profits— much greater, in fact, than what they had with cotton. Not only did we survive, but by trying something different, we thrived.

"The boll weevil was great opportunity disguised as great disaster. And that's why, in 1928, the county erected that monument to the little creature that had destroyed everything in its path, only to create space for something new, something better, in its place."

He paused again. He looked out into the audience. He met the eyes of the people he knew.

"I think a lot about that story," he said. "I think about how it applies today. As you know, there are new opportunities on the horizon. There is some fear about those new opportunities. They're different. They go against some of what we've been told in the past about what's wrong and right. But I believe, and I hope you believe, that our prosperity as a county is likely to turn on our ability to grasp those new opportunities. What seems scary now might turn out to be a great boon for us.

"It's an exciting time for farmers. Change can be scary, but I believe these new opportunities will be good for us. And my commitment to you is very simple: I will not stand in your way. To the contrary, as County Commissioner, I will do everything in my power to ensure that our farmers, our businesspeople, our community as a whole, are in a position to take full advantage of whatever opportunities arise. Moreover, I promise to spend my time listening, and not talking. I promise to represent your desires, your interests, and not to impose my own desires upon you. If you'll give me a chance, I think you'll find that I'm a good fit for this job, and I sure look forward to the chance to earn it. Thank you."

When he had imagined giving this speech, he envisioned applause rising up at this final word. Instead, there was now silence. He gathered the microphone cord and stepped toward the metal stand. The speakers thumped and thudded in the silence as he worked the mic into the holster at the top of the stand. He could feel his face grow flush; he hoped he would not faint. He heard a single, faint clapping arise from somewhere in the crowd. Another soon joined in. He looked out into the audience. Slowly, like a gathering storm, others joined. The applause began from the right side of the crowd, then gradually spread to the left, until the sound filled the entire space. He heard a single *whoo!* rise up. A whistle. He looked out at the group. Most everyone was clapping now, some with great enthusiasm. He detected huge, appreciative smiles on the faces of a few. He smiled a genuine grin and looked out into the audience. He waved his arm. "Thank you!" he said.

# 9

IT RAINED the night of Daniel's speech, and it was still drizzling the next morning. The long, light rain had turned the dirt trails that wound through the woods and across the pastures into a firm sort of clay. The clay was perfect to be gripped by the tread of a four-wheeler tire. Amber rose early, strapped on her helmet, and rode out to a particularly muddy spot she knew, a place out on the edge of their neighborhood where the developer had cleared away the trees for more houses but had never built them. She came out here a lot to open up the throttle and feel the mud splashing all around her and spin doughnuts. Sometimes she brought a shovel to dig up earth and pack it into ramps and slopes.

Now, she eyed a slope of red clay, once a pile of roots and fill dirt, that she had been shaping into a ramp over the months. She squeezed the clutch with her left hand and stomped the gear-shifter down with her foot. The low rumble of the engine rose suddenly to a high-pitched, angry growl. She planted her boots on the foot-platforms and stood, knees bent, leaning toward the incline. She pushed the throttle with her thumb, and the machine careened forward. In only a moment, the front, then the back wheels gripped the incline. She straightened her knees and pulled back on the handlebars, a carefully measured amount of force, enough to keep the front end of the vehicle up, not so hard as to flip it backward.

The wheels lifted off the earth, and the precious moment of weightlessness was achieved. She inhaled deeply, lessened the pressure on the throttle, relished the thrill of the jump. In moments like these, brief as they were, the confusion of life occasionally came into clarity.

More and more, the separateness of her relationship with Jackie and her relationship with her new friends bothered her. In her first weeks and months here, Jackie had been the anchor that kept her from drifting into loneliness. Jackie had always been happy to do mundane things with her, like go to the Wal-Mart or the Ingles Supermarket to buy groceries, to jog around the track at the high school, to sit around and listen to rap music, to drink cheap pink wine and eat popcorn and watch reality television and occasionally smoke weed. Jackie had saved her from isolation, and Amber had done the same for Jackie. But now, Amber was finding shelter elsewhere, in a place that didn't feel safe or inviting to her friend. She was putting distance between herself and her friend, and she did not want to be, and she couldn't decide what to do about it.

As she rose into the air, the September rain in her face, the weight of the machine beneath her, the ecstasy of the jump in her heart, it occurred to her that it was her lack of power that prevented her from resolving the dilemma. Her place in this society remained tentative. She was new, frankly, and each interaction was a sort of audition. She could ill afford to say something controversial, or turn down an invitation, or give someone a cross gesture. In hindsight, back at the Gardner picnic, she knew that Donna Pinkerton's many probing questions to Jackie had been mildly rude, yet she had smiled and played along as if nothing unusual was happening. When Jackie had declined the invitation to come shooting, Amber could have insisted and made a special effort to ensure she felt included and respected. But she hadn't done that, unwilling to expend social capital for Jackie, because she wanted to appear unqualifiedly agreeable and fun to her new companions. She had been wary of making even the smallest of waves, wary of disturbing the delicate structure that she was trying to build.

She was annoyed and ashamed at her lack of courage.

If they won this election, it occurred to her, she wouldn't have to decide between friends. She wouldn't have to defer to others. She would have capital. People would want and need to be her friend, and not the other way around. They would be working to gain her favor. And when she was at the top, she'd keep Jackie right there by her side, and, she felt sure, anyone who wanted to be in her good graces would take special caution not to be rude or condescending to her friend.

If she was to have any role in undoing the prejudice and division that made her friend feel bad, if she was to fit in here while keeping a clean conscience, if she was to no longer feel compelled to follow others, they had to win.

She crouched back down again, prepared her knees to absorb the encroaching impact with the ground. The vehicle landed, back wheels first, then front, its shocks helping her knees to lessen the jar. She accelerated a few yards forward, then twisted the handlebars right, squeezed the brake, shifted her body so that the vehicle spun as it decelerated. It came to a stop, now facing the back of the ramp, maroon dust rising around her. She turned the key, silenced the engine. She took off her helmet, held it under her arm, shook out her hair. She stood on the foot platforms, straddled the worn, duct-tape covered seat, looked back at her conquest. "Damn," she said. "That was higher than I remembered."

She looked at her helmet. There was a particular splatter-drop of mud there that moved her. It was the most beautiful, perfect shape she had ever seen. The rare, fleeting, inexplicable sensation of artistic inspiration struck her. She took out her phone, placed the helmet on the seat, angled it so that the morning light caught it fully, and took several photos of it. Satisfied that she had captured it, she put the helmet back on her head, climbed on the four-wheeler, pushed the ignition switch, and blasted off back toward home.

Back in her studio, she studied the photograph. What could she do with this? She thought about the campaign signs they had reviewed. They had been so generic, so plain and uninspired. This shape, formed by the random, natural forces of the rain and earth and her own movement among them, the shape of letting go and letting happen, said something, she thought. Maybe they could use this instead.

The thickest strand of outsplash extended from the top right-hand side of the central dot, a narrow arm topped by a dramatic curling crescent like a solar flare. Almost exactly opposite this strand, a perfect triangle jutted out from the bottom left of the shape, a muted counterpoint to the flourish of the top strand. Many more little shapes emanated along the perimeter, each one in pleasing proportion to the central object. A few hair-thin strands, barely perceptible, extended out now and then, each one as delicate as it was mysterious. Breathtaking.

She plugged her phone to her computer, imported the images, loaded them into her design software. She scrolled along the images, picked the one that best captured her initial impression of the shape.

She used the software's *vectorize* tool to convert the image to a digitally malleable shape.

She chose a blue background that was almost white.

Now, the text overlay. She checked the notebook paper where Daniel had scrawled the chosen slogan. She typed it upon the top layer. She experimented with many different fonts until, in a single click, she found it. Something called *Centurica*. Classic, but a little unusual. She made little adjustments to the size and placement of the text, then took several steps back and examined her work.

She took a single, long step back to her computer. She adjusted the color of the text very slightly, bringing in a tiny fraction of purple for richness. *Flatten*, she clicked, then left the room without another thought.

"No, this is it," Daniel said.

"This is the sign? I don't even know if the printer can make these!" said Michael.

"Well, we're going to have to find someone who will."

"This looks weird, man!"

"It's a little unusual, that's for sure. But I think it looks cool. I think it'll make an impression."

"Maybe the wrong impression! The impression that you're cuckoo!"

"It's a bold statement. We need a bold statement."

"Do we? I think we need to communicate reason and sobriety, not wacky and psychedelic."

"It's not psychedelic. It's just. . . impactful!"

"Dude, please. Take this back to her. Ask her to make something more mainline. Or I can just get the sign guy to put together a traditional design, something basic."

Daniel looked at his friend with a sternness in his eyes. "No. This is the sign. She's passionate about it. Whether we win or lose this election, she is going to be with me. She's given and given and given to make all this happen. I'm not going to take this from her."

Michael looked at his friend, looked down at the image again, closed his eyes, took a deep breath, released a deep sigh. "Alright," he said. "Alright. These are going to be expensive as hell to print, though."

Daniel marched through the gravel toward Ed's office-trailer, holding a heavy cardboard tube across his body at an angle like a bazooka.

"Come on in, boy, let's see what you got."

He helped Ed push some chairs to the edges of the space, then set the tube on the ground. Ed squatted down and held one end of the tube while Daniel strained to slide the thick, rolled up sheet of vinyl out of the other end. Formaldehyde fumes rose off the fresh vinyl, the noxious though strangely pleasant smell of new plastic. Daniel unrolled the sheet across the floor, then stood back, watching Ed inspect it. It took some time before he said anything. He tilted his head, squinted his eyes.

"Well. . . it certainly is. . . unusual! Are those letters purple?"

Daniel gave a nervous chuckle. "Yeah, I think they turned out a little more purple than she had intended."

"Mm hmm," he said. He looked at Daniel curiously, then back down at the sign for a while. "It's different," he said. "But there is something. . . appealing about it, ain't there?" He shrugged his shoulders.

"I thought so!"

Tyler rapped at the door to Darby's office, then let himself in. Darby was sitting at his desk, a steaming cup of coffee before him, the *Macon Telegraph* obscuring his face.

"Good morning Tyler!" said Darby from behind the paper. He appeared to be in a good mood.

"Good morning," said Tyler.

Darby lowered the paper, looked at Tyler. "You look displeased," he said. "What's the matter with you?"

"Have you driven by Ed Gardner's grain bins this morning?" asked Tyler.

"I haven't. Why?"

"Why don't you just come and see for yourself."

"Is something wrong?" Darby seemed excited by the prospect that something bad might have happened to Ed Gardner, who he did not particularly like.

"You just need to come and see."

Tyler was silent as he drove the Commissioner down the Beeline, then the county road toward Gardner's bins.

"You're starting to worry me," Darby said. "What is it?"

"You'll see."

After a little while, Ed Gardner's two towering aluminum bins came into focus on the horizon. The structures truly were majestic. These bins were reserved for the largest of producers; they were the only two in Goshen or any surrounding county that could accommodate an industrial-level output of feed corn. As the Regal moved closer, the men could discern against the grey surface of the bins a large, light blue rectangle, the same size and directly below the enormous American flags, with what looked like an enormous bug splatter in the middle. There was some text there, but Darby could not immediately make out the words. As they moved closer, and the text became clearer and clearer, Darby began to fidget in his seat. His breaths grew loud. Ed Gardner's glorious grain bins announced, to all of Goshen County, in huge purple letters:

ELECT DANIEL RILEY
COUNTY COMMISSIONER
FOR PROSPERITY

Had Darby been a man with any self-control, any sense of diplomacy, he would have taken a deep breath, returned to his office, and began forming his plans to counter this young challenger. But Darby was not such a man. He was impudent and impulsive. After decades of supremacy, he had become reduced to a child used to getting what he wanted, with no frame of reference for how to respond appropriately if something did not go his way. He was unable to accept or understand a world in which anyone would challenge his hold on power.

He commanded Tyler to drive up to the front office of Gardner's Granaries. He was almost hyperventilating. He was twitching and grabbing at the door handle, as if he was ready to jump out of the car that very moment as it coasted along the county road.

"I don't recommend you confront Ed Gardner at this time," Tyler said.

"Dammit, I said go!" screamed Darby.

Tyler complied. *I'm definitely going to bill for this*, he thought.

Ed heard the gravel crackling outside his office-trailer. He looked out the window, and a mixture of fear and glee came over him as he made out Tyler's Buick, with Darby's angry face in the passenger-side window. Ed stepped out the front door onto his deck and stood with his hands on his hips, watching the car settle into the driveway. A late- September breeze blew across his face, and he thought how nice it felt. He was truly amused at the thought that he had upset Leon Darby, but he also hoped he was not about to be shot and killed.

Darby, disheveled and agitated, struggled to extrude himself from the vehicle. He opened the door violently and began to exit, but had forgotten to remove his seat belt. The belt pulled him back into his seat, and he flopped pathetically. He unhooked the belt. He grabbed the door handle to pull himself out, but instead pulled the door back on him again and fell once again into his seat. Tyler, stone faced, watched his bumbling client struggle. Ed did his best to maintain a somber and concerned face, even as he grinned in his belly.

Once Darby had made it out of the car, he was so agitated he couldn't think straight. He looked as if he was on the brink of a heart attack.

"Are you out of your goddamn mind!" he shouted up at Ed. "What in the hell do you think you're doing! You look like a fool with that goddamn sign hanging there! Who the hell made that anyway, it looks ridiculous! Is that tie-dye? I'll put you out of business, you son of a bitch!" He stumbled toward the steps that led to the front deck of the trailer. Tyler hung back next to the Buick.

Ed watched the bellowing madman cautiously as Darby stepped onto the first of four creaky wooden steps. Ed moved his large body forward, blocked Darby's way. "I'm going to remind you, Commissioner—you're on my property. I suggest you calm down before you come any closer."

Darby peered his sweaty red face up at Ed's, disbelieving. "The goddamned *audacity!*" he said.

Darby was in no position to push further. What could he do, really? He was old and weak. A tussle might cripple him entirely, not to mention cause a tremendous scandal. Darby gradually caught his breath and backed away, his jaw clenched. As he staggered down the steps, he glared into Ed's eyes with warning. He turned and walked back toward the car.

Jeff Jessup displayed a huge sign on each of his cattle barns, which were visible from the Dixie Beeline. While not as significant as Ed's bins, Jessup's big barns were prominent, and the presence of the signs there made an impact. News of the signs, with their unusual but somehow compelling design, on the properties of two respected, long-time residents, reverberated throughout the community. The phones at Drummond & Riley, and at the Riley home, rang through the remaining week and into the weekend. A handful more farm-owners offered their support. The campaign had ordered a few hundred smaller, corrugated plastic signs that could be displayed in one's yard on metal stakes, and by the end of the week, thirty households had taken one. Five farmers had brought checks for one hundred dollars each to Daniel's law office.

For nearly two full weeks after the signs went up, Daniel's efforts seemed to go totally unanswered by Darby. For a brief moment, Daniel allowed himself to believe that Darby was giving up, that he wouldn't fight back. Had it not been for Michael, Daniel might have allowed himself to sink into this complacency. Michael, for his part, viewed Darby's silence with great apprehension. Some calculation was being made, some plan being developed, he knew. The Riley campaign was sitting in the center of a storm's eye, the winds spinning violently around them, the storm preparing to set in.

# 10

DARBY's long hold on power, his economic might, his many years at the helm of the county, afforded him certain advantages that Daniel had not fully appreciated. Over many years, Commissioner Darby had developed a network of business associates, friends, acquaintances, and fellow Baptists who were unbudgingly loyal to him. Most knew that Darby was a snake, but he was a snake they knew, and he was a snake in whom they were personally invested. People liked knowing the County Commissioner, they liked being in his good graces. They liked the feeling of importance they got when he shook their hands and said their names. In many cases, their businesses depended on him—they sold him chemicals, or fertilizer, or trucks, or parts to repair irrigation rigs or tractors or sorting machines or assembly belts or roofs or any of the other thousand things that were a part of his operation. In many other cases, their paychecks depended on him—they were his farm laborers, his drivers, his bean-counters, his middle management, his machinists.

So, while Daniel was shaking hands and delivering yard signs, Darby was making a quiet effort—with phone calls, personal visits, conversations in the church narthex—to gently remind these people who he was and how nice it was to be friends with the boss. In this way, Darby was able to generate more support than a hundred glossy campaign signs.

In the Thursday, September 22, edition of the *Telegraph*, whose pages were read closely throughout the area, Darby took out a full page advertisement, which appeared on page three, visible right as you turned past the front page:

Leon Darby has been proud to serve Goshen County for the past 15 years. Leon and Linda Darby would like to thank their friends, families, and neighbors who have supported them over the years. They are pleased to announce their first list of endorsements for re-election to the office of County Commissioner.

What followed was a daunting, almost jaw-dropping list. There were over one-hundred names, and they included the owners of most of the medium and large-sized farms in the county, people who had lived here for generations. The list included the county's only pediatrician, two well-known and well-loved pastors, every attorney save Michael and Daniel, and four out of five members of the school board. The list included people who had invited Daniel into their homes, had shook his hand and smiled as he spoke, and whose support he believed he had earned. The list's placement in a forum so public as the *Telegraph*—the primary source of news for most of Goshen County, *especially* its older residents, the ones who voted—made it all the more intimidating. By publishing the list, Darby was speaking to every person who had wondered whether the Commissioner's day might finally have come. He was saying, my time has *not* come. He was saying: all of *these* fine folks are still *for* me, now who shall be against me?

For those whose approach to politics was to see which way the wind was blowing, and then to move in that direction, the list would be a powerful motivator. It showed that Darby was supported by the county's most prominent citizens, that this Riley kid was a nobody, that the show was finished, let's get this election over with and get on with our lives. The list was a reminder of the power of incumbency, of the powerful resistance that always meets change in a rural community like this one.

The morning of the list's publication was a difficult one in the Riley home. As Daniel sat reading the paper, he held a spoonful of Cheerios and milk suspended in the air before him, its movement toward his mouth thwarted by his concentration on the list. As he read through the names, drops of milk fell down onto the newsprint, absorbing into the paper, blurring the words. A nauseous feeling churned in his stomach. He had bitten off more than he could chew, he realized, and now he was choking on it. He had been tilting at windmills, stupidly driven by his own delusions of grandeur, trying to defeat an incumbent leader without the credibility or the stature to do so, and now, he felt, he was finally being hit with the reality of his mistake.

Amber watched Daniel, observed his slumped shoulders and his sullen face. She felt that her fears were being realized. His ambition had outpaced his ability. She put her own spoon down into her cereal bowl and rose from the table. She walked to the sink and stared out the kitchen window, looked out toward the road, thought how nice it would be if she could just get in the car and drive away and not come back.

As Michael read through Darby's list, he imagined, with great accuracy, the turmoil that must be brewing in the Riley home. He called Daniel, suggested they skip the office that morning and meet at Daniel's house. He kissed Jackie goodbye on her way to drop Zoe off at daycare and head into work, then got dressed and headed west down the Beeline.

Michael knocked on the door, and Amber answered. She stepped in for a lingering hug then led him inside and to the back porch where Daniel was sitting at the table poring over the list.

"Do we have any chance?" Daniel wondered aloud, speaking to no one in particular.

Michael had come over this morning in a strategic, professional mood. While Michael once looked at Daniel's campaign with skepticism, even indifference, he had grown to care about it very much. He cared about it because he cared for Daniel, but also because of the stakes it held for his own dreams. A victory for Daniel could provide a huge, unanticipated windfall. It would almost certainly mean Michael becoming County Attorney, the most coveted, lucrative position available for a country lawyer. On the other hand, failure could spell disaster. The name "Riley" was now posted at the front door above his law office, and a loss, especially by a large margin, might stain his reputation forever. It could dash any hope Michael had for expanding his practice beyond his current clientele. No prominent businessman, no wealthy person, no one who valued his social capital, would bring important work to the law firm of the young gadfly who had insulted and distressed the county leader, much less his negro partner.

It was with this in mind that Michael had kept a keen ear to the ground as the campaign progressed. He had listened to people's talk. He had requested polling data from previous races. He had retrieved voter registration information from the Secretary of State. He had pulled census information. He knew things.

"You need to calm down about that list," he said. "You should've written off every name on there to begin with. Those are Darby's people. You should never have expected any of them to support you in the first place."

Daniel said, "Really? A lot of these folks are businesspeople. People in the farming community. That's the support we've been relying on—those who have something to gain from legalization. Without them, where are we?"

"Sure, but. . . Relationships have everything to do with business. We don't exist inside some dry equation where you plug in the numbers and the most efficient solution comes out. People like to deal with someone they *know*. Compared to Darby, you're still an unknown commodity. For all these people know, you might just up and leave if things don't go your way. You *say* you'll be good for business, but why should anyone believe that? Why should they pull up stakes from something that's been steady and reliable over time for an untested element like you? Sure, there are people who have been burned by Darby. But there are still many who benefit from him."

Michael paused and watched Daniel, to see if his words were sinking in. He hoped he wasn't being too harsh, and he looked for signs that he was losing his friend's confidence.

"Then what am I doing here?" Daniel said, to himself as much as to anyone else.

Michael looked over at Amber, who was looking out into the yard at a flittering bird, possibly trying to distract herself. He reached into his back pocket and pulled out some papers, which he unfolded onto the table before him. "I've been doing a little research," he said. "This," he said, "is a list of farmers and farm businesspeople who *aren't* on Darby's list. I got this from the voter rolls, so I know these folks vote. Now, keep in mind, a lot of these people will still probably go along with Darby anyway, especially if they think there's no chance of you defeating him. But even if we cut my list in half, that leaves us with a good number of farm people who Darby either did not ask—or could not get to agree—to publicly support him. You need to take *this* list and focus on *these* names in your outreach over the weeks ahead."

Daniel looked down at the list. He scanned it and nodded. "Lot of familiar names here," he said.

"But that's not the most important thing I want to tell you about," Michael went on. "Notice anything significant about Darby's list?"

Daniel studied the newspaper for another moment. He shrugged his shoulders.

"It's all white," Michael said "And so is the list I just handed you. Not a single black voter on either one."

Michael brought out a separate document. He put it on the table and flipped dramatically through the stapled pages, from the first, to the second, to the third, all the way through to the seventh page of the document.

"These 489 names," Michael said, "are registered black voters. Or at least, they were registered as of the last election. And not a single one with any allegiance to Leon Darby. You get these votes, and a big chunk of the non-committed white voters, and you're dangerously close to winning."

Michael watched Daniel read through the names. He saw no nods of familiarity, no indication of anything other than bewilderment. He could tell Daniel had no idea who any of these people were.

"How are we going to get them?"

"You're going to knock on their doors and shake their hands, same as you did on this side of the county."

Daniel took a deep breath, put on a brave face, and nodded in vigorous agreement.

North Goshen was home to most of the county's farmland, and all of the north-side farms were owned by whites. On the northwest side of the county, closest to old downtown, were a number of old Victorian homes, some built before the Civil War. Vast estates surrounded these homes, and the county's wealthiest residents lived there. These were multi-generation farm families, the inheritors of antebellum estates, the local pediatrician, a couple of lawyers, the Gardner family, the Darby family, Tyler's parents Will and Pat King, and others. Some of the homes maintained intact former slave quarters, now used for storage or as chicken coops.

Eastward down the Beeline, beyond this cluster of Victorian homes, were numerous farms, dirt or concrete drives cutting through the tillable acreage and leading up to neat farm homes and yards covered by barns, tractors, toolsheds, pickup trucks, animal pens, and other mainstays of an agricultural economy.

East of farm country and just north down a county road were a series of residential subdivisions. Here resided the county's well-off but less wealthy whites and the ones who didn't farm. Along a series of wide, winding roads, nice-sized homes were set inside spacious yards full of tall pine trees. The development had filled up over time with a mix that included a number of farm supply salesmen and other non-farming agriculture businessmen, upper management at Darby Tobacco, real estate investors, a pharmacist, and a few career military men and women who commuted to Robins Air Force Base. This was where Daniel and Amber made their home.

Further east, and farther to the north, behind a large tract of Darby-owned land, were clusters of quiet residential streets, cracked but acceptable rock-and-tar roads, lined with respectable middle-class ranch homes and bungalows with big enough yards for kids to play.

Scattered even further north, in a rocky, woodsy area that pressed up against I-16, were several trailer parks, each separated from the interstate by a narrow section of trees. Here, poor whites lived, and a handful of blacks.

South Goshen was poor and almost entirely black.

If you turned south down the county road just east of old downtown, you would first pass two weather-beaten churches, one right across the road from the other. Hephzibah Baptist and the Holiness Temple were the lifeblood of the southside community. Hephzibah was a traditional Baptist church with old-time Gospel music and a conservative theology. Holiness Temple was a wild Pentecostal affair that attracted searching souls from throughout the region, who writhed and spoke in tongues while contemporary praise music blasted through the PA system.

As you passed by the churches, you would notice an abrupt change in the road, which became rough, craggy, and broken as you moved into South Goshen. For years, the county and state had spent their limited resources on maintaining the roads on the north side—the white side—leaving the south side neglected.

Along this craggy road, you would pass a number of small, black-owned farms, roughly 20 acres each. Some of these bordered on subsistence farming, where a group of families worked together to plant and harvest sweet corn, tomatoes, sweet potatoes, greens, squash, and other garden foods. Much they ate or preserved, and the rest they sold at farmer's markets or roadside produce stands. A few small tobacco farms sold their meager returns to Darby Tobacco.

Along the county road, and scattered throughout South Goshen, were trailer parks and old, dilapidated residential roads. Some roads were paved, some covered in gravel, some dirt. Here resided farm workers and laborers of all sorts in small, flimsy houses. The homes were mostly well-kept, but they strained under the weight of their age, struggled against the pine roots that pushed up through the floorboards.

White people found little occasion to visit South Goshen. There were no major trade posts here, no businesses that a white person would patronize. The seed suppliers, grain bins, farm equipment retailers, restaurants, the big white churches, the public school, all sat in North Goshen. Not surprisingly, the electoral strategy of Goshen politicians—that is, Leon Darby and the crackpots on the school board—never much involved South Goshen.

Historically, voter registration in South Goshen had been very low. This region of the state had voted overwhelmingly and reliably Republican since the 1970s, and no Democratic politician saw much use spending time or money catering to black votes here. For years, thoroughly jaded by generation after generation of disenfranchisement, few of the residents on this side of the county bothered to vote.

That is, until the 2008 and 2012 election years, when Barack Obama was on the ticket, and black registration skyrocketed. And then, in 2018, when Stacey Abrams ran for governor, and in the years that followed, through the efforts of her New Georgia Project, black registration had steadily risen. Court challenges from Abrams and her camp had disrupted efforts by Republicans to remove voters from the polls. These factors gave the Riley campaign hope.

Yet, the challenge remained to mobilize these voters, to convince them that Daniel Riley was worth their time and allegiance. Daniel would have to persuade them that he was not just another Leon Darby in disguise. He would need to cross the Beeline and walk the roads and knock on doors.

Michael had gently encouraged Daniel not to go by himself at first. He could benefit from an introduction by a familiar face, Michael had said. But Daniel thought he knew better. The more he looked over Michael's list of registered black voters, the greater his confidence grew. True, he felt foolish not to have realized the potential in South Goshen before. But now that he had the list, now that he realized the treasure trove of voters that lay south of the

Beeline for the taking, the less he worried about his chances for victory. It was not possible for him to lose these voters. He held educated, egalitarian views. He believed in equality. He had many black friends. He didn't need Michael's help to communicate any of that. It would be apparent to the people he met. Their support for him would be obvious.

Michael hadn't pushed back very hard after Daniel expressed this confidence. He bid him good luck and told him his door was always open if he changed his mind. Smiling inside to himself, he wished he could be a fly on the wall to observe that first day of canvassing.

In later years, Daniel would recall that first day on the South Goshen campaign trail as one of the most difficult of his political life. He was greeted by deeply wary, sometimes hostile residents with little to no desire to converse with him. His experience at Ray McMillan's home was illustrative. Ray was 54 years old. He had been a farm laborer since he was a child. His foot had gotten caught in a grain separator and ground into mush several years ago while he was working on the back of a combine. Between that and a longstanding back injury, he was often in pain and totally unable to work, grateful for the Social Security funds that allowed him to feed himself and go to the doctor. He was a gruff man with little patience for nonsense. He had voted for Obama in 2008, simply for the election's historical significance, but he stayed home in 2012 and thereafter, and in general had no interest in politics. He just wanted to be left in peace. His wife Marcy worked nearly every day, all week, cleaning houses in North Goshen, and she was away when Daniel came to visit.

Daniel tried to open the screen door to the McMillans' home, to knock on the wooden door behind it, but the screen was latched. So, he banged on the hard metal frame of the screen, which made a hollow rattling sound that added to his discomfort and sense of intrusion. Ray opened up the wooden door and stared blankly at Daniel through the screen.

"Yes?" he said.

"Hi, Mr. McMillan?"

"Mm hm."

"Hi, Mr. McMillan, my name is Daniel Riley, I'm running for County Commissioner."

Silence.

Daniel cleared his throat. "Well, I sure would appreciate your support. Do you have a couple of minutes?"

McMillan grunted. "Ok," he said. He stood there.

Daniel swallowed hard. He cleared his throat again. "Well (cough), as you know, Leon Darby has been County Commissioner for nearly 16 years. I'm hoping to bring some changes to Goshen County."

McMillan stood there, hoping Daniel would go away.

"As you might know, the Georgia legislature has legalized the cultivation of recreational marijuana, and . . ."

"Marijuana?" McMillan interrupted. He shook his head. "I'm not trying to get in no trouble, now."

"Oh, no. No, sir. No trouble. You see, the state is about to *legalize* cannabis. Meaning, there won't *be* any more trouble. It will be a great opportunity for the people here. It will cut down on some of the pointless arrests we see now."

"Well, it don't make no difference to me one way or the other."

"Yes sir, I understand. I. . ."

"Listen, you got a card or something?"

"Well, yessir." Daniel fumbled in his pocket. He pulled out his wallet and a business card for his law firm. He handed it to Ray. Ray took the card and glanced down at it.

"Alright," he said. "Daniel Riley. Ok. Good luck to you. You have a good one," and he closed the door. Daniel stared at the door for another moment, wanting to knock again, wanting to give his pitch another try. But, he realized, the man did not want to hear any more from him. He turned and sulked away, back toward the road.

After that, Daniel walked toward the home of Monica and Malone Perry, who lived in a neat but dilapidated house on Paul Street, a well-worn dirt road that ran parallel to the Beeline, separated from it by little more than a hedge of varied weeds and bushes. Among the bushes were many wild scupadine vines, each filled with clusters of grape-like fruits, now fully ripe. Daniel stopped and picked some of the fruits as he walked. He squished the tough skin of the fruits between his molars and the semisweet goo burst into his mouth. They were good, but not as good as he remembered from childhood.

Malone Perry was a night-shift associate at the Wal-Mart distribution center east of the county. He had been a farm laborer in his younger years, but sought the opportunity for a decent-paying indoor job when the distribution center opened. Monica Perry, for years, had operated an unlicensed, informal daycare in their home, watching neighborhood children while their parents were at work. As the population had aged, and fewer young, working families stayed in South Goshen, business dried up.

Daniel knocked on the door. Monica Perry greeted him with a curious, concerned look on her face.

"Hello, Mrs. Perry?"

"Yes?"

"My name is Daniel Riley. I'm running for County Commissioner. I wondered if I might have a moment of your time."

"Who is that?" Mr. Perry shouted groggily from the back of the house. "Tell him I'm trying to sleep! I just worked an all-night shift!"

"It's a politician!" shouted Mrs. Perry to the bedroom.

Malone Perry sauntered out of the back room into the living area, where Daniel stood in the doorway. "What are you running for again?"

Daniel opened his mouth to speak. At that moment, a baby began to bawl from somewhere behind Mrs. Perry. She turned and said, "hush!" The baby kept crying. Mrs. Perry ducked back to tend to the child. Malone came into the doorframe and looked sternly down at Daniel, who wanted very much to run away.

"County Commissioner," Daniel stuttered through the baby's cries. "Leon Darby has held the office for nearly 16 years. I'm trying to bring new leadership to the County. I'd really like your support. Darby has neglected South Goshen. I'll represent *you*." He tried to give an optimistic sort of smile at this last word.

"So you're trying to get the black folks on your side," said Mr. Perry.

Daniel chuckled nervously. "I guess I am. That's why I'm here. I can guarantee you Leon Darby won't be campaigning here on this side of the Beeline," Daniel said proudly.

"Yeah, and when's the last time *you* came over here, before today?"

Daniel stammered.

"That's what I thought. Who's to say things would be any different with you? Darby's stayed in office all this time without ever coming here. Why should I believe you'll be any different?" His voice grew in volume and intensity. "We had us a black president, and look what happened after that! Ain't nothing changed. The backlash to it made things worse, in fact. Black people are as poor today as they were when I was a young man. My children struggle to get ahead, just like I did. And these politicians out here selling snake oil, creating false hope. If you manage to get elected, you'll forget about us before you even take that oath of office, I guarantee it."

Daniel struggled to respond. "Well sir, my law partner, my best friend—you know Michael Drummond? He grew up over here. Just down the way there. I've spent a lot of time listening to him. I'm doing my best to understand your perspective. I can't promise I'll fix everything, but I'm asking you to give me a chance."

This was a fair response, Daniel thought. Still standing in the doorway, he looked at Monica Perry, who was standing just behind Malone, rocking the baby against her shoulder. She seemed sympathetic to the young man, both for his views and for the fact that he was now enduring Malone's famous temper. But Malone had worked himself up, and was barely listening anymore.

"Oh sure," he said. "I'm sure you got all kinds of black friends. I saw your crazy signs out there on the County Road. But you won't see one in my yard. I'm fed up with your kind. You want to do something to help us? Get these damned streets fixed. Can't nobody hardly drive over here. Help us get our church fixed. Hephzibah Baptist has been crumbling for years, with not a penny's help from the white churches who claim to be our brothers and sisters. But you and I both know you ain't planning to do nothing of the sort. So until you're ready to do something to actually help, instead of just making promises, just leave us alone."

Malone closed the door in Daniel's face.

Daniel's mouth hung open, his words caught in his throat. He turned away, defeated and embarrassed.

As the day grew warmer, Daniel continued his long walk through South Goshen. Behind each door, he faced reactions ranging from total indifference, to skepticism, to anger, to the very worst—fear. Of course, there were exceptions. A few people knew who Daniel was from his work with Michael and were enthusiastic to support him. He got a few smiles, a few hugs around the neck. Though these welcoming arms were few and far between, each one seemed to come at the very moment he was about to give up, and they fueled him to keep going.

By the time the sun had begun to make its way toward the horizon, Daniel had visited 54 mostly unsympathetic South Goshen homes, and shook about as many hands.

His legs tired, his feet sore, he walked back to his car, which he had parked in the lot of the Hephzibah Baptist Church. He drove over the Beeline back to old downtown and dragged himself through the doors of the Bank & Trust, a tired, beaten expression on his face. He passed through the dark lobby, walked down the hall toward his office. He noticed a light coming from Michael's office. He looked inside and saw Michael sitting at his desk, flipping his pen around in his hand, reading under the light of a single lamp.

Michael looked up curiously. "How did it go?"

Daniel wanted to cry as he looked into the eyes of his friend. The events of the day flickered in his mind: the indifferent stares, the hostile voices, the smell of cynicism, the worry.

"If our strategy is to win by way of the black vote," he said, "I fear we are hopeless."

He felt childish and ashamed. This morning, he had imagined himself standing gallantly in the doorways of happy black families grateful and enthusiastic to see him. He had fancied himself an enlightened white man, a progressive thinker from Atlanta, someone who would be received with open arms. He had imagined a scene from a campaign advertisement, with him as the handsome politician shaking hands with smiling voters, inspirational music playing in the background. He had been naïve, he realized. He felt like a little boy who had thought he could fly, and who had wrapped a blanket over his shoulders like a cape and jumped off the couch into the air, only to hit the floor face-first.

Michael saw the despair in his friend's face. He stood and walked to Daniel and opened his arms. He pulled him in and gave him a hug. Daniel put his eyes on Michael's shoulders and began to groan.

"Oh my God, man. What the fuck. What. The. Fuck. What the fuck."

Michael laughed. He patted his friend on the head.

"What happened, my man? Did you get robbed over there?"

"No."

"Nobody wanted to talk to you?"

"Ugh."

"Dude, get off my shoulder. Sit down. Have a drink."

"Ughh."

"Seriously, sit down. Sit." Michael chuckled and gently pushed his friend away. He walked behind his desk, leaned over and opened a drawer, pulled out a bottle of scotch and two glasses. He poured one for himself, one for Daniel. He took his glass and sat in his comfortable leather seat, leaned back and propped his feet on the desk.

Daniel sat in one of the two guest chairs in front of the desk. He took several quick, hungry sips from his glass. He sank into his seat and let the scotch trickle into his brain. After some time, he spoke. "Near-about nobody that I met today had any interest whatsoever is talking to me. Most everybody was anxious for me to leave. Everyone was uncomfortable in one way or another. *I* was uncomfortable. It was miserable."

"Maybe it was *your* discomfort, rubbing off on them? You ever think about that?"

Daniel thought. "Maybe," he said. "But I'm pretty sure most of it was coming from them, not from me. Not at first, at least. By the end of the day, though, I'm sure I did look pretty pitiful."

Michael sat quietly for a moment, taking in his friend's glum countenance. "You knew this would be hard though, didn't you? How did you think this would go? That you would just show up at their doorsteps, and they'd be taken by you, and they'd just lift you into power, just because you want it?"

Daniel hung his head.

"If you want this job, you've got to convince the boss—the voters—that you're the right man for it. That you're a *hard worker*, your 'views' be damned. How are you going to convince any of these black people, who have been living under white supremacy for generations, to throw their emotion and support behind you?"

Daniel's heart drooped into his stomach. He felt nauseous. He felt angry at himself for being so naïve. He felt stupid, but grateful that Michael cared enough to be honest.

"So what are you going to do?" Michael asked firmly. "How are we going to win this election?"

"I don't know," Daniel said. "I'm not good at the retail politics of it all. Put me in front of a group of people, and I can shine. Something about the energy of a crowd, the intensity of that focus upon the stage, brings out the best in me. I can work a room, or a jury, or an audience. But face-to-face, I'm weak. I feel disingenuous. I feel uncomfortable. It's something I can work on, but my fear is that I don't have the time."

"You *are* good in front of an audience." Michael said. "I've known that since we were kids, since I saw you debate in big championship rounds. You feed off the energy. You were great at the Ag Fair."

There was a moment of quiet contemplation. Then Daniel said, "I have an idea. I met a man today—he wasn't too happy to see me—but he said something that reminded me of something you and I talked about once. I remember you telling me how you'd like to give some money to Hephzibah Baptist once you get your fee in the Everett case. It got me to thinking. . . what if the campaign made a big donation?"

Michael was taken aback. "Might be some legal problems with that."

"Well," he said. "What if we just did it through the law firm. Just count it against my draw."

Michael raised his eyebrows in thoughtful surprise, then slowly, gradually, he began to nod. "We could do that," he said.

"Let's pledge $10,000."

Michael thought some more, shrugged agreeably. "Okay. Let's."

"And," Daniel said, then hesitated. "Maybe I could address the congregation."

At this, Michael's eyes widened once again, surprised and questioning. He lowered his head and shook it softly for a little while, then relented. "I'll speak to Pastor Reid tomorrow. No promises. But. . . let me see what I can do."

"Thank you, Michael," said Daniel, warmth and affection in his voice. "Thank you for everything."

Michael knew that Pastor Reid would require some softening up before he would accept Daniel, even with the substantial gift he proposed. He knew his pastor would feel an instinctive skepticism toward the gift, would expect strings attached, and would want to know what those strings were. Michael was wary of creating the perception that Daniel was trying to buy off the black community, that he was treating their support as a rude commodity, something to be purchased. He knew this would be a delicate task, that the wrong impression could easily outweigh the good will they hoped to build.

So, sitting in Pastor Reid's kitchen Tuesday morning, Michael poured himself out.

"Daniel Riley is a good man, pastor. He's not perfect. But he is my friend. He's my business partner. I trust him. Our families have dinner together. Our children play together. Our wives shop together. I don't think he'll let us down."

Pastor Reid listened.

"He believes in the same things I do. He knows what a great thing we could have here in this county, if we had a government that represented us. We have a beautiful countryside here. Fertile land, clean air. This could be a wonderful place for black people to raise our families. There is wealth here, if only we could access it. Darby and his people are getting old. They have become lazy because no one has challenged them. Their grip on power is loosening. They will kick and flail to stay in power, but I believe we can win. And if we can get someone into office who answers to us. . . It will make a difference.

"Our church is falling apart," Michael said. "The roof hasn't been replaced in nearly a decade. There are leaks in the stone. It needs to be treated for mold. It needs to be painted throughout. So, let Daniel Riley give the church this money. Let him address the congregation. And help him to win. Help *me* to win."

Pastor Reid nodded. He was empathetic toward this young man. The pastor had watched Michael play in the churchyard as a boy. He had watched with the same wonder as the rest of the congregation as young Michael spoke in church, as he debated scripture and theology in great detail and with a higher intellectual capacity than most adults he knew. He had watched the young man grow into a father, seen the love in his eyes as he held his daughter's hand and walked her to Sunday school. The pastor had been so pleased to learn Michael would return to the county. It had given him hope that there was a future for the people here. And he had been so grateful for the legal help Michael offered his parishioners, fighting debt collections and evictions and bogus criminal cases *pro bono* for those who needed it. He had been so proud to see him succeed.

"Michael, I would do anything in the world for you." Pastor Reid said. A big, earnest smile opened onto his face. "Does your boy want to speak this Sunday?"

"Yes, sir, if that won't interfere with your message, of course."

"Nah," the pastor said. "I've been working on something, but it can wait for next week."

Michael smiled. Pastor Reid embraced him. "Thank you, Pastor," Michael said.

On Wednesday, Daniel was back out on the streets, knocking on doors in South Goshen. But this time, Michael was by his side.

As the two friends stood together in the modest doorways of South Goshen, most neighbors smiled at the sight of Michael, whom they knew from his childhood. The entire community knew about this Drummond fellow, this great mind, this great promise. Even those who didn't recognize him naturally opened up to his smiling, friendly face. Michael did most of the talking. Daniel said as little as he could. He smiled and shook hands and showed gratitude and said "thank you for your support."

By the end of the week, "Daniel Riley for County Commissioner" signs dotted the landscape of South Goshen. Nearly every street had at least four or five.

Daniel did not sleep well on Saturday, the night before he was to address the congregation of Hephzibah Baptist Church. All week, as he walked along the roads of South Goshen, as he stood listening to Michael talk to its residents, he had been writing, editing, reworking the speech in his mind. In the moments of silence that arose while they traipsed along dirt roads between houses, he would become lost in his thoughts, imagining the words he would say, rearranging sections of the speech, practicing different ways to phrase his points. He had written nothing down; that was his way. But on this Saturday, he finally reduced something to paper. He drafted a rough outline, not a full text, but a series of reference points to the text already in his head, something to remind him how he should organize the words he had rehearsed so many times in his mind.

Only a week ago, the prospect of speaking to a black congregation might have played out in his head like a TV movie. He had envisioned himself a white Barack Obama, the other side of the post-racial coin, a white man who could effortlessly connect with black people. He would have pictured an adoring, appreciative audience, looking up at him as he spoke, sunlight pouring in from the stained-glass windows, casting colorful light over his smiling face. He had imagined himself as Joel Osteen, a man so seemingly pure and earnest in his words that an audience drew magnetically to him.

But now, he imagined himself a stumbling fool, anxiously struggling through a speech, with a stomachache, talking to an annoyed, possibly offended crowd of people just hoping for him to finish.

He whispered the speech quietly to himself in the car on the drive to church, while Amber offered occasional critiques. "Don't say that; not that word; that part sounds good." He had a solid sketch of the text now, but he knew the final words would not come into existence until he actually spoke them.

The Rileys sat in the front pew, little Johnny wedged between mother and father, the Drummonds beside them. Daniel felt intensely nervous through every moment of the service. He strained to smile through each song, to maintain the appearance of a neutral sort of pleasantness on his face. But in his gut, he felt terror and anxiety, emotions he hoped were not apparent on his face.

After much singing and the weekly prayer requests, Pastor Reid finally said, "Brothers and sisters, I come to you today with an exciting announcement." Daniel felt a sinking in his stomach. He became light-headed.

"Daniel Riley is a young man who grew up here in this community. He went to the University of Georgia with our very own Michael Drummond. They are law partners now, and their firm has been serving our community well. As some of you also know, Daniel is running for County Commissioner. He has pledged a generous contribution to our church, as many of you already know. I'd like to give him an opportunity to speak to all of you. And I hope you will welcome him warmly."

Pastor Reid gestured down to Daniel, who arose from the front pew. His heart pounded, and he drew in long, steady breaths. Adrenaline poured through his body as he approached the front of the church. He snapped into a deep, unconscious sort of focus. All anxiety, all fear, left him, its energy replaced by the energy of performance. His mind took over; it would not let him fail.

He climbed the steps to the pulpit. He peered out at the vast congregation before him, hundreds of curious, expectant faces staring up at him. He cleared his throat. "Good morning," he said.

"GOOD MORNING," the congregation boomed. It startled him. He had not expected any reply at all, and the thunder of the congregation's response reminded him that they were paying close attention to his words.

"I think you all know my friend Michael." He smiled and looked down at the Drummonds in their pew. "He has been instrumental in helping me to understand more about your community and the things that are important to you in this election. So I want to thank him, first and foremost, for that. I also want to thank Pastor Reid, and to thank all of you, for allowing me to be here today. I truly appreciate it, and I feel humbled and Honored."

Daniel looked down briefly at his notes. He looked back up toward the congregation, scanned the audience and made eye contact with as many as he could. His face spoke earnestness, humility. He could see his expression reflected in the faces in the audience.

"I have to be honest with you all, I'm feeling very nervous right now." There was light, airy laughter from the congregation. "You all probably can understand why. I'm embarrassed to admit it, but today is the very first time I have been to a service in an African-American church. I lived here in Goshen County—just a couple miles from this church—since I was a little boy. But I hardly ever came over to this side of town. I feel a little bit ashamed over that now. And, as I look out at everyone here today, I wonder what you must think of me. You might be thinking, what have I done to deserve your support?"

There was rapt silence in the crowd. He had gripped their attention. He was speaking candidly, and that was disarming.

"I know I have prejudices, subconscious biases. I won't try to convince you otherwise. What I'd like to do instead is make a logical argument to you. I'd like to appeal to reason.

"Leon Darby has been the Commissioner here for a long time. He was born during the time of segregation. His tobacco corporation is the direct descendant of a century-old farming operation that was built on the backs of slaves. His business has been the centerpiece of an economy, and a society, that has remained largely segregated even to this day. He's never had any interest in expanding opportunity beyond himself and those who look like him and think like him, and he's never going to. He is comfortable with the way things are, and so are the people who keep him in power."

Daniel caught Michael's eyes, which had widened considerably, a crooked smile forming on his face. Daniel was crossing a line. He was calling Darby an outright racist. He was dispensing with all sense of politeness. It was a bold and risky move—the kind Daniel couldn't resist, the kind that had gotten him into this mess in the first place.

"I come from a different generation," he went on. "I've got the same biases hard-wired into me as anyone else. But I do *believe* in equality. In the idea of it. I'm conscious of the tremendous gap between white people and black people in this county—in this state—in this country, for goodness' sake. And I cannot, and will not, promise I can make it go away—I certainly can't. But I can promise that I will never deny it exists; I will never ignore it.

"There are economic opportunities on the horizon that could be a boon for all of us. You all know what I am talking about. New investors from different parts of the country, investors who are interested only in buying the best product from the best growers, and who have no interest in preserving some antiquated economic structure here. I believe this new crop will help us to create a clean slate, one on which South Goshen can write a new history.

"I will work toward concrete gains for this community. In county employment, in contracting, in licensing, in every element of county business. And the *first* thing I will do is to fix the doggoned roads on this side of the Beeline!"

The audience issued genuine applause. A big, pleased smile formed on his face.

"I will not be perfect. I can almost guarantee you that I will disappoint you as many times as I will please you. But I will try my very best. My *very best*." His voice shook as he emphasized his words.

"And I will make Michael Drummond, my good friend, the County Attorney, and I know he'll hold me to all of this . . ."

He was interrupted by more applause.

"He will keep me in check. He will keep me fair. He will make sure my decisions are made with *everyone* in the county in mind, without prejudice."

He took another moment to look over the audience and meet his face with theirs. He looked down once more at his notes to ensure there was not some important point he had missed. There wasn't. His speech had been brief, and well received, and now it was time to wrap it up.

"I am so grateful for your attention," he said. "And I will work hard to earn, and keep, your support. You all know where my office is, and you know my number. Please call me if I can help you in any way. Thank you."

He nodded, almost bowed, and waved. The audience continued to applaud as he moved toward the steps that led down from the pulpit. Daniel smiled shyly as he moved from the pulpit area back to his seat. Michael rose and shook Daniel's hand, pulling him in for a hug, as the audience continued to cheer. Daniel looked back up at the congregation once more, turned to the left and the right, and waved. He felt like a candidate. He felt like a force in the room. He bowed once more, turned his back toward the congregation, and took his seat next to Michael.

Michael leaned forward, crossing his body over the wives. He whispered, "damn good job, my friend. Damn good job."

# 11

WORD of Daniel's successful speech and his donation spread quickly to the ear of Leon Darby. He sat stewing in his office, his face red with frustration. "Got the goddam blacks all riled up," he said, looking across his desk slack-jawed at Tyler. "Here it is end of October, election coming right up, and I gotta say I'm not feeling too good about the whole goddam situation. We need to figure us out some kind of insurance policy, just in case this thing goes sideways. Some kind of contingency plan, if you know what I mean."

"I know what you mean," Tyler said. "I've been thinking about this, actually. I think we've got an ace in the hole."

"And what is that?"

"I've got two words for you."

"Let's hear em."

"Meth Cop."

Darby's expression was blank. "What in the hell are you talking about."

Tyler waggled his eyebrows up and down.

"I haven't the slightest idea what you are . . . Oh. Oh Lord, no. You can't be serious. Are you serious? That peckerhead is still a deputy?

"He is. And if anyone owes us a favor, it's him."

Russell Tibbits was a young, cocksure Sheriff's deputy. He was tall, strong, and slightly overweight, with greasy, unkempt brown hair. He grew up just down the road—in Emanuel County—in a little house with an angry, bitter father and no mother because she had left when Russ was very small.

Several years back, Russell had been the star villain in a regional scandal after he pistol-whipped a young woman named MacKenzie Sanchez, punched her in the face, and knocked out four of her teeth in the course of arresting her. She sued the deputy, the county, and the Sheriff for excessive force but hired a local lawyer with no experience in federal court and an ever-worsening drinking problem. The county eventually got the case dismissed, but not before the litigation surrounding it yielded some incredible—the county claimed dubious—testimony regarding Deputy Tibbits.

Numerous witnesses—fellow residents of the trailer park where the young woman lived—testified that Tibbits was known to spend quite a lot of time "checking in" on certain female residents. An old lady who lived nearby testified that she had seen Tibbits' car parked outside MacKenzie's home on more than one occasion, and he often went inside and did not emerge for over an hour. MacKenzie's on-again, off-again boyfriend testified that, once, while he was at work, a friend called and told him that Tibbits' car was parked outside MacKenzie's trailer again. The boyfriend went to check it out, and sure enough, Tibbits was there, emerging from the home just as the boyfriend arrived. The deputy had said that he was just "checking in," and nobody was naked, and besides, the boyfriend was a felon with some warrants looming, so he wasn't about to confront the deputy. But when the deputy left, the boyfriend went inside and found a little bag of *chicken*—the parlance *du jour* for crystal meth—right there on the coffee table next to MacKenzie's pipe, as usual, and she was as high as ever. How could it be, he wondered, that a police officer was in the house and had not seen this, or had seen it and done nothing?

But the most explosive testimony came from MacKenzie herself, who testified that the deputy frequently allowed her to smoke in front of him and had, on more than one occasion, taken a hit from the pipe himself. She testified that, on the day of the incident, Deputy Tibbits had given her the bag of *chicken* that he later supposedly arrested her for possessing. Unfortunately, she had been up for days—three, four, who knew how many—at that point and could hardly remember any details of the event. But her best recollection was that they had been smoking together when something set her off and, in a paranoid fit, she had freaked out and threatened to expose him, and he had snatched her phone away, beaten her, and put her in cuffs. Of course, the footage from Russ's body cam showed her thrashing and attacking but showed nothing of what led up to that moment, so there was no evidence to corroborate her admittedly fuzzy account.

At Tyler's recommendation, the Sheriff did not ask Deputy Tibbits to take a drug test. After all, the county was defending him and had taken the position that the young woman was lying. Tyler knew, in fact, that quantities of the drug had gone missing from the evidence room right around the time of these events. Tyler had not disclosed that fact to opposing counsel, of course, and he saw no benefit to investigating it further.

In the course of the case, several neighbors testified that Russ's indulgence in the stuff—or at least the rumor of it—was well-known throughout the park. But other than MacKenzie, no one claimed to have personally seen him using it. There had been several eerily similar accounts of strange behavior—on some days, he was manically enthusiastic, highly magnanimous, the friendliest cop you ever met; but on others, he stalked angrily about the park, harassing people about trivial matters like a broken-down car parked in the yard or a dog off its leash. He was unpredictable, and folks were afraid of him. And they had given him a nickname—*Meth Cop*.

Tyler had gotten the case dismissed on the grounds of officer immunity, because it was uncontested that MacKenzie had been thrashing insanely about, delirious on meth, when the incident happened. The body cam footage was bad for her. It could not be clearly established—at least not according to the highly deferential standard of the Dublin Division of the U.S. District Court for the Southern District of Georgia—that the force employed had been excessive under the circumstances.

It didn't help that her lawyer was half-drunk the whole litigation. In the deposition transcripts, the text next to his questions often read: [Unintelligible].

Though the outcome to the county had been favorable in the courts, it was not so favorable in the press. The deposition transcripts, with all their colorful, salacious details, were obtained by a curious blogger out of Soperton, and he posted them online. Shortly, the story of Meth Cop was plastered all over local social media, and, perhaps due to the catchy name, and also perhaps due to the fact that the story confirmed people's worst, most comical caricatures of the rural South, the story spread from there, hitting trashy tabloid style blogs and message boards throughout the country. The story was in the *Macon Telegraph*, the *Atlanta Journal-Constitution*, and even, for some reason, the *Miami Herald*. Sad to say, but for a while there, the story of Meth Cop was Goshen County's most prominent export.

Eventually, people lost interest in the story. Russ returned to his job. He was put on desk duty for a while, but returned to full patrol once the Sheriff and the Commissioner became comfortable that the scandal had died down. The Sheriff had questioned the wisdom of this but Tyler had reminded him how good it was to have someone who owes his livelihood to you. Russell Tibbits certainly did. And now here was a perfect time to cash in some of those chips.

"Come on in, deputy," said Tyler. "Sit down." Tyler gestured to the sitting area of Darby's office. Melanie Stewart was there on the couch, visibly nervous at the sight of Russ Tibbits, straining to issue a pleasant expression. Darby was in his usual seat, blank-faced, almost like he was annoyed at all the company.

Russ sat opposite Melanie on the couch. He nodded to her, and she nodded back.

Tyler pulled up a chair. "Listen, Russ," he began. "I'm glad you could be here. This is all going to seem very unusual. But we have a bit of a problem on our hands." He paused for a moment, as if troubled by his thoughts. "You know about this young man running for County Commissioner, right? Riley boy."

Russ nodded.

"He's got the blacks whipped up into a fervor. A few of the farmers as well. Making all kinds of promises. Now I don't think the boy's got a chance in the world. But, we can't exactly take that for granted. All of us sitting here today depend on the Commissioner here," he gestured to Darby, "for a whole lot. Someone like Riley comes in, someone young and inexperienced, with no idea who made this county what it is today, he's going to want to bring in his friends and family, he's going to want to bring in the blacks who got him elected, you understand? All of us have worked too hard to make this county what it is today. Do you agree with me?"

The deputy looked straight ahead at Tyler, nodding only vaguely. He shifted a little in his seat. He cleared his throat and thought for a moment. "Well," he said. "I don't want him to win, I can tell you that." He looked to Tyler for approval. Tyler was unmoving. Russ cleared his throat again. "Sheriff told me yesterday that I'd been assigned to monitor the polls," he said. "I guess that has something to do with this?"

Tyler began to nod, ever so slightly.

"Just tell me what to do."

Tyler smiled broadly.

"Our friend Melanie here was just promoted chief deputy of the Clerk of Superior Court, isn't that right, Melanie?"

She gave an uneasy, shallow titter. "Yep. Yes. Very nice."

"Old lady who'd been there for a while was due to retire, and we helped move that along, didn't we?" He gave her a sickening wink.

"Now deputy, Melanie is going to be one of two poll workers at the north side precinct on Election Day. She'll be the one checking ID cards, giving voters their ballots, checking them off the list. I need you to work closely with her, you understand. She has a job to do, and I need you to make sure nobody interferes with her, or even sees what she's doing."

"Yes, sir."

"Unfortunately, we don't have much control over the southside precinct. The blacks control that. Who knows what kind of shenanigans they'll be pulling. Hell, any votes we steal will probably be cancelled out by the votes they steal, plus some. So, we've got to be aggressive."

Russ nodded enthusiastically.

"Now, this ain't like the old ballot-stuffing days. We've got these machines the Secretary of State makes us use. Now, we thought about getting some whiz-kid to hack into the thing and screw with the code or whatever, and I've looked into that, but it's really not that simple."

"What about your nephew?" Darby interjected. "What's his name, Dennis or something? He's real good with computers."

Tyler drew a breath and shook his head. "Right," he said. "Again, it's not that simple." He turned to Melanie. "I know we've been over this before, but just so the deputy here understands, let's go over the plan one more time."

# 12

WHEN Daniel woke up on the morning of Election Day, he found himself possessed by an unexpected lightness of heart. He jumped straight out of bed, no snooze button, ready to seize the day, excited yet calm. Why did he feel so light? Perhaps it was the fact that, after today, the thing would be over. Win or lose, the uncertainty would be resolved, the unknown would become known. He ate his breakfast with ease, his stomach calmed by the promise of a finally finished task.

Daniel and Amber dropped Johnny off at school then drove together to the First Baptist Church, the site of the northside poll. They parked in the lot of the little baseball field across the street. They walked up the concrete steps into the front doors of the fellowship hall, hand in hand. Daniel could feel his heart pounding as they strode together across the linoleum and approached the voter check-in table. He saw before him, at the table, what he imagined to be an illustration of the challenge he would face that day: an older black lady smiled with recognition and checked his ID; a middle-aged, agitated-looking blonde lady, seemingly uncomfortable in his presence, handed Amber her voting card. *Which sentiment will rule the day?* he wondered. He looked at the white lady's name tag. "Hey there, Ms. Stewart," he said. "I recognize you from the clerk's office, don't I? I think I've filed a couple of things there with you."

She gave a forced, half-hearted smile. "That's right," she said. "Have a nice day," then looked back to her work. His attempt to lighten her mood had failed, it appeared. Oh well.

He took his voter card to one of several booths lining the back wall of the fellowship hall and clicked his card into the slot of a little metal box. The screen flashed to life, and there was his name. An unexpected sense of elation welled up inside him. He could not explain why the sight gave him such grand satisfaction. *Why do I need this?* he wondered. *My name on a screen. Why do I crave validation? Why do I yearn for attention? Why do I seek approval so desperately, so openly? What love was ever deprived me, that I seek to amass the affections of strangers?*

He realized he had probably been standing there for too long. He took a deep breath and pushed aside his thoughts and pushed the button on the screen. *One vote for Daniel Riley.*

Amber was waiting for him near the exit doors, a fresh "I Voted" sticker with a nice looking peach on it attached to her sweater just below her collar bone. Daniel caught her eye and issued a big smile that caused her to smile back. She held her hand forward, gestured for him to take it, and he did.

"Give me that sticker," she said. She took his "I Voted" sticker, pulled it off the paper, and smacked his bottom with it.

"Woo!" he said. He turned around to the ladies at the table. The older lady was laughing, the white lady looking as sour and sad as ever. "Did she get it on there?" he said.

"Oh yeah, she gotcha good. Right on the back pocket," said the older lady.

He waved, then turned back to Amber. They kissed, held each other's hands tightly, and walked out into the cool November air. Across the church parking lot and just across the road in front of the baseball field, they saw Jacob and Margaret Riley, next to Ed and Velma Gardner, all of them waving "DANIEL RILEY FOR COUNTY COMMISSIONER" signs and cheering as the young couple emerged. It brought a smile to Daniel's face. He knew there would be others like them—the Jessups, Ed's Episcopalians, family friends from the Presbyterian church—staked out in strategic locations throughout the county, waving signs of support. What a day it would be.

They smiled and waved to their family and friends and climbed into the Explorer, where Daniel pulled out his phone and brought up a custom GPS map he had created. He had pinned the home of every north side supporter who might have trouble making it to the poll on their own. Older people, a few disabled folks, some folks whose spouses might be driving their only car to work. He pressed the screen at the nearest target location. They buckled their seatbelts and Amber backed the vehicle into the road on a mission to deliver as many favorable voters to the north side polling place as they could.

Meanwhile, on the south side, Pastor Reid had loaned Michael the church's clunky old van, which could transport up to nine people at a time on a good day. Michael drove the van up and down the south side's craggy roads. At each stop, he got out and walked among the houses, knocking on doors and pulling back anyone who would come and vote. The south side precinct saw a steady stream of voters all morning.

Around 10 a.m., Michael pulled a van full of voters into the parking lot of the Hephzibah Baptist Church, only to see a tan police cruiser parked carelessly out front, sideways over two handicap spots. Deputy Russ Tibbits leaned his chunky frame against the cruiser, arms crossed, glaring at the van as it pulled into the lot. He appeared to be chewing gum. The people in the van, who had been laughing and talking the whole ride there, grew suddenly serious and quiet. They looked out at the chubby, pale man in his pressed brown uniform, firearm at his hip.

Michael tried to keep the group calm. "Alright, folks, we're here," he said. He got out of the van and opened up the sliding door. The people inside emerged cautiously.

"What's the police doing here?" someone muttered.

"Oh, I'm sure he's just doing patrol," Michael said. He guided the group past the deputy and his cruiser. The deputy gave an unsettling nod to the group. Michael kept his eye on the deputy, who glared back at him. Michael walked the voters up the front steps and held open the door. When the last voter had stepped into the church, Michael waved and said, "thank y'all!" He closed the door behind them. He turned to the deputy and walked down the steps to meet him.

"Deputy," Michael said.

"Mr. Drummond."

"Everything ok here?"

"Well," began the deputy. He spit onto the concrete. He pulled himself up from the cruiser. The car creaked as it rose off its shocks. "I'm afraid we do have a bit of a problem." He nodded over to the van. "You can't bring people here in that van."

"And why is that?"

"That van's church property."

Michael looked back at the deputy, unmoved, as if waiting for more. There was no more. "And?" Michael asked.

"Can't use church property to campaign."

"Says who?"

"That's the law."

"Are you a lawyer?"

Michael could see anger creeping into the deputy's face. The man was not used to being talked back to, especially not by a black man. Michael took slow, calm breaths, even as adrenaline raced into his body and caused his scalp to tingle.

"Sheriff's office says so," the deputy finally growled.

"Sheriff don't make the law," Michael said. "I'm an officer of the court. And I am telling you that everything we're doing here is above board. And we're not going to stop."

The deputy took off his sunglasses. He leaned his face into Michael's and looked sternly in his eyes. "Well," he said. "You and I are going to have a disagreement then."

Michael did not move. He looked back at the deputy with calm, knowing eyes that did not blink. Conviction burned in his chest. His heart pounded. Yet, he controlled his exterior. His body was placid and unyielding. "I guess we are," he said.

The small group emerged from the church doors, their voting finished. The people paused to watch the two men, who stood frozen, glaring at one another.

Finally, the deputy broke his stare. He looked over at the group and met their eyes. He turned his head back to Michael. "How about you let this be your last load. Then, we won't have any more trouble."

Michael looked down at the deputy's badge. He made a crooked, almost mocking smile as he looked back up into the man's eyes. "Tibbits. I think I saw you in the news a while back, didn't I?"

Russ returned Michael's glare with intense, boiling hatred, now mixed with a modicum of fear. He glared for a moment more, then put his sunglasses on. He turned and ambled back over to his car. "I'll be back with warrants," he said, loud enough for the group in the doorway to hear.

Once the deputy had dumped himself inside his car and closed his door, Michael turned to the group and said, "Ain't gon' be no goddamn warrants. Trust me on that."

Michael turned back to the cruiser and watched the deputy drive away. He turned back to the group. "Y'all vote?" he asked, smiling.

Everyone nodded.

"Great," he said. "Who needs a ride back?"

Having just dropped an elderly couple off at First Baptist, Amber sat waiting in the car, a sense of impatience creeping in, a sense that there must be something more she could do. Each time they pulled into the church lot, she would see a few cars parked, a few voters trickling in and out of the front door, but there had not been the sort of energy she expected. There was certainly no sense that a revolution was taking place, no sense that the hoards were coming in to tear down the institutions of power. Instead, it seemed like an ordinary, tepid country election.

As she was thinking this, her phone began to buzz, and Jackie's name and face appeared.

"Hey girl."

"Hey girl. I need your help. We're out here in this rickety old van, and some of our voters live out in the damn woods. Like dirt roads and shit. We'll never get the van out there, and I ain't about to walk. I'm thinking that four-wheeler of yours could be quite useful right about now."

"Oh yeah? I can be there shortly. I've been driving old fogies around with Daniel all morning. I'm about to fall asleep. There's no reason he can't do this on his own." She looked at Daniel and rolled her eyes at him.

He held up his hands. "But I need you here!" he said. "These people like you better than they like me! You're the only reason they're agreeing to come along!"

"Too bad, Commissioner," she said. "I'll be there in a minute, sugar. I'll just come out to the Hephzibah church? Alright then, see you soon."

Daniel's jaw was agape, half-joking, half-truly hurt. "You'll be fine," Amber said. "You want me to sit here keeping you company, or go wrangle some more votes?"

He smiled. "When you put it that way. . ."

Amber had bought a passenger trailer some months ago to ride Jonathan and his friends around, and it was outfitted with plush seats, guard rails, and off-road tires. She secured the trailer to the hitch, filled the tank with gasoline from a can she kept in the garage, straddled the machine, primed the engine, and pressed the ignition with her thumb.

During high school, and then again over the last year or so, she had spent countless hours exploring the land. She knew the location of every deer trail and cow path. She knew the topography of every field, knew the places where the ground stretched flat for hundreds of yards so she could sustain a sprint, knew the sinkholes to avoid, knew the location of every fallen tree. She knew the wide, shallow spots in every creek and stream where she could cross over, knew the broken spots in the fences where she could cross property lines, knew the slopes that could sustain the longest jumps. With this knowledge, she made her way quickly from her home, to the Beeline, into South Goshen, and to the church.

Jackie told her where to go, and she trekked along narrow, dusty paths littered with mud holes. She traveled roads that had not been repaved in many decades and were now little more than trails of broken tar-rocks. She bumped along trodden footpaths to ramshackle homes in the woods. She rumbled from place to place, picking up amused, surprised old country people and rattling them along to the poll in her trailer hitch. She relished the chilly November air, the brilliant oranges, reds, and yellows in the trees all around her, the smell of exhaust, the excitement of enfranchisement.

Daniel turned off a county road and drove down a long dirt driveway onto the Crick property. Dusty Crick was a mechanic who often worked on the Riley family farm when Daniel was a boy. Today, he worked much less than he used to. He had an older brother who nobody ever saw, but who everybody knew Dusty took care of for some reason or another. People respected him for that.

As a boy, Daniel hung around Dusty when he was on the farm to work. He was soft-spoken and unperturbed and patient, and Daniel looked up to him. To this day, Daniel considered him a family friend and someone whose vote was secure.

He got out of the car and walked past a small pen that enclosed seven fluffy chickens. He could smell the dung inside the chicken coop. It was a soothing, familiar smell. The wind had picked up, and he listened to the sound of the breeze in the silence of the country. He walked past an array of stray machine parts surrounded by grass and brambles, to the modest farmhouse. He knocked, and Dusty answered. He looked surprised. He had not been expecting a visit, but he gave a tired, patient smile and invited Daniel in. He looked surprisingly old to Daniel, who had not seen him face to face in some time, and who, until this moment, had in his mind's eye the image of the strong young mechanic he had admired as a child.

The door opened into a kitchen lit only by dim light through dirty windows. There was an old stovetop with two cycs, a clean tin pot on one, the other full of rust and looking as if it had not been used in years. The sink was full of dishes. A tall stack of Mountain Dew cases sat next to the refrigerator.

"Come on in," Dusty said, and walked through the kitchen, gesturing for Daniel to follow. "You want a Mountain Dew?"

"Sure," Daniel said. "Thank you."

Dusty pulled a warm can from a plastic ring at the top of the stack and handed it back to Daniel and moved deeper into the house. Daniel felt uneasy but followed Dusty inside into a smoky living room. The curtains were drawn, the furniture lit dully by the occasional flicker of the television. "Divorce Court" was on the set.

Dusty flopped down onto his Lay-Z-Boy. He picked up a Mountain Dew from the floor next to his seat and took a long drink. "Ah, that's good," he said. "Love the Dew."

"Heh heh," Daniel said and took a shallow sip from his own can. "It's a good one."

Against the wall was a long, filthy-looking orange couch. A grey man sat on the far end of the couch, his watery, lifeless eyes pointed toward the television. He seemed unaware of Daniel, possibly unaware of his own existence. The man wore a clear mask over his face. A tube ran out of the mask into an oxygen tank sitting on the floor. A pack of cigarettes and an overflowing ashtray sat on the table beside him.

"Have a seat," said Dusty. He signaled to the orange couch.

A pang of horror struck him, and he knew it showed on his face. Luckily, Dusty was engrossed in the justice being delivered on television and didn't notice. *Just act natural*, Daniel thought. He maneuvered himself onto the couch, as far away as possible from the specter on the end. *Make your pitch and get out of here*, he thought, suddenly beginning to panic.

"Dusty, have you gone and voted today?" he asked. Dusty kept looking at the TV. He didn't answer for a moment. Daniel swallowed.

"I have not. I don't know that I'll make it down there."

"Well, Dusty, we sure would appreciate it. This cannabis bill is a big deal. We could bring big opportunities here to Goshen County."

"I don't know," he answered. "I just assume let the tobacco industry die a natural death, without bringing the dope in."

"How do you mean?"

"Tobacco contracts are reaching their term. A lot of people getting out of the business no matter what. More folks growing soybeans now. Hell, I hear blueberries are supposed to be big business. Ain't your daddy doing that? Anyway, there are other things out there besides the marijuana." He took a long sip of his soda.

"Tobacco's killed a lot of people," he said, still looking at the television. "Weed won't be no better. You smoke it just the same. The companies pushing tobacco today are the same ones going to be pushing marijuana tomorrow. They'll be after that money. I'm afraid we might be jumping out of the frying pan and into the fire on this one, buddy bear."

He paused and looked over at his brother on the couch, who had begun to weakly flick a lighter under a cigarette.

Daniel had struggled very little with the morality of commercial marijuana. To him, weed had always been something romantic and natural, something unconnected from the crass commercialism surrounding cigarettes and booze. He had fond memories of sitting in dormitories, blowing bong-smoke out the window, laughing hysterically and listening to Smashing Pumpkins on the stereo. He had smoked very little since Jonathan was born, but he had not protested when the opportunity presented itself and the moment was right. Like when the Toadies came to Atlanta and played "Rubberneck" all the way through, or when his buddy offered him a gummy right before the opening sequence of *Infinity War*, or last winter on the beach at Seaside, Florida, when he and Amber shared a vaporizer pen he brought back from Las Vegas and they had incredible sex. These had been wonderful moments. Weed had always seemed like something pure and harmless, all upside and no down.

But now, he looked over at the man on the couch. He looked down at the pack of cigarettes at his side. *Basic*, the box said. What happens when they're selling joints in little packs like that? he wondered. Low-dose joints so that you can smoke a pack a day and still function? What happens when they start selling "tobacco blends," adding nicotine to make pot more habit-forming? What happens when marijuana becomes as commercial as tobacco, as crass as lite beer at the supermarket? Would the laughter in the dorm room become less magical? Would the love-making become less intense? Will people start dying of pot-induced emphysema? Will we all sit sunken into our couches for eternity, unproductive forever?

Daniel shook his head and awoke from his thoughts. He stood and said, "Well, I hope you'll come out and vote. I can give you a ride if you'd like."

"Good luck, Daniel," Dusty said, his eyes transfixed on a commercial for some kind of mop.

"Thanks."

Daniel walked back through the kitchen to the front door. When he opened it, the light poured into his eyes, the air into his lungs, as if he had been trapped underwater and had finally emerged. He bounded through the yard back to the Explorer.

* * *

Michael was driving a fresh load of voters to the poll when his phone rang. He looked down at the screen. "King, Tyler," it said. Bizarre, he thought. He hadn't realized the man's name was saved in his phone.

"Can y'all give me a second?" he projected to the people in the back. "I need to answer this." They quieted their talking. He pressed the "accept" button. "This is Michael," he said.

"Michael, how are you?" Tyler had a sweet friendliness in his voice. "This is Tyler King."

"I'm just fine, sir. How are you?"

"I'm ok, Michael, I'm ok," said Tyler, a tone of fatherly concern in his voice. "Listen, Michael, I don't know if this is a good time for you to talk . . ."

"It's fine."

"Good. Listen, I heard what you've been doing today, and lawyer to lawyer, I have some concern. I've got a pretty good pulse on this election we're having here, and your boy just ain't got a chance, Michael, and I'm just trying to be honest with you. I'm telling you this because, well, you've started to build a good reputation for yourself. I'm afraid you may be making a mistake that you're going to regret. When your boy loses, you're going to wish you had not been so gung-ho in delivering votes against the Commissioner. That's the sort of thing a man like Leon Darby won't forget. And I'm telling you this because. . . well. . . it might not be too late to seek redemption, if you know what I mean."

Michael took the phone from his ear, held it to his chest. "This man thinks he's slick," he said, just loud enough for his passengers to hear. He brought the phone back to his face. "Maybe you're right about our chances. But then again, maybe you're not," he said.

"Listen, Michael, I don't know how to say this other than just to say it. There's a big infrastructure project on the horizon. We're knocking the roads out over in the commercial district, adding lanes. Going to be updating the watershed system at the same time. It's a multi million-dollar project. Lots of state money. There's going to be lots of legal work to be done. The whole bid process, insurance, all kinds of opportunities. Your name has come up more than once. I'd like to see you get some of that business."

Michael smiled broadly. He tried to contain his laughter.

"I don't need your money," Michael said. "Remember, once the Everett appeal is wrapped up, I'll be rich as hell anyway."

The people in the van looked at one another with intrigue.

Tyler's tone changed. "Boy, this thing is going to blow up in your face, and I'm going to be there to watch when it does. Your life's not ever going to be the same after this thing is over. You'll never get another client, I'll be sure of that. I'm also going to have the Secretary of State on your ass over this electioneering you're doing. I know it ain't legal."

Michael had maintained his cool throughout this conversation. But something about this threat, this raw attempt at intimidation, caused him to snap. He finally lost his cool. He said, "But what happens when we win? What happens is, you lose everything. Because you've put all your eggs in one basket, counselor. When Daniel Riley is County Commissioner, you will lose a degree of control that you've come to take for granted. So, I can understand why you're trying so hard to defeat us. Because when Riley wins, your whole world will come crumbling down around you. Your greatest privileges will evaporate. And personally, for me? I personally *cannot wait* to see that happen. So I'm going to keep trying my damnedest to win this election. Good bye." He hung up the phone.

Michael turned to the people in the back. Their mouths were slack, their eyes wide. "Anyone need help getting out?" he asked. Every eye looked to Michael with deep, abiding respect. The man closest to the sliding door opened it up, and the group poured out toward the church to vote. Michael took out his phone and called Jackie, then Ed, then Jeff, then every other volunteer they had. *Step on the gas*, was his message. Don't let up. Don't let a single supporter miss the poll. Don't let a single voter go untouched.

He continued his work through the day with an angry sort of determination. Through his efforts, Jackie's, and Amber's, by 4 p.m. every southside household had been greeted with a knock on the door, a request to come vote, and the offer of transportation. Even after every household had been touched, Michael insisted they go back through the biggest neighborhoods a second time to make sure everyone had voted.

The air outside the church became electric as the afternoon went on. A steady stream of voters poured in and out of the double doors that led into the church lobby. It was a level of turnout unprecedented in the history of the precinct.

Tyler phoned Deputy Tibbits, who stepped outside the narthex of the First Baptist Church to take the call.

"Now," Tyler said through the receiver. "There's no time to wait. We need these votes *now*. As many as you can get. No fucking around."

Russ ambled back into the front doors. He caught Melanie's eye. He nodded and gave her an instructive look.

Melanie took a deep breath. She looked out the corner of her eye at Mrs. Folds. Mrs. Folds had worked as a filing clerk for decades. She was a sweet lady who Melanie knew and liked. Melanie announced, "I've been having some trouble with these cards." She held up one of the sturdy electronic cards voters were issued before they stepped into the booth. "Miss Folds, can you cover for me for a minute?"

Mrs. Folds nodded.

Melanie found a random name on the screen of her workstation and selected it, as if that voter had just arrived and presented his ID. She put the card into the little device beside her, and the device clicked. She took the card out. She stood up and walked back to a voting machine. She turned her head, ever so slightly, to see if Mrs. Folds was watching, but she was greeting a voter and did not seem to be paying attention. Melanie put the card into the machine, and the ballot flashed onto the screen. She touched the box next to Leon Darby's name. The card popped back out. Her heart beat loudly. She felt dizzy. She had just cast a ballot for someone who wasn't there.

Melanie walked back to the check-in table and said, "Hmm, that one didn't work. Maybe there's something wrong with that machine." While Mrs. Folds was checking in another voter, Melanie repeated her process. She clicked on a voter's name, put the key card into the device, took the card back and voted. Mrs. Folds still seemed not to notice. Melanie did it a third time. Then a fourth.

Melanie's heart began to calm itself. She could still feel it thumping, she could hear it in her head, but she no longer felt like it would burst. The bile that had been boiling in her stomach began to simmer down. She still felt light-headed. Her hands and arms felt numb. She felt as if she were floating above herself, watching herself, somehow disconnected from her body. She was casting fraudulent votes, one after the other, and she seemed to be getting away with it.

Then, in a single, terrible moment, Melanie saw Mrs. Folds look down at her fingers on the keyboard. Mrs. Folds looked at the computer screen, then looked at Melanie's face. The older woman furrowed her eyebrows. Melanie grew pale.

"You get the card worked out?" Mrs. Folds asked, still looking intently into Melanie's eyes.

Melanie gave a nervous chuckle. "Yes, ma'am. I think I did." She looked away from Mrs. Folds and back at her computer screen.

Melanie had a recurring dream where she had killed someone, or done some other horrible thing, and it was always unclear how or why she had done it, but she had gotten away with it. No one had known. But in her dream, people were starting to ask questions. Someone was starting to piece together what she had done. She was struck by great dread that she would be found out. In the dream, she was never sure whether anyone really knew she had done it, or whether it was her own paranoia. She would try to act as if there was nothing wrong, would go about her business, calm as possible on the surface while intense foreboding boiled underneath.

It was a classic stress dream, and the feeling she had then was the feeling she had now. She saw in Mrs. Folds' eyes the judgment of the righteous upon the wicked. She swallowed hard. She felt as though she might vomit.

Deputy Tibbits had been watching this exchange. He had seen the strange look that Mrs. Folds gave to Melanie. He went over to the table and said with an affected sternness in his voice, "What's going on over here?" Melanie kept her eyes on the computer screen. Mrs. Folds looked up at the deputy with some relief that there was a man with a badge taking interest in something that seemed suspicious.

"Show me what the problem is," he said to Melanie, and gave her a wide-eyed look that said he was acting.

"Well," Melanie said. She clicked on a voter's name. "I put the card in." She put the card in the device. The device clicked. "And then I take it out." She took the card out of the device. "And when I take it over to the voting machine here. . ." She stood up and walked over to the voting booth, the deputy following behind. "I put it in the machine here." She put the card in. The screen lit up with the ballot.

Goshen County Commissioner

___ Leon Darby

___ Daniel Riley

Russ moved close to her, obscuring any view that Mrs. Folds might have of the screen. Melanie pushed the box next to Darby's name. She confirmed her selection. Vote number five. "See there," she said, loud enough to be heard by anyone in the room. "Nothing comes up."

"Let's try again," said the deputy.

The card popped out of the voting machine, and she carried it back to her station. By way of this charade, she and Russ delivered four additional votes to Darby by 4:30 p.m. Nine in total.

Russ looked down at his cell phone, which had just issued a loud ding.

Tyler: looking good?

Russ: 9 votes

Tyler: !!!!!!!

Tyler: not enough. Not even close. Get the lead out.

Tyler: need 100

Tyler: at least!!!

Russ's heart raced. He looked around the room. Two old men waited in line for their turn to vote. Melanie fiddled with her computer screen, probably checking in another phantom voter. That would be ten. But that's not nearly enough, he thought. He had to act fast.

"I'll be right back," he announced.

Russ walked through a pair of double doors in the back of the fellowship hall. The doors led him down a dark hallway deeper into the church. His mind raced. He looked into each room he passed, trying to find something, anything, that he could use as a distraction. His patrol boots clomped on the linoleum and echoed along the empty walls.

Finally, he peered into an open door and saw the church kitchen. He went into the kitchen, scanned the room, and his eyes rested on the electric stovetop. He walked over to it, looked down at the eyes and thought for a moment. He reached down and turned a knob, spinning it until its arrow pointed to a red band labeled "HIGH." The grey-black coil of the stove popped and lurched. A faint heat rose onto his face.

He turned and saw a little wicker basket lying on a countertop. The basket was filled with a stack of old church bulletins. He walked over to the basket and pulled out some bulletins. He walked back over to the eye and lay the bulletins on top.

Russ went back to the basket. He picked up another bulletin, and tore off a small strip of paper. He picked up a tiny pencil that was lying nearby—the kind of pencil left in the pews for people to write down their prayer requests. He wrote something on the little strip and put it into his pocket. He walked out of the kitchen, through the hallway, and back through the double doors to the fellowship hall.

"You figured it out yet?" he said to Melanie as he came back into the lobby.

"Still working on it," she replied.

"Well, call the Secretary of State's office if you can't get it working," he said. "Or just tell folks not to use that machine."

"Alright," she said.

Russ returned to his post at the front entrance. He put his hands into his pockets. He sniffed the air intermittently, hoping for smoke. He thought he smelled a faint burning. He pretended not to notice. He wanted Mrs. Folds to notice first. She didn't seem to. He walked toward the table where Melanie and Mrs. Folds were working. He sniffed loudly. "Y'all smell something?" he said.

Mrs. Folds lifted up her head and sniffed the air. "Oh," she said. "Goodness, is something burning?"

The deputy feigned a casual air. "Does kinda smell like something burning," he said.

Mrs. Folds turned her head to one side and sniffed twice. "Something's burning," she said, assuredly.

The old lady standing in line held up her nose and whiffed the air. "I smell it, too," she said.

Russ shook his head and pursed his mouth skeptically. "I don't think so," he said. "But let me look around." He looked at Melanie, and their eyes met, knowingly. As he walked past her, he handed her the little strip of paper. She looked down at it. "Need 100," it said. "Pronto!"

The deputy walked back through the double doors into the hallway. He turned into the kitchen and looked at the bulletins lying there on the stove. The eye was red. Smoke rose from underneath the bulletins and lifted into the air in thin white ribbons. He looked up at the ceiling. A little green light shone from the smoke alarm. He leaned against the counter near the door and watched the smoke rising from the stovetop. He knew the smoke would soon turn to flames and the alarm would sound.

The volume of smoke increased. Then finally, a flame. Even still, the alarm was silent. Russ found himself growing impatient and pushed himself off the counter, ready to fan the flames. But then, as if on cue, the fire alarm sounded. A shrill ring pierced the air. He could feel the sound bouncing around the walls of the kitchen. It hurt his ears. He knew this would do the trick.

He left the kitchen and ran down the dark, empty hallway, back through the double doors into the fellowship hall. "There's a fire," he said. He hardly needed to make the announcement. The alarm in the fellowship hall had begun to sound as well. The room was full of confusion and panic.

"Let's evacuate," he said. He moved urgently to Mrs. Folds and put his hand on her back. "Let me help you up, ma'am." She rose from the metal folding chair and shuffled her feet toward the door, guided by his pushing hand. "C'mon, folks," the deputy said, loud enough for everyone in the room to hear. Three older people followed him as he pushed the front doors open and guided Mrs. Folds outside.

As he pushed Mrs. Folds out the door, Russ turned his head and met eyes with Melanie. He gave her a stern, desperate look. Mrs. Folds turned her head as well, just as the doors were closing. She saw Melanie standing there behind the table, unmoving, while the deputy pushed everyone else out the door.

Melanie's hands began to shake. The shrill cry of the alarm rang through her ears. Her throat tightened. She turned down to look at her screen. She clicked the next voter on the list with an urgent, unsteady hand. She pulled herself out of the seat and strode to the voting machine. She cast a vote. Her body shook. She ran back to the check-in counter. She did it again. Her conscious mind turned itself off as she continued her terrible work. Her animal brain carried her legs from the table to the voting machine and back, over and over, in fearful obedience.

After some time, Russ came back into the lobby, alone. "Election superintendent's coming," he said.

Melanie looked up from the computer screen, where she had been about to check in another voter.

"All good?" Russ asked.

She nodded her head jerkily, sniffing and catching her breath. In the ten minutes between the evacuation and Russ's return, she had cast 77 more votes for Leon Darby.

.

# 13

DANIEL AND AMBER stood across the street from the First
Baptist Church, next to their little boy and the elder Rileys,
watching the troubling scene unfold before them. They had heard
the sound of a fire alarm emerging from the church. They had
watched Russ Tibbits escort several older voters outside in a hurry.
It appeared the church had been totally evacuated, and even though
the fire alarm had now stopped, nobody was being asked back into
the church to vote. Now, they watched a disheveled-looking man
with white hair and a beige jacket—the regional superintendent for
the Secretary of State's Office—walk inside the front doors, a
manilla envelope in his hands, probably there to collect the ballots.
So, it was over.

Daniel felt that he should say something poignant. He thought
for a moment, but could find no inspiration. He was exhausted. The
relief he had felt that morning, knowing that the election would
soon be over, had melted away. He was now filled with worry more
acute than ever before. Very soon, he would know whether he had
achieved his goal, or whether he had failed. But first, there would be
several more hours of uncertainty.

The air was growing cool as the sun went down. Daniel said, "I
need a beer."

Daniel opened the back door to his family's farmhouse and stepped
into the warm hearth of his mother's kitchen. The heat from the
furnace, the familiar food smells, caused him a moment of relief.
Amber followed behind him.

Johnny and the elder Rileys had arrived before them, and
Johnny was now sitting on a big ottoman, too close to the
television, watching *Spider-Man 2*—the Sam Raimi one with Toby

MaGuire as the wall-crawler. Jonathan turned quickly as his father walked into the door. The boy's face lit up, and he ran to Daniel, and Daniel crouched to embrace him. The boy wrapped his arms around his father's neck and pressed his wooly head into his cheeks. Johnny lingered there for a moment, then pulled away and ran back toward the screen, where he became transfixed by the plot of the film.

Daniel sauntered over to the kitchen table and sat. He pulled out his phone and texted Michael. Michael texted back, said that he was going to the Secretary of State's office to watch the election results come in.

Amber brought Daniel a bottle of Budweiser. He took a long gulp, released a satisfied *Ah!* and set the bottle back down on the table. He looked at Amber and gave her a tired smile. "Thanks," he said. "I needed that." He tipped the bottle back and took another long drink.

Amber looked down at the bottle. She saw that Daniel had nearly emptied it in only two drinks.

He took the bottle back up and finished it. He set it down and drew in another long breath. He relaxed into his chair and let his head hang back. He closed his eyes, felt the alcohol pour through his blood. He opened his eyes and looked up at the little clock on the microwave above the stove. 6:44. "Is that clock right?" he asked to no one in particular.

"Yes, more or less," said his father.

Daniel pulled out his phone. 6:42. He took a long, deep breath. "I need to step outside," he said.

Daniel walked out the back door into the cool evening air. He wandered away from the farmhouse, through the yard and to the fence that separated the yard from the empty cornfields beyond.

Harvest time was long over, the fields barren now except for rows of dry stalk-scrap and overturned dirt. He leaned his forearms onto the smooth, cool coil of wire stretched between the fenceposts and looked out into the darkening landscape before him. The field ran back 300 yards or so. In the distance, he could make out the trees that formed the eastern boundary of his family's property. The tops of the trees formed a jagged line, visible in contrast to the clear, star-lit sky. The night was quiet. In the summertime, the pulsating rhythm of locusts and crickets and frogs would have beat against his ears, but these creatures were now asleep in the ground or warming their buggy bodies somewhere farther south. He was surrounded by silence. His breath, and the sound of beer sloshing around in his bottle, was all he could hear.

He did not think about the election, not consciously so. It was there in his brain, jumbled and confused among the noise of his thoughts. But in his conscious mind, he thought about his little boy, the peace and neutrality in his face, his divine unawareness of the things that caused Daniel so much anxiety. He wondered whether there was any particular moment in his own life when he had transformed from that sweet little animal, concerned only with cartoons and snacks, into one of the sad and stupid beasts we call an adult.

As he stared into the darkness, it struck him that he ought to go back inside. What if the election results had been announced? What if his family was sitting in there just waiting for him to return? Yet, if he had won, someone surely would have burst the doors open and shouted his name and urged him to come inside. That had not happened. Maybe he had already lost. If so, he wished he could just hide away until the morning, that he could skip the hours of consolation, the innumerable, pointless statements about how hard he'd tried.

He pushed his arms off the fence wire and finished his beer. He turned back toward the house and as he walked past his father's old tractor barn, he thought he remembered something that might be in there.

He opened up the little door on the side of the barn. It was completely dark inside and smelled faintly of grease. It smelled like childhood. He'd spent so much time in here as a boy, playing with his Ninja Turtles, reading his comic books. As a moody teenager, he hid himself here when he needed refuge. He felt his way through the darkness to where he remembered there being a little tool cabinet. His hands touched upon the cold, smooth metal of the cabinet, right where it had always been. He moved his hand toward the middle of the cabinet and opened one of its drawers. Inside was a little plastic flashlight just where he expected it to be. He pushed the switch forward with his thumb and a beam of light cut through the darkness.

He shined the light upon a wooden ladder built into the barn's back wall. He walked over to it and put the flashlight in his pocket and climbed up the ladder. The flashlight shined up into his eyes as he climbed. He made it up onto a platform and walked along it to the corner of the barn. In that corner lay a stack of scrap-board crates that had once held mason jars or mousetraps or something. Daniel took the top crate off the stack, then the next, and then the next, until the very bottom crate was exposed. He pulled off the dusty lid and shone his flashlight down inside. There, he saw the little orange plastic box his grandfather had given him for fishing tackle or whatever other things a boy would like to put in a box.

A smile of anticipation came upon his face. He took out the orange box and sat down on the platform. He set the flashlight down next to him. He flipped up the little latch and opened it, then picked up the flashlight and shone it inside. He smiled broadly and laughed to himself, quietly, not daring to let anyone else into this moment.

Down in the box he saw a dusty zip-lock bag filled with some very dry, very old marijuana. He picked up the bag, and the pot shook loosely inside. Sitting amidst the shake was a thin, crooked joint. Next to the bag was a cigarette lighter that, amazingly, still worked.

He opened up the bag and pulled out the joint, delicately. It was dry and stiff and yellow. He thought it might disintegrate in his hands. He wondered if it would evaporate at the touch of a flame. He put the joint into his mouth and held it there between his lips and flicked the lighter. A flame appeared, and as he sucked air through the paper, the flame transferred to the joint. He held it out before him and blew softly onto the flame. The flame disappeared, and a thin bright circle of orange surrounded the circumference of the joint. Daniel put it into his mouth and inhaled. The orange glow pulsed. Smoke rose from the end. He felt the smoke hit his throat— dry, tasteless, harsh. He coughed uncontrollably. He put his free hand over his mouth and held his head down low, trying his best to keep the coughs quiet, not wanting to be discovered.

Finally, he gained control of his lungs and took in several deep breaths of fresh air. Smoke continued to rise off the dry old joint. He brought it to his mouth again and pulled in a careful, measured hit. He coughed a little once again, his throat still reeling from the last hit. He composed himself. He cleared his throat and took another small hit.

He felt a sensation he had almost forgotten, but which now seemed so familiar. That first euphoria. That rush of satisfaction. So wonderful, so pure and good. He cut the flashlight off and relaxed his back against the wood behind him. He closed his eyes and listened, aware now of the barn's many little sounds, the tiny creaks and pops as the wooden planks of the structure settled. He heard a scratching, a fluttering up above his head from the opposite corner of the roof. He remembered the owls that did their hunting here; he realized he was in the company of one this evening. He heard faint skittering and squeaking sounds from down below, the mice that his owl friend would chase tonight. His scalp tingled as the cool air crept in between the hairs on his head. For a moment, the struggles that had occupied his mind so completely vanished into that cool, quiet barn.

Then came the flood of ideas and realization that often accompanies a good marijuana high. It struck him, perhaps for the first time, that tomorrow, he could be the Commissioner-elect of Goshen County.

It was almost unbelievable that he actually had a shot. His chances, he realized, had little to do with his own efforts. Had Amber said no, which she very reasonably could have done; had the state never moved to legalize marijuana; had another, more deserving candidate declared; had Ed Gardner not taken an interest in the race; had his father never blessed the campaign; had Michael—dear Michael—never decided to help him, he would have crashed and burned more spectacularly than he had back in Rosewood.

*If I win, I have to do a good job.* That statement rang through his head. *If I win, I have to do good.*

He sat thinking on this for a little while. Before very long, the euphoria faded into a comfortable sort of numbness. Daniel recognized this feeling as well, the inevitable phase when the elation recedes and worry creeps back in. He remembered that his family was sitting in the house, yards away, probably wondering where he was. It struck him that the results must be in by now. He wished he could stay right here. He put the baggie back into the orange box and put the box back into the crate. He stacked the crates just as they had been before. Maybe in another ten years he'd come back for the shake in the bag. He turned the flashlight on and climbed down the ladder.

He opened the door to the barn and stepped out into the cold. The door closed behind him and he heard its sound emanate through the night. He heard his wife say his name and he walked toward her voice.

While Daniel was sitting in the barn, Michael was waiting inside the fluorescent-lit lobby of the Secretary of State's regional office. He wanted to know the result before anyone else, before it was posted online, before the news sites reported it. He sat in a metal chair beside a plastic fold-out table, a cylindrical metal coffee pot, a short stack of Styrofoam cups, and some cardboard tubes full of sugar and non-dairy creamer. He drank powdery, bitter coffee and waited for the returns to be counted.

Goshen County's little election had been pushed to the back of the line. Toombs County had a contentious race for school board seat. A fundamentalist pastor had been on a scorched earth campaign to unseat the school board's chair after the board rejected a curriculum that rejected evolution and taught that the earth was about 4,000 years old, and dinosaur bones had been placed into the ground by the devil to lead us astray. "I didn't come from no monkey!" was his major argument, and it had been persuasive to many. Toombs County was larger than Goshen, and turnout for that election had been high, so the S.O.S.'s office was backed up tallying those returns. In addition, the City of Vidalia had a referendum on Sunday liquor sales. Vidalia had four precincts, and a lot of votes to be counted, so they got put in line ahead of Goshen's little race for Commissioner.

A squat lady waddled out from the tabulation room. "Goshen," she said, half announcing, half mumbling. Anxiety seized Michael's heart. The lady walked the few feet from the tab room to the bulletin board. She pressed a sheet of paper onto the board with a thumbtack. Michael set down his cup. He stood and moved toward the bulletin board. From a distance, he saw two narrow lines of text. He drew closer and was able to make out the shapes of the names on the paper, but not the numbers. He drew closer, and there it stood in black-and-white:

Leon Darby  787
Daniel Riley  771

He stared at the numbers, processed what they meant. He felt his vision blur. He could not deny what it said there on the paper. Daniel had lost by 16 votes. Sixteen votes, he thought. *Sixteen votes.*

Amber had been in the kitchen, loading and reloading a page from the Secretary of State's website on her laptop when she heard Daniel's phone buzzing on the kitchen table. He had left it there when he went outside. She looked at it and saw Michael's name on the screen. It was 7:34. She knew why he must be calling. Something seized her heart and she could not answer. Daniel was still outside. She wanted him to take this call, not her. The buzzing stopped. Then, from the other side of the room, she heard the little jingling sound of her own phone. She couldn't ignore it. She picked up the phone and touched "Accept." *Accept*, she thought.

Michael told her the news.

She hung up the phone and walked out into the front yard.

"Daniel?" she called. She listened, did not hear him, did not see him. She walked around to the back of the house and through the back yard to the fence that separated the yard from the acreage. In roughly the same spot where Daniel had stood moments earlier, she leaned her arms on the coils of wire and looked out into the night.

There was this terrible moment from childhood that came into her mind now and then, seemingly out of nowhere, and over time she had come to recognize it as a manifestation of subconscious anxiety. She had been shy and awkward in grade school—smart and well-liked by her teachers, but never accepted by the more self-confident girls in her sixth grade class, the ones to whom puberty had been kind, the ones who stayed pretty and eased into young adulthood while Amber was plagued by acne and cheap haircuts and chub. One day, Belinda Parsons—probably the prettiest one, the one whom Amber most envied—passed Amber a note as she was quietly doing her math drills. The note said something to the effect that Belinda was so sick of Lisa Crabtree—who Amber knew to be Belinda's best friend. Lisa was so stuck up, the note said, didn't Amber agree? Lisa needed her butt kicked!

Amber felt such hope, such exuberant happiness, to get that note. Belinda was confiding in her, gossiping with her, passing her notes in class! She felt pride in this new, unexpected acceptance. She smiled and looked over at Belinda, her new confidant, who smiled back. Amber wrote (she remembered exactly what she wrote because she put a lot of thought into what she would say): "Yeah what a bitch," and passed the note back.

Later that afternoon, during snack break, Amber was swinging on the playground because that's what she did, even as a sixth grader, lost in her own thoughts. She was jarred suddenly from behind. Her head snapped back on her neck, and she stumbled out of the swing, and there was Lisa Crabtree, scowling, the note in her hand. Belinda was standing a few yards behind Lisa, grinning. Lisa called Amber a fat turd and pushed her into the dirt and ran away laughing with Belinda. Amber kneeled there in the dirt on her hands and knees, her head and neck aching, her heart breaking. She had been set up. The worst part of it was that it had been her fault. She was in the dirt now because she had run her big mouth and said something that she shouldn't have, something mean. In a single moment, she went from believing that a new day of friendship and acceptance was upon her, to realizing that she was just as stupid and ugly as ever, and now it was about to get even worse.

That memory played in her mind now as vividly as it ever had before, and this terrified her. She was about to cry, but she stopped herself. She took in several deep breaths, steadied herself, pushed herself off the fence and turned.

"Daniel?" she called, louder this time. She heard the sound of the barn door opening and closing again. She looked toward the barn and, shortly, Daniel emerged.

"Come in, Daniel, it's cold," she said.

He looked at her with flat affect. "Have you heard anything?" he said.

"Daniel," she said. She reached out her arms and moved toward him. He moved toward her, allowed her to wrap her arms around him. She put one hand on the back of his head and pulled his face onto her shoulder. She felt his hair in her fingers.

They came together through the back door into the warmth and light of the house. Daniel looked at his family standing in the kitchen before him, his cheeks red from the cold, his eyes red from the exhaustion and the weed. His mother approached him and hugged him around the neck. His father reached out his hand. "We're proud of you, son. Don't let this get you down." Daniel took his father's hand and pulled himself in close. Tears began to well up in his eyes. He gripped his father's shirt tightly at the shoulder and steadied his breath. He pulled away. "Thank you," he said.

Nobody said anything for a few moments. Daniel looked down at his son, who was now at his legs looking up into his eyes. Daniel crouched down to hold the boy in his arms. Johnny laid his head on his father's shoulder and held him.

"Why don't you have something to eat?" his mother asked.

"I'm ok," he responded. Then he said quietly to his son, "Let's go watch Spider-Man." He stood and guided the boy by the hand to the couch. The movie was paused, and the screen showed a frozen image of an angry Doctor Octopus swinging his metallic arms toward a leaping Spider-Man as the two fought atop a racing subway train. Jonathan nestled beside his father, and Daniel pointed the remote at the television and pushed play. Doc Ock's arm finished its swing, missing Spider-Man and crashing into the brick wall beside the train. Bricks flew through the air. A smile came upon Daniel's face, and the two lost themselves for a moment in the fantastic battle on the screen.

Michael sat in his sports-model Cadillac, driving down the Dixie Beeline back to Goshen County. An old CD of Earth, Wind & Fire played lightly through the speakers. It was a comforting, familiar sound.

His phone buzzed from the passenger's seat. He expected to look down and see Daniel's name there. Instead, it was a number he did not recognize. A local number. He picked up the phone. "This is Michael," he said.

"Um... yes... Attorney Drummond?" said an older woman's shaky voice.

"Yes ma'am?"

"Yes sir, I'm sorry to bother you," the lady said. "Pastor Reid told me I ought to give you a call. My name is Lurleen Folds."

Michael listened. What the woman said made his heart race. He asked her to come to his office. He dialed Daniel.

# 14

SOME MONTHS EARLIER, it had occurred to Daniel that the election could be close. He figured that maybe, just maybe, there could be a challenge to the results—one way or the other—and that he should be prepared. He had spent one weekend researching the law and drafting the shell of a recount petition, just in case, complete with a legal brief. He had almost forgotten about it, but tonight, he pulled it up on the computer screen and scanned its contents and smiled at how good it was.

It was nearly 10 p.m. on the eve of his defeat, yet he and Michael sat side by side, hope in their hearts, typing vigorously.

Michael wrote:

"County of Goshen

State of Georgia

Affidavit of Lurleen Folds

"1. I am a resident of this County. I am under no disability that would render me unable to give truthful and accurate testimony.

"2. The statements contained herein are truthful and are based on my own personal knowledge, observation, and experience.

"3. On November 5 of this year, I was employed as a poll worker for the north precinct of Goshen County, Georgia, during the election for County Commissioner.

"4. On this day, I observed a number of irregularities in the conduct of my fellow poll-worker, Ms. Melanie Stewart, which has caused me to become concerned that the vote total for the election for County Commissioner was not accurate."

And the document went on. In concise language, the affidavit described the suspicious behavior of Melanie Stewart and Deputy Tibbits, the sudden fire alarm, the numerous voters left disenfranchised.

As Michael wrote, his mind raced, his blood boiled, his heart spun in his chest. He had asked Mrs. Folds to come to the office that very evening, and soon she would arrive.

While Michael drafted the affidavit, Daniel worked on the brief. He pulled from his desk a file labeled "Election Challenge—Legal Research," a compilation of all the election contest cases he had studied. He turned to *Branch v. Anderson*, a 2012 case laying out the proper procedure to petition for a manual recount of electronically cast votes. He pulled *Hindman v. Paul*, a 2019 case holding that, in an election where the poll worker had not properly required voter identification cards, the judge in a recount may review voting data for irregularities.

He had what he needed. He pulled the shell brief he had previously constructed. He typed rapidly, but calmly, inserting the cases he needed and the facts he hoped to prove. He became absorbed in his work. He was tired, but the words flowed effortlessly from his mind, to his fingers on the keyboard, and onto the screen, because he knew that what he was writing was brilliant and true. Adrenaline rushed through his veins as he typed.

There was a knock at the front door. They looked up together, startled from their reverie. "That must be our witness," Michael said.

While Daniel and Michael plotted their demise, Leon Darby and Tyler King stood laughing and drinking among their allies on the Darbys' front porch. They swayed to an old Garth Brooks song and sang: *"I've got friends in low places."* Another favorite, *The Thunder Rolls*, would come on next.

Deputy Tibbits, large and heavy, sunk precariously into the swinging chair on the end of the porch. He drank a Budweiser and stared groggily ahead. Linda Darby watched him nervously, expecting at any moment for the hooks holding the chains into the ceiling to rip out or the wooden seat simply to break in half, causing the deputy to flump onto the floor. Also, he was wearing his full uniform, gun and everything, which Mrs. Darby found rather off-putting. She figured he'd been too lazy to go home and change clothes.

Darby went over to the deputy and put his hand on his shoulder. "We thank you for all your help, young man," Darby said. "Truly outstanding." He looked at Tyler, who stood bow-legged and proud next to the Commissioner, then back to the deputy. "You've got a big future ahead of you. There'll be an election for Sheriff next year," he said. "It may be time for ol' Sheriff Milligan to think about retiring. I may even encourage it. You'd make a mighty fine successor."

Russ grinned and nodded his head. "Thank you, Commissioner," he said.

"No, thank *you*," the Commissioner replied.

Linda Darby and Cathy King chatted across a wicker table and drank mint juleps. "I almost feel sorry for that little girl, the Riley girl," said Linda. "Her husband has made a fool of her. If she'd had any sense at all, she would have talked him out of doing such a thing."

Cathy King, a wiry, always frightened-looking woman, said, "And going around town talking about marijuana. My goodness. Imagine her children hearing that kind of talk."

"I imagine they'll have to go back to Atlanta, or wherever they came from," Linda added. "They've got no place here, as far as I'm concerned."

"And what about that colored girl she spends so much time with?" Cathy said.

"*Lord*, Jackie Drummond," Mrs. King continued. "Married to that black lawyer. I guess they've got some money or something. Uppity as all get-out. I see her over here on the north side all the time. She and the Riley girl are quite a sight together."

"Coexist!" said Linda Darby. She leaned in and slapped her knee. Cathy burst into laughter. This was an inside joke. One day, the two of them had driven into Macon to go shopping, and had seen this comically absurd bumper sticker on a car in front of them in the mall's parking lot. The word "Coexist" had been spelled out with various religious emblems—a cross, some kind of Muslim crescent thingy, a "ying-yang," as they called it, a Jewish star, and some other mess too, probably a Satanist symbol or something. They had watched two frumpy-looking women get out of the car. One had a nose ring, and the two women were holding hands! It was shocking and ridiculous. From that moment forward, the term "Coexist" had come to symbolize that hilarious, awful sight. The word could be uttered to signal scorn toward any stupid, sinful, or weird thing that floated around outside of God's country, in big cities like Macon.

In the ladies' collective mind, there was very little to separate those nose-ring wearing, areligious lesbians from the sight of a wealthy Negress shopping on the north side of their county with a marijuana-pushing white woman from Atlanta. In any case, Cathy and Linda knew, those girls' days of showing their faces in polite society were over.

Back at his office, Michael asked Mrs. Folds about several details of what she had told him on the phone. He made some changes to the affidavit, added some things, corrected a few points he had misunderstood. When he was through, he printed it out for her to review.

Mrs. Folds read over the document slowly. She asked for a pen. Michael smiled and handed her the pen he had been spinning around in his hand. She took it without looking. As she drew the pen to the signature line, she shrieked. She dropped the pen suddenly and looked at Michael with horror in her eyes.

"What's wrong?" Michael asked.

"My goodness, have you been *chewing* on that pen?"

Michael drew in a sigh of relief. He closed his eyes and smiled. "I'll get you another one," he said.

The germaphobe witness went into the bathroom to wash her hands. When she returned, she signed the affidavit, and a powerful legal instrument came into being.

It was late, almost midnight. Daniel and Michael thanked Mrs. Folds kindly and each gave her a big hug and walked her to the front door. Outside, they saw her husband sitting behind the wheel of an old station wagon, asleep. He'd been waiting there for her this whole time. They watched them drive away down the Beeline.

They went back into the office, and Daniel put the final touches on his "Emergency Motion for Temporary Restraining Order." The Motion asked the court to decertify the election results pending further review. He proofread his "Petition for *Quo Warranto*," which sought an immediate hearing to determine whether the election results had been obtained through fraud or abuse. He printed three copies each of the documents. He laid them out on Michael's desk and stood there for a moment, admiring them. Here, in the form of paper and ink, was truth. Here was justice, shining like the purest gold, wrought from his own hand. He felt that rare pride, that supreme confidence a lawyer gains when his position is unqualifiedly correct.

"Ready for your signature, counselor," he said. "Can't be representing myself in court."

Michael drew his signature on each document and returned them to their neat stacks. He looked at Daniel, a question in his eyes. "You ready to do this?" he said.

"Got nothing to lose at this point," Daniel said behind a sleepy smile. He held his hand out to Michael. "I'm going to stay here a while longer," he said. "I've got a little more to do. Why don't you go and get some sleep. You're going to be the one arguing tomorrow, after all."

Michael stood from his chair, shook his friend's hand. "I'll take you up on that. You try to get some sleep yourself."

"I will." There was a moment of silence. "You've done so much for me, Michael. I've done nothing to deserve any of it, and I'll never forget it. No matter how this thing turns out, just know that I am so thankful. You need anything, just ask." His lip quivered as he spoke. He was exhausted, and still a little high, and his emotions were laid bare.

Michael pulled Daniel in and gave him a tight hug. "Don't you worry about that," he said. "I'm already thinking of some real good favors to ask." He laughed, but his voice was sincere. "Don't you stay too late," he said and flicked off his lamp and picked up his briefcase. "Big day tomorrow."

After Michael left, Daniel drew out by hand a memorandum setting forth all they needed to do tomorrow in pursuit of their goal. They would file the petition first thing in the morning and insist to be heard by Judge Roundtree. They would present Mrs. Folds' affidavit and, hopefully, get the restraining order. They'd ask for a full hearing on the *quo warranto* petition without delay. They'd get the clerk to issue subpoenas for Melanie Stewart and Russ Tibbits to come and testify. They'd get a separate subpoena for the Secretary of State's regional superintendent. They'd have to get everything served, which would be dicey, because it was the Sheriff's Office's responsibility to serve documents of this nature, and he wouldn't be too thrilled about it, but he'd have to do it. After the hearing, Daniel would drive over to the regional superintendent's office to get the readouts from the voting machines.

Everything would have to go just right for this to work. He looked at the list before him, shrugged his shoulders and sighed. "Here goes nothing," he said.

He rose from his seat and clicked off the lamp, and the office grew suddenly dark. He walked out of his office and down the short hallway to the lobby and out the front door into the deep, cold darkness outside. It was still and so quiet. He looked into the sky at the expanse of stars, closed his eyes, took in a lingering breath of the cool, clean air.

He turned back to the door and pulled the keys from his pocket to lock up. As he jingled the keys, looking for the right one, he was suddenly gripped by the sense that someone was behind him, watching him. A pang of fear struck him. He cocked his head and listened. Silence. He turned around and the old square came into view. It was as empty as it could be, not a soul in sight, not a movement anywhere. But something was looking at him, watching him—he could feel it. He looked at the marble column in the middle of the square, up to the little iron boll weevil sitting on top. Its pointy little head looked down upon him. Had it turned? He stared back at it. The two watched one another for several moments before finally, Daniel turned back to the door, locked it, and marched off to his car.

# 15

IT WAS 7:04 the next morning, Wednesday, and Daniel lay asleep in the bed. Amber had gotten up already and gotten Jonathan ready for school. Daniel was thankful she had let him lie there for a little while. He hadn't gotten home til nearly two and hadn't fallen asleep til three, his mind still racing even through his exhaustion. He moaned and buried his face deeper into the pillow. He pulled a second pillow onto his head, down over his ears. Through the fluff, he could hear his wife's voice. "Daniel, you've got to get up!" she said. Finally, he fought off the desire to stay there sleeping and threw off the covers with a broad swing of his arm and swung his legs over the side of the bed.

He dragged himself into the kitchen in boxers and a t-shirt. His legs were heavy, his eyes groggy. He hadn't brushed his teeth, and his breath tasted awful. He saw that Amber had made a pot of coffee, so he poured himself a cup and drank. His zombie brain crept slowly to life. "I'll take him to school," he said. "That'll force me to go ahead and get dressed."

"Dressed for what?"

"Court."

"Court?"

"We're going to try and overturn the election."

Amber drew in a long, deep breath and sighed. "This your idea or Michael's?"

"Both. We have a good witness. I'm too tired to talk about it now. Let me get some more coffee in me."

Daniel got quickly dressed and had Jonathan in the car and off to school by 7:40. He drove up to the front of the schoolhouse, where the vice-principal smiled and greeted him, same as ever before, and Johnny opened up the door and crawled out with his lunchbox. The lady waved amiably goodbye and guided the boy into the building. Maybe she didn't know about the election. *Maybe she did, and she doesn't care.* That possibility was comforting, but almost disappointing—it belied his fantasy that everyone in town was tuned into his political fate.

He drove to the courthouse, where the parking lot was empty. He was exceedingly early. He pulled his notes out from his briefcase and began to tick through the tasks before him. He sipped coffee from a large thermos. He took off the lid and held the vessel to his face and inhaled the aromatic steam that rose from it and listened to rap music on the radio.

After a while, he looked up and saw Michael pacing up the concrete walkway in front of the courthouse's front doors, looking down at his papers, talking to himself. Daniel sat there a moment or two longer, watching Michael pace, then got out of his car, gathered his things, and moved quickly up the walkway to the courthouse entrance. "What's up?" he said.

"Yo. What's up with you?"

"Ah, nothing," Daniel smiled. "Just reeling from a humiliating public defeat, that's all."

Michael chuckled. "Well, we'll see about that," he said.

"Courthouse open yet?"

"Nah, it's still locked. Still got a couple minutes."

A brown patrol vehicle pulled from the street into the courthouse parking lot. They saw Russ Tibbits inside. The deputy looked out at them as he pulled into his reserved space. "Look who it is," Michael muttered. "I bet he's wondering what the hell we're doing here."

Daniel felt a nervous excitement. He was about to kick the hornet's nest, and here came one of the hornets.

The two kept an eye on the deputy as he walked from his car to the Sheriff's office next door. The deputy gave them a stern-faced nod. The friends nodded back. Daniel knew how suspicious they must look there in their suits and ties, the morning after the election, talking and conspiring, waiting for the courthouse to open.

A moment later, they heard the lock turning inside the courthouse. The heavy wooden door opened, and a lady invited them inside.

In the main courtroom, the bailiff was pouring himself a cup of coffee from a plastic carafe. He looked up with surprise in his face. "Y'all sure is early, ain't ya?" he said.

Michael smiled. "Got important business," he said and walked through the little gate that separated the gallery from the lawyers' tables and the bench.

Daniel sat down on the front bench of the gallery. He was accustomed to sitting at the lawyers' table, behind the separating wall, but today he was the client.

Michael approached the bailiff, shook his hand. He was taking advantage of the emptiness of the courtroom, which allowed him to chum it up with the courthouse staff as much as he liked. "How's the judge's calendar look this morning?"

"Take a look." The bailiff handed Michael a single sheet of paper. "Civil Motions Day," it read. There were the captions of four civil matters—three of which Michael recognized as divorce cases (because the last name on each side of the "v." was the same). These were probably contempt motions because somebody hadn't paid their child support. The fourth looked like an auto accident pending a motion for summary judgment. That could take some time, Michael thought.

"Looks like a pretty slow morning," Michael said, questioningly, as he looked up at the bailiff.

"You not on there?" the bailiff asked.

"Not exactly. We've got an emergency motion. We're asking for a TRO. I'm actually hoping to address the judge first thing this morning. Is he here?"

"Gimme one second." The bailiff picked up a phone receiver and pressed a few buttons. He sat waiting as it rang. "Marcy?" he said. "How you doing, this is Henry. Listen, I've got Attorney Drummond here, and he's got some kind of emergency motion. He's wanting to see the judge this morning."

Henry was quiet for a moment, and Michael could hear the muffled outlines of Marcy's voice from the receiver. It sounded friendly. His heart thumped in his chest, though. *What if he won't hear us today?* he thought.

"Ok. Ok, then. Thank you ma'am." Henry put his hand over the mouthpiece and looked to Michael. "Just one minute. She's talking to the judge." He continued to pause, waiting for Marcy to come back on the line. Henry looked over at Daniel sitting on the bench, then back at Michael. A smile formed in the corner of his mouth. "Whatchy'all up to, anyway?" he asked. Michael grinned deviously. Just then, Marcy came back on the phone.

"Yes ma'am? Ok, then. I'll tell him." He hung up the receiver. "She said wait just a minute, she's gonna come out and get you."

Judge Roundtree was sitting at his desk, scratching some notes on a paper before him when Michael and Daniel walked into his chambers. "Have a seat, counselors," he said, without looking up from his work.

Michael could feel the authority in the room, the hallowedness of the space. He found his seat and cleared his throat and sat with his back up straight, as if he was prepared to address God himself. The judge looked at Michael, then Daniel, expectantly.

"Good morning, your Honor," he said. "Thank you for your time today. As you may know, the election for County Commissioner was held yesterday. Daniel Riley here lost the final vote tally by only 16 votes, and . . ."

The judge interrupted. He said dryly, "Goodness, that *is* close." His tone seemed to suggest that he knew all of this—of course he knew—but he was making an effort to sound like he didn't.

Michael cleared his throat. "Yes, your Honor. Now, we've brought with us today a motion for a temporary restraining order, and along with that I've got a brief. I have a copy for you here, your Honor, if you'd like one."

Michael leaned down and pulled some papers from his bag in front of him. The judge leaned forward to take them. Michael handed him the motions, the brief, and the Affidavit of Lurleen Folds.

"Your Honor, in Georgia, unlike some other states, there is no provision for an automatic recount, even when an election is very close. But there is a case, *Branch v. Anderson*, which I've cited here in our brief, your Honor, in which the Georgia Supreme Court held that a court can order a recount in a local election under special circumstances."

The judge nodded as he looked over the papers. Michael looked up to the judge to see if he might have a question. The judge was still looking through his bifocals at the pleadings, so Michael just continued.

"Your Honor, there are extraordinary circumstances that have led us to file this motion. You have there before you the affidavit of one Lurleen Folds. Mrs. Folds was a poll-worker here in the north precinct. As you can see, your Honor, Mrs. Folds observed what I think any person would find to be some highly disturbing irregularities."

The judge shuffled through the papers until his found Mrs. Folds' affidavit. He brought it close and began to read in silence. His eyes squinted with concern. "Goodness," he said.

"We have cited the case of *Hindman v. Paul*, your Honor. The Supreme Court in *Hindman* held that, where there is evidence of significant irregularity, the court may order the results be decertified pending further review. In this instance, we are asking to be heard on that issue as well, your Honor. We want to subpoena the data from the voting machines; we want to check the voting rolls."

The judge continued to read Mrs. Folds' affidavit. He took a deep breath, issued a long sigh. "You have a draft order for me?" he said.

"Yes, your Honor." Michael pulled out another paper from his bag and handed it to the judge. The judge looked it over, then took his pen to the signature line.

Michael's heart almost exploded.

"Can you get everybody served and be ready to make your case tomorrow?" said the judge.

"Yes, your Honor. I believe I can."

"See you tomorrow," he said, and looked down at his work.

"Yes, your Honor. Thank you."

The judge did not look back up. The young men scrambled out the door. They almost ran out of the courthouse, almost jumped out of the front doors. Daniel leapt into the air and swung a punch toward the sky, Judge Roundtree's order gripped into his fist. A wide, open-mouthed smile appeared on his face.

# 16

COURT BEGAN at promptly 9 a.m. Thursday morning. The news of the hearing had spread, and the gallery was now filled with supporters from both sides of the contest as well as a handful of curious onlookers.

Pastor Reid of the Hephzibah Baptist Church sat on the back pew, his arms crossed, examining those in the room. He wondered what each player was thinking. He watched Michael furiously writing upon his pad. He watched Daniel, who seemed oddly relaxed, smiling and waving to his supporters in the gallery. He watched Leon Darby, his face permanently fixed into a constipated frown, sitting straight and uncomfortable in his chair. He looked at Tyler King, somehow disgusting in his handsomeness, a wicked man in an attractive body.

He recognized Ed Gardner and Jeff Jessup; they were on the front row of the gallery directly behind the petitioners, wearing coats and ties, which was unusual for them. He saw Amber and Jackie on the second row, right behind Ed and Jeff, whispering to one another.

There were Linda Darby and Cathy King sitting behind their husbands on the first row of the opposite gallery. Linda held her head down, reading something in her lap. Cathy looked furtively about the courtroom, her eyes darting around at every creak and step, keeping inventory of everyone in the room.

"Oyez, Oyez!" said the bailiff. The Superior Court of the County of Goshen, in the State of Georgia, will now come to order. Presiding is his Honorable Evan Roundtree. All rise!"

All rose.

Judge Roundtree walked out from his chambers and scaled the few short steps to his seat. He sat down and scanned the room and issued a friendly smile. "Good morning, everyone," he said.

"Good morning," the room issued back.

"We are here this morning for the matter of Daniel Riley, Petitioner, against Leon Darby, Respondent. This is a petition for *quo warranto*." He recited these procedural facts with businesslike neutrality, no editorial position apparent in his voice. "Do we have everyone here, counsel?"

Both Michael and Tyler started to rise, but Michael rose quicker. "Michael Drummond, for the petitioner, your Honor. We have everyone here, your Honor. We do have a number of witnesses, some of whom are here under subpoena. We would like to invoke the rule of sequestration."

"Very well, counsel. Any objections?"

"Good morning, your Honor," Tyler drawled. "Tyler King, for the Respondent, the good Leon Darby, the long-standing Commissioner of Goshen County, I . . ."

"Save your case-in-chief, counsel, let's stick to procedural matters for now." Judge Roundtree said.

Tyler cleared his throat. "Yes, of course, your Honor. We have no objection to invoking the rule."

"Alright then, the rule is invoked. If anyone here intends to give testimony, or has been served with a subpoena, I'd ask you at this time to wait outside the courtroom. Someone will come and get you when it's your turn. Ok?"

Michael and Daniel both turned and looked about the room. Mrs. Folds walked outside. So did Melanie Stewart.

Deputy Tibbits, who had been standing near the courtroom door, stood still as a sentry. Michael watched him as the double doors closed back up. It seemed he intended to stay.

"Anything else before we get started?" asked the judge.

Michael stood. "Um, your Honor. There is a witness who has not left the room. I don't mean to be rude to him, but . . ."

"Who is that?"

"Mr. Russell Tibbits, the Deputy Sheriff." Michael signaled toward the deputy in the back of the courtroom.

"Mr. Tibbits, have you received a subpoena to testify in this case?" the judge asked, his voice raised to travel to the back of the courtroom.

The deputy stuttered. "Well, I . . . Yes, your Honor. But I . . . I'm the deputy assigned to this courtroom, and . . ."

"Well, sir, you are a witness in this case. We have the bailiff here. I'd ask you to please step outside until such time as you are called. If we have an emergency or something, we'll holler for you." The judge issued a good-humored grin.

"Yes sir." The deputy turned and shuffled out of the room.

"Mr. Drummond, you're the petitioner. Make your case."

"Would you like to hear opening remarks, your Honor?"

"I've read your petition, I know what the case is about. I'll hear closing remarks after the evidence. Call your first witness."

"Your Honor, I'd call Mrs. Lurleen Folds."

The judge nodded to the bailiff. The bailiff walked out of the gate into the gallery and back through the double doors. A moment later, he re-entered, with Mrs. Folds following closely behind him.

Mrs. Folds was wearing a floral dress that seemed oddly colorful for the occasion. She looked rather younger than her 74 years, but her face gave off an aura of knowledge and experience. Most everyone in the courtroom that morning recognized her. She had been a mainstay of county business for decades and had volunteered as a poll worker in every election anyone could remember.

"Just step right around here, ma'am, and take a seat behind the witness stand," said the judge. Mrs. Folds nodded and worked her way over to the witness stand. She sat in the chair behind the stand and looked out nervously into the courtroom.

"Have you ever testified in court before?" the judge asked.

"Uh, no sir."

"Well, just try to relax. The bailiff is going to issue the oath, and then the lawyers will ask you some questions. All you've got to do is answer the questions as best as you can, and tell the truth. Ok?"

She nodded.

"Raise your right hand!" the bailiff boomed. Mrs. Folds jumped a little, startled. She raised her right hand.

"Do you solemnly swear that the testimony you shall give today shall be the truth, the whole truth, and nothing but the truth, so help you God?"

"I do," she said, and nodded.

"Mr. Drummond, your witness," said the judge.

Michael greeted Mrs. Folds good morning. He proceeded to ask her a series of short, basic questions about her experience at the poll on November 5. He walked her through the day, and she testified just as she had in Michael's office the evening of the election. She told of the strange behavior of Melanie Stewart, how she had gone back and forth from her check-in screen to the voting booth so many times in the last minutes of voting. She told about the curious fire, how Melanie had stayed behind when Deputy Tibbits evacuated everyone else outside. She told about the last remaining voters who were forced to leave and never got to cast their ballots, and the several who drove up to the precinct but were turned away because the doors were never reopened.

"Now, Mrs. Folds, you are here on your own accord today, is that right? Nobody has required you to be here today, correct? Nobody has served you with a subpoena?"

"Yes, that's right."

"And why is it that you decided to testify today?

"Because it all seemed so suspicious. And the election was so close. I feared that something . . ." she looked for the right word. "*Untoward* was happening."

"Remind us how long you have been a poll worker?" Michael asked.

"Been doing it right at 26 years now."

"And how many elections have you worked?"

"Oh goodness. More than I can remember. I missed one back when Harold got sick."

"And in your experience, have you ever witnessed anything similar to what you saw this past November fifth? Anything like what you've testified to today?"

"No sir. Nothing like it before."

"Thank you, Mrs. Folds. Your Honor, I have nothing further at this time, but I'd like to reserve the right to re-direct."

"Very well."

"Mr. King, cross-examination?"

Tyler was leaning across the arm of his chair, whispering with Darby. He looked up at the judge's inquiry. He smiled, but the smile turned to concern, and he stood. "Your Honor," he said. "There is a great deal at stake here in this proceeding. The question of who shall hold the highest office in this county, the integrity of our electoral process. Yet, we only received notice of this proceeding yesterday; we've only now had the opportunity to review the petitioner's brief, the affidavit of this witness. To be very honest, your Honor, we do not feel we have had a fair chance to prepare ourselves. I would like to cross-examine this witness, I certainly would. I have grave doubts about what she has said today. But due process demands that we have a little bit of time. We are requesting a recess, your Honor. We are humbly requesting that this hearing be stayed for a period of 14 days, at the least, to allow us some basic discovery, to do our own investigation, to research the law. Otherwise, your Honor, I feel we are being ambushed here."

It was the most calm and cogent argument that Michael had ever heard Tyler King make. And it made sense. Michael had been excited by the element of surprise this quick hearing allowed him— but, he realized, it *was* fundamentally unfair.

"What do you say, counsel?" said the judge to Michael.

"Your Honor, I agree that the stakes are high. And for that very reason, a delay of fourteen days is unconscionable. The people of this county deserve to know who has won this election. And if there has in fact been fraud, its perpetrators need to be brought to justice without delay. I propose that we continue forward as planned, your Honor. We are ready."

Judge Roundtree thought it over for a moment. "Mr. Drummond," he said, "I agree with you that we do not want to prolong these proceedings unnecessarily; the people *do* need to know who won. And honestly, I'd like to get everyone on the stand as soon as possible, while memories are still fresh. But even a criminal defendant gets time to prepare, gets some basic discovery. There is a due process argument to be made here."

He looked to Tyler. "Mr. King," he said, "I am going to reschedule the remainder of this hearing for this coming Monday, November 11. That's not very long, I realize that. But I am going to instruct Mr. Drummond here to produce to you *today* every piece of evidence he has. Mr. Drummond, I want you to give Mr. King a comprehensive witness list and a basic description of the testimony you expect each witness to provide. Mr. King, I realize that is not a whole lot of time to prepare, but this is an urgent matter, and we must get on with it. I do not intend for this to become a protracted piece of litigation. Does everyone understand?"

"Yes, your Honor," said both attorneys in unison.

"Alright then," said the judge. "I will see you on Monday at nine. Be prepared."

"Yes, your Honor."

The judge banged his gavel.

# 17

THAT AFTERNOON, Tyler sat in Darby's office and flipped absently through a crusty old farm journal while he listened to the Commissioner curse and spit.

"You have got to get these people under control!" Darby said. "This Folds woman is dangerous! She's got to be dealt with! What about the woman from the clerk's office? Stewart? Is there any risk she'll turn on us? Dammit, Tyler, this situation has got to be nipped in the bud *now*!"

Tyler listened. "Stewart is in our camp. I feel pretty firmly about that. I'll make sure, though. Folds, I don't know what to do with. I'll see what I can dig up on her; I'll get to cross-examine her first thing next week. I can discredit her."

"*Discredit* her? What the hell does that mean? You heard the woman. If she comes to court on Monday with that same story, Judge Roundtree is going to eat us alive. She needs to be convinced—in whatever way necessary—to *stay away from the courthouse*. Put her on a bus out of town, for all I care! Make that woman disappear!"

Tyler kept his gaze on the pages of the magazine. He hated Leon Darby so much right now. Even as he labored to appear calm and unworried, he simmered inside, angry that the plot he had designed might be exposed, angry at the consequences it could bear for him—public humiliation, disbarment, prosecution—and most of all, angry that he had done it all in service to this awful fucker. And not an ounce of appreciation for any of it. Just blame, and a demand for more.

"I'm on it, boss," he said, his contempt veiled as thinly as possible. He dropped the magazine onto the table, stood and left the room.

* * *

That evening, Deputy Tibbits sat in Tyler's office, a dumb, half-scared expression on his face. Tyler said, "Russ, you have done a great thing for this county, helping us to win this election. But as you probably realize, our victory has been placed at risk. And we need you to help us protect it. You've already gone above and beyond the call of duty, but now I'm asking you to go even beyond that. These witnesses—Melanie; the colored lady, Folds—we've got to get a handle on them. This whole thing could slip through our fingers, Russ. My job, your job, everything we've built, is at risk."

"What do you want me to do?" Russ asked.

"Talk to Melanie. Make sure she is solid. Make sure she'll stick to the story. The very worst thing that could happen is she turn on us. She is our Achilles' heel. She knows everything. If she breaks, we are finished. You and I could *go to jail*, Russ." Tyler leaned forward as he said this, capturing Russ's eyes, capturing his imagination.

The deputy was startled, indeed. He hid it poorly. His foot kicked reflexively against Tyler's desk. His eyes, his skittish manner, betrayed the visceral fear he felt at the prospect of being found out, of being held accountable for his actions. "What about the colored lady?" he asked.

"She could be as dangerous to us as Melanie. You weren't in court when she testified, but she came across well. I haven't cross-examined her yet, but. . . The judge seems impressed by her." He paused, clearing his throat. "It sure would be nice if she didn't show up for court next week. If only someone could persuade her."

"She won't listen to me," Russ said, protesting now. "Can't we offer her some money? Maybe you know somebody from that side of the road who can talk to her? Somebody she trusts?"

"Ain't nobody on that side of the road gonna do me any favors, I'll tell you that. Paying her off is a good idea, but that could backfire on us, especially if she says *no* and it gets out that we had offered it to her. Yep, Folds does pose a much more, shall we say, *complicated* challenge. I can't tell you exactly how to deal with her. All I can say is: Russ, I need you to make sure she is not in court next week. How you accomplish that, I'll leave to your discretion."

Russ began to jitter. He shook his leg nervously.

"Do whatever you have to do," Tyler said. He looked sternly into Russ's eyes, and Russ glared back. The hairs of his mustache stood on end.

Finally, the deputy rose from his chair, nodded his head and said, "Understood." He turned swiftly toward the door and goose-stepped out of the office.

The next morning, Friday, as he prepared himself to carry out his work, Russ had an epiphany. Up until lately, he had looked at the MacKenzie Sanchez situation as a wake-up call. He had been smoking meth, beating ass, banging women on the job, and had basically gotten caught, but had miraculously escaped any consequence. When the federal judge dismissed that case, he felt as if he had been given a sort of undeserved second chance from God. He had been doing so many things that he should not have been doing, and he expected to be punished for it; yet somehow, it had all gone away, save for the nickname he would probably never escape. The dismissal had been an opportunity to get himself right. And he had. He had been doing a lot better. He hadn't been using drugs. He had stopped messing with the women on his patrol routes. He was more cautious with his use of force.

But now, he realized, that had all been a mistake. It wasn't a miracle that he had escaped the consequences of what he did to that girl. Getting away with it was a perk of this job. Now, he finally realized, the rules did not contain him; he contained the rules. The

Boll Weevil

Sheriff's Office and the Office of the Commissioner were the highest authorities here. There were higher authorities, of course, outside of the county, but none with any interest in this place so isolated from the world outside, so far from the mind of anyone who might have a problem with what went on here. He was hidden from view; the county was a world unto itself. He could do whatever he wanted, so long as he pleased the Sheriff and the Commissioner. And if *he* were to become Sheriff, something that now seemed bizarrely feasible, he could do whatever the fuck he wanted, *period*. What a wonderful feeling. *What a wonderful fucking feeling!*

These thoughts raced through his mind, and a powerful ecstasy of purpose filled him as he watched thick, milky smoke rise in delicate ribbons from the bowl of the glass pipe in his hand. He exhaled, and a great mass of smoke poured out, filling the cab of the police cruiser. His favorite album—*Creed's Greatest Hits*—was playing through the car's stereo system. He cranked up the volume as the chorus to "One Last Breath" poured over him, so beautiful, so profound, so perfect, Scott Stapp speaking to him directly. A tear poured from his eye. *God*, this feeling of clarity, this feeling of power, so pure and so good. The delightful tingle that sizzled along every inch of his body. And the focus. *The goddamn focus!*

He rolled down his window, let the smoke escape into the cool air outside, put the cruiser in reverse and backed out of his driveway, en route to the courthouse.

That same morning, Melanie reported to work at the County Clerk's office as usual. She did her best to act normal, to behave as if nothing was wrong. She avoided eye contact with her co-workers and occasional residents who came to seek some document or pay some fine. She didn't want to talk about the election or yesterday's hearing. She felt her culpability would reveal itself in subtle, unconscious ways. Her guilt tortured her. Her pain came not so much from the knowledge that she had done something wrong, but from her certainty that she would soon be caught. She could not imagine explaining herself in court, in any believable way, without telling the truth. In fact, she rather wanted it over with. She rather wanted to shout from the rooftops what she had done, to remove the boulder of this heavy secret from her chest. The next court date would almost be a relief; it would be her chance to end the misery of this anxiety.

Around noon, she went out to her car to smoke a cigarette and eat some crackers. She sat in the car with the window cracked and took big, deep drags from a Virginia Slim. She had quit smoking last year—for good this time, she thought—but the urge this morning had been too great. No nicotine gum would do. She had picked up a pack on her drive into work, and now, she closed her eyes and breathed in the tobacco smoke, let it relax her racing mind.

Suddenly, she heard Russell Tibbits' voice in her ear. She jumped. She opened her eyes and saw his face, inches from her own, on the other side of the window.

"What the hell, Russ! You scared the shit out of me." She rolled down the window some more.

"Sorry," he said. He crouched down and looked at her through the open window. He had a friendly, frankly elated smile on his face. "How you holding up?"

She was silent for a moment. Then she said, "not good, to tell you the truth." She looked past him, then turned and looked out the other window, as if someone might be listening. She said, "I'm scared as I can be, Russ. Miss Folds done told them everything. How the hell am I supposed to explain myself? I've got to swear on a Bible and everything, Russ! I can't do this!"

"Calm down, calm down," Russ said. "Remember, I'll be testifying, too. I'll back up everything you say. There was a malfunction with one of the machines. All you were doing was checking it out. I was right there with you. I saw the whole thing. You and I were just trying to fix the machines, that's all. Easy breezy."

She took another long drag from her cigarette. She shook her head. "I don't think it's that simple," she said. "Can't they prove that machine wasn't broken?"

"No, no, no, they can't open up those machines. All they've got is that old black lady, and all she's got is suspicions. Trust me on this."

Melanie didn't answer. She smoked her cigarette. "Well, anyway," she said. "I've got to get back to work." She tried to roll up her window. Russ held it down with his powerful arm.

"Melanie," he said. His eyes were serious now. "I ain't messin' around. We could go to jail. You ain't takin' this seriously."

"You need to calm your jitters before the hearing, I'll get you something from the evidence locker. We got all kind of Xanax in there." He raised his eyebrows, gave her a dumb, overly friendly smile.

"Russ, get your hand off my window. What if Tyler found out you were talking to me like this? What would he think?"

Russ issued a huge, frightening grin at this, held his glare for several moments too long. Finally, he moved his hand from the window. He put his hands up in a surrender pose. "Sorry," he said. "Sorry. But think about what I've said. Don't screw this up."

She rolled up the window and looked straight ahead, avoiding his face, which still appeared behind the glass. She waited, and eventually he stood and turned and walked back toward the Sheriff's Office. She watched him until he was gone inside. She waited a little longer, and finally she got out of her car, locked it, and walked quickly back to the clerk's office.

That evening, she got into her car and began the drive home. Once she had made it past historic downtown, she lit a cigarette and drifted into the lull of driving in the country.

She looked into her rearview mirror and saw a car approaching in the distance. She could see it was coming fast because it got larger and larger in the view of her mirror. She made out the color—brown—and she made out the shape of the lighting structure on the top. It was a police cruiser; she could see that. She looked down at her speedometer; she didn't think she was speeding, but maybe she was. She was cruising at around 67 miles per hour, not too high over the speed limit. Nobody followed the speed limit out here in the country, anyway. She looked again into the rearview. The cruiser got closer. The lights came on. "Shit," she said. She slowed down and pulled over onto the shoulder.

She came to a stop and the cruiser pulled in slowly behind her. She looked back into the rearview. She could see it was Russ. He got out of his car, the flashing lights still active. He walked up to her window, and she rolled it down. "What is it, Russ?" she said. She was scared now.

"You was going a little fast back there, weren't ya?"

She gave him a look of disbelief. "I don't think so, Russ. Did you pull me over to harass me about the election again?"

He looked away from her, out over the road, and took a deep breath. He sighed. "Melanie," he said. "I don't know how else to say this: I can't take no for an answer. I need to know for damn sure you're not planning to turn on us."

"Dammit, Russ, leave me alone!" she shouted. "I've got a lot to think about! Whether I confess or not, there's a big chance we're going to be found out! And then all of us are going to be in even worse trouble! To be honest, I'd like to get on the right side of the law sooner rather than later! I suggest you do the same! Now get the hell away from me!"

Russ stood there very calmly for a moment. He looked dumbly inside the car at her for several uncomfortable moments, silent. She wondered what the hell he was doing. Then, she heard the sound of a car approaching. The car zoomed by, behind Russ's back. After it went by, Russ turned his head to watch it go off into the distance. Then, he grabbed the door handle. She pushed the lock just in time. She lunged into the passenger's seat, where her phone was lying face down. "I'm calling 9-1-1!" she said. Russ dove into the car, over her body, and struggled with her for the phone, his legs waggling out of the driver's side window. He grabbed the phone and yanked it back. His elbow smashed into her jaw as he extracted himself from the window.

Her face showed shock as she reeled from the sudden blow. She held her jaw and looked at Russ with frightened, outraged eyes. She grabbed the transmission bar and put it into drive. Russ punched her in the side of her head with all his might. She slumped forward onto the wheel. He took the transmission bar and pushed it back into park.

He stood there for a while, looking into the car at Melanie's unconscious body, the drugs and his adrenaline racing through him. He held still and calculated. His chest rose and fell with deep, rapid breaths. A few more cars passed by. He realized he could not stand here forever; the facade of a traffic stop would only hold for so long. Before long, some driver would pass by twice and wonder what was going on, or another officer would come along and stop to assist. He needed to get her out of there, out of sight, for at least long enough to buy himself some time to think. He looked all around, listened closely to his east and west, made sure no one was approaching. He moved his way around to the passenger's side of Melanie's car. He opened the door and leaned inside and unbuckled her seat belt and grasped her armpits and pulled her out onto the dry grass. She moaned; her head moved.

Russ could hear a car coming from the east. He ducked down behind Melanie's car, hid himself from the view of the passing vehicles. He hoped desperately that the driver would not see him crouched there next to the unconscious woman. The car zoomed by; he watched its wheels poof past beyond the undercarriage of Melanie's vehicle. Another followed almost immediately after. Then another, from the west. Finally, quiet. He peeked out from behind the car. No one was coming. He looked at Melanie. Her moans were becoming more like speech. Her arms were moving now, her hands searching for something to grasp. Her eyes began to open. Russ's heart thumped. He looked once again to his east and his west, then back down at Melanie. She opened her eyes and looked at him. "What did you do to me?" she groaned. Her face twisted into a terrible, horrified sob. "What did you do, Russ?"

Russ grasped the asp baton from his belt. He raised it into the air. The black steel rang in the blue-grey of the overcast sky. Melanie put her hand on the grass, turned onto her stomach, tried to push herself up. Russ held his breath. He swung the baton down, smashed it onto her skull. She dropped onto her face, now totally and utterly still.

Russ had felt her skull collapse under the force of his baton. He had felt the cylinder sinking into the soft material of her brain. As he drew the baton back up, numbness shot through his arm, shock through his entire body. His legs buckled, his arm became rubber, his grip became weak. His stomach quivered, he felt that he would vomit. He dropped the baton. He bent down, ducked again behind the car. He looked away from Melanie, looked out into the empty cornfield. He closed his eyes, tried to steady himself.

It was amazing that no one had stopped yet, that no one had called anything suspicious into dispatch, that no other law enforcement officer had come onto the scene. He held Melanie by the armpits and dragged her the ten yards or so back to his cruiser. He opened the back door and hoisted her in, head and shoulders first. He pushed her torso and her legs in by her hips. He folded her legs over so that her feet fell into the floorboard. He closed the door. He looked down at his boots; there were fat, pregnant drops of deep red blood on the black leather. He looked at the path where he had dragged Melanie; maroon liquid painted the dry blades of grass.

He went back to Melanie's car. He pulled the keys out of the ignition and dropped them in the seat. He picked up her phone and powered it off and put it in his pocket. He got into his cruiser. He drove a few miles farther east, then turned north onto a little-used county road. A few miles down, he turned onto a logging road he knew of, one where he knew high school kids sometimes parked and drank beer and made bonfires. He drove about half a mile down the road, just before it became too craggy for his cruiser to navigate. He stopped the car and drug Melanie from the cruiser, pulled her body into the woods among the crunchy fall leaves. He pulled and pulled until his cruiser was almost fully obscured from view. He let her go; she flopped down onto the ground. He gathered pine needles and leaves from all around, covered them half-heartedly over her body. He walked back to his car.

He drove to his home. He stumbled into his door. He pulled out a bottle of cheap whisky and drank it down as fast as his body would allow. He drank until he vomited. Then he drank some more until finally, at long last, he passed out.

It rained that night, a cold November rain. It was the best luck the Darby campaign had had in some time. By the time someone finally stopped to investigate Melanie's abandoned vehicle, the rain had washed the blood away. It seemed she had just parked there and vanished.

# 18

RUSSELL AWOKE. His head pounded, his stomach churned, his face was planted in the depths of his couch. Over a torn piece of fabric and a loose spring that rose from the dirty surface of the couch, he gazed into his filthy living room. A wave of horror and nausea—one of many more to come—washed over him, and he retched.

As his consciousness crept slowly back, it struck him that perhaps he was awakening from some terrible dream. He felt a tiny, fleeting moment of hope that perhaps the events of the evening before had been a delusion, something he had imagined. Then, he heard a banging at his door. An urgent banging. At the sound, he knew instantly that it had not been a dream, that it had been real, that now there was someone at the door to ask him about it.

He looked down at his right hand, which still throbbed from his blow to Melanie's head. His back ached, as did his shoulders and his biceps, from pulling her from the car and dragging her through the woods.

With much effort and great discomfort, he rose from the couch and gimped over to the door. He opened the door, and the light of the day poured into the room, blinding his eyes and causing his head to pound. He squinted and covered his face. After a moment, the image of Tyler King appeared before him. Tyler was wearing a clean-looking linen suit and a mint-green tie. Russ looked flatly out at him. Tyler said, "Do you know what time it is?"

Russ said, "No."

"It's damn near 2 p.m. The Sheriff's bitching and moaning about you not showing up for shift this morning. Add to that, the Stewart woman is gone, and there's quite an uproar about it. It's

Saturday, Russ. We go to court in two days. All this commotion could be a little. . . distracting."

Russ just looked at him, a dull expression on his face.

"What are you, drunk?" Tyler said.

Russ hesitated for a moment, as if processing the question. "Something like that," he said.

"Jesus, deputy."

"You can come in if you want." Russ turned his back and walked into the house.

Tyler stepped inside. He closed the door and followed Russ into the kitchen. He watched Russ amble to a cabinet, open it up, pull out a bottle of aspirin and dump several capsules into his hand, then pour a big glass of water and drink down the medicine. Then, he watched him pick up a half-empty bottle of whisky and pour it into the same glass where the water had been and drink that down, too.

"What's going on with you, buddy?"

Russ did not respond. He just stood there, looking down into his glass, reeling from his headache and the pain in his body and the tremendous, crushing guilt.

"Listen, Russ. . . you wouldn't know anything about what happened to the Stewart girl, would you?"

Russ stood looking at his glass.

Tyler looked at Russ for a little while longer and said nothing. He glanced about the dark, filthy room. He let the silence linger. He knew Russ had done something bad. He felt a mix of guilt and accomplishment. Mostly accomplishment, because he didn't know for a fact what Russ had done, and he had never outright told him to do any specific thing, so he had plausible deniability, a rare and beautiful thing. This made him want to smile, but he had to keep a serious face now, for Russ.

After some time, he said, "You know, Russ. There is still the black woman. Lurleen Folds."

Russ was silent for a while. He braced himself against the surface of the kitchen counter. He looked as if he was trying to keep from throwing up. Then he said, "Can you do me a favor?"

"Sure," said Tyler.

"Tell the Sheriff I've got the flu. And get me a case of Bud?"

Tyler smiled and said, "Of course, Russ. Of course."

Melanie had not shown up to her ex-husband's house that Saturday morning to pick up the kids. He had gone looking for her and saw her car there on the Beeline.

The news of her disappearance spread quickly. When Daniel heard, he was angry, but more than that, he was afraid. Afraid because no one with any authority seemed to care much about it. He had put in a call to the Sheriff's Office seeking more information, but no one there would tell him anything. They seemed indifferent. A woman had vanished—a crucial witness in a pressing legal matter, no less—and her car had been abandoned on the side of the road; yet, for all he could tell, there was no search, no investigation, no concern, nothing.

It was a terrifying thing. Maybe Darby's determination to stay in power was grander than he had imagined. Would the man kill for his office? It was a grotesque, unbelievable idea, but not an impossible one.

It was cold and still wet from the rain the evening before, and he paced around the house, looking frequently out the windows, checking now and then to make sure Jonathan was still there playing with his Legos on the rug in the living room. Of course he was, but this nagging paranoia compelled him to keep checking. He had wanted Amber to stay inside, too, just so he'd know where she was, but she had refused. She was angry and agitated and said she needed some air and had hopped on the four-wheeler and disappeared into the country. Maybe she was looking for Melanie, Daniel wondered, though he hoped that was not what she was doing. She seemed to be taking the happenings of the previous week harder than he was. Together, they had experienced the unique trauma of having great hope result in great disappointment, only to be followed by a tantalizing renewal of hope, only to result in a new, more terrifying disappointment, the disappointment of learning that the forces working against you may be far more determined and far more lacking in conscience than you had imagined. And while Daniel at least had a court date coming up, and therefore someplace to channel his nervous energy, Amber felt powerless, with no place to pour out the rage and worry boiling inside her.

Court was Monday—the day after tomorrow—and Daniel had so much to do. He had started working on a supplemental brief with some new cases he found, but he couldn't concentrate under the weight of his fear. He found himself looking constantly out the windows, checking his doors to make sure they were locked, his mind racing at the horrible possibilities of what could have happened to Melanie Stewart, what plot might be brewing against him.

He called Michael. "You hear anything?" he said.

"Nothing. I heard Melanie's ex-husband got a group of guys together to scan the area where her car was found. They went the length of the highway, checked with anyone that lived there alongside the road. But nothing. I asked if anyone had thought to call in the Georgia Bureau of Investigation; big surprise, no one had. I put in a call myself, but they say she hasn't been missing long enough to bring in state resources. So, it seems there is no great urgency to find her. Nobody cares but us.

"And get this: no one has seen Russ Tibbits all day. Apparently, he didn't show up for shift this morning. Official word is, he's sick."

"What the. . ."

"On the bright side, I spoke with Mrs. Folds. She's fine as she can be. Hasn't seen or heard anything unusual. So, to the extent someone is out there picking off our witnesses. . . she's safe."

"Thank God."

"She's got my home phone and my cell phone number, just in case. I offered to let her come stay with me and Jackie, but she won't do it. She knows to call me if there's any trouble."

"Ok," was all Daniel could muster.

"Listen, why don't we get the families together tonight? We'll have dinner, put our heads together, strategize over this hearing on Monday. I'm feeling pretty behind the ball. This whole thing with Stewart has thrown me off. We need to get our ducks in a row. I looked at the data from the voting machines. Some interesting stuff in there. I think you'll be intrigued."

"That's a good idea," said Daniel. "Y'all want to come over here?"

Russ spent the rest of the afternoon and the early part of the evening watching a marathon of *The Real Housewives of Atlanta* and drinking the Budweisers that Tyler had brought him. With the help of the alcohol, the pain in his head and the nausea in his stomach eventually subsided, blanketed over by a warm sort of numbness, a welcome unawareness.

Even through the enveloping haze, he knew what Tyler wanted him to do, and he knew he had to do it. If the Folds woman testified, Darby might lose his position after all, and there'd be nobody in power with any interest in protecting poor Russ, and he'd be found out for what he'd done to Melanie Stewart. Ten beers into the case, he finally felt he was drunk enough to set out on his mission. He peeled himself off the couch, took a piss, put on his utility belt, checked for his gun, and stumbled out the door to his cruiser.

He fired up the engine. He could tell it was cold outside— despite his numbness, that basic signal made it to his brain, plus his breaths turned to mist. His hand went down to the heater knob; then, he allowed it to open the little compartment directly below the climate controls. There was the little glass pipe and the little plastic zip-lock, a few crumbs of powdery crystal inside. He picked up the pipe, poured the remainder of the bag inside, drew it to his mouth and flicked the lighter over the bowl. He received three lungfuls of smoke, more than he had expected from the crumbles there in the pipe. Motherfuck, now he felt good. *Let's do this damn thing, let's be the hero that no one else can be, let's take what's yours, let's kill, let's fuck, let's CRUUUUSSSSHHHHHH.*

With this new, brilliant focus, Russ remembered that he had programmed Mrs. Folds' address into his GPS. He had actually followed her home on the night of the election, just to keep an eye on her. It was actually a real pain in the ass getting to her house, which was deep inside South Goshen, past the homes along the county road, off a bumpy dirt road and out in the woods. A pain to get to, but really an ideal location for what he had to do, an isolated place within an isolated place.

Thanks to the alcohol and the amphetamine, he now experienced a beautiful mixture of disconnection from the world around him and a complete, intense awareness of it. He was numb to the horror that resided deep inside his brain, yet possessed by an acuteness of sensation, an intensity of feeling that would allow him to perform his task effectively. He aimed his cruiser in the direction of his next travesty and stepped on the gas.

He swerved along the Beeline—wide, dramatic swerves, with minutes spent in the oncoming lane before overcorrecting onto the shoulder and into the grass when another vehicle approached. He lacked any fear of consequence, partly because there was no authority here other than himself and partly because he had drunk and smoked himself beyond the concept of consequence. He rumbled down the rough county road into South Goshen. The beer in his eleventh bottle sloshed and splashed onto his uniform as he bounced around inside the car.

He turned off his headlights before he turned onto the dirt road that would take him to the Folds' home. He rolled slowly down the road. He recognized the mailbox with the street address on it. He parked there on the road at the entrance to the drive. There were no streetlights here, and he was concealed by the darkness of night. He killed the ignition. He rolled down his window and looked out at the house and finished his beer. The air remained completely quiet. He listened for any signs of startle from the home, but heard none. He could see a little light on in one of the rooms; he guessed Mrs. Folds and maybe her husband were getting ready for bed, that they wouldn't be expecting any trouble at all. He thought about drinking his last Bud, which was lying down in the seat next to him, but he decided to save it for the second phase of his task. He looked into his backseat, checked for the shovel and tarp there. He opened his door and hobbled out of the car.

Mrs. Folds had just gotten out of her bath and wrapped a towel around herself. Harold was working a night shift, so she was alone. She walked out into her living room and grabbed a book she'd been reading and was on the way back to her bedroom when she heard, she thought, a thudding sound outside, like someone falling to the ground, followed by the muttering voice of a man. She froze and listened. She held still, perfectly still and quiet. A moaning slur of speech, closer this time. She moved quickly into her bedroom, panicked but somehow calm, and picked up the wireless handset sitting next to her bed. She dialed the number of the man she trusted the most. Her heart racing, the line still ringing, she crept into her hallway and peaked out through the kitchen to the door. She wondered where that shotgun was, tried to remember how Harold had showed her to load it. She saw a man in a mask. She gasped for air and stuttered into the phone. Her body shook with fear.

Michael answered.

"Someone is here!" she said, a scream contained inside a whisper.

Michael was sitting at the Rileys' kitchen table, papers spread out before him, explaining rows and columns of data from the voting machines, when he saw Mrs. Folds' name and number appear on the screen of his phone. He answered, then jumped up from his seat. "There's someone at Mrs. Folds' house!"

Panic gripped the room. "We've got to get over there!" he said. "I've got the address in my phone." He tapped on the screen. "Here it is. Butter and Egg Road. Where are my keys!"

"Give me your phone," Amber said, stern but strangely calm. She stepped quickly to Michael, took the phone from his hand.

"What are you doing?" he said.

But she had disappeared out the back door. Michael, Daniel, then Jackie all ran after her. "I have no idea what she's thinking," Daniel said, panic and apology in his voice. They had barely made it outside when she blasted past them on the four-wheeler. She was standing in a straddle over the seat, leaning into the air, her hair blowing out behind her, determination on her face.

Amber had in mind a nearly straight-line route from her home, southeast across the Beeline, to Butter and Egg Road where the Folds' home sat. It was a rough one, though. There was a patch of woods separating her neighborhood from the farmland just west of it, with a bumpy trail cutting through. She found the trail and kicked the vehicle into low gear and the engine screamed. She remained standing as she roared ahead, pulling the handlebars back to keep the thing upright, to keep it from flipping frontward as it bounced over the mud holes and crevices. She made it out of the woods and tore along the fence bordering the neighboring farm until she found a weak spot where a post was leaning. She turned into the post, and it folded to the ground, but a frayed length of barbed wire snapped, and she felt a sharp pop against her face just along the socket of her eye. She winced, but ignored it and throttled to maximum acceleration as she sped southwest through the empty cornfield. She had a moment to put a finger to the spot where she was struck, and when she looked at the finger it was covered in blood. With this awareness, she could now feel it trickling down her cheek. She gritted her teeth, growled, then lowered the gear and pushed the accelerator with her thumb and shot forward even faster.

She exited the farm at its driveway, blasted down the Beeline for several yards, then turned at a forty five degree angle to a slope that ran along the other side the road. There was a narrow plateau at the top of the slope that formed a path parallel to the road. She boomed down the path for a distance, then turned into the decline on the other side, zipping down the hill and across an empty field.

Soon, she arrived at a shallow creek. She moved east along the edge of the creek for a short while, then turned gradually down its banks into the water. Cold water and mud splashed up her pant legs, soaking her shoes, but she felt no chill, her body so hot with effort and the air rising off the nearly-overheating engine. Finally, she reached the place where the creek passed through an old concrete tunnel under the county road. She went up the slope onto the county road and then directly across it onto Butter and Egg Road. She sped down the dirt road, still wet from the morning's rain, allowing her tires to grip and the vehicle to gain speed as she up-shifted gears. Her LED illuminated a police cruiser in the distance.

Despite the illusion of focus created by the drugs in his brain, Russ was actually being quite sloppy, quite inefficient, and raising an enormous ruckus. He had given up trying to kick in the heavy hardwood door, which Harold Folds had thankfully outfitted with a heavy bolt and sturdy hinges. He thought about shooting through the bolt, but figured that would be too much noise and could attract attention even way out here in the country. His plan was to beat the lady in the head, just as he had with Melanie. She was screaming now, though, and he was starting to worry. This was taking too long. He found a big sturdy stick in the yard, and a fragile-looking side window, and he thrust the branch into the pane. It didn't break right away, which he had not expected. He took several steps back, ran forward, and thrust the branch once again into the glass. This time, it shattered.

"Get away! Get away!" the lady was screaming.

He approached the window, prepared to climb inside. Then, he heard something. The roar of an approaching engine, like a motorcycle or a four-wheeler. *Goddammit*, he thought. He took his gun out of the holster and crouched down in the darkness and looked toward the sound. He could see a light reflecting on the back of his cruiser and illuminating the foliage that bordered the dirt road. He aimed his gun in the direction of the light. Suddenly, the vehicle appeared behind his cruiser and turned quickly in his direction. The light of the LED blinded him, and he winced. He closed his eyes and pulled the trigger. The sound was deafening. He opened his eyes. His ears were ringing, his scalp tingling. He had hit his target. The four-wheeler was now tumbling forward, end over end. In the chaotic dancing of the light, he saw the vague outline of the vehicle's driver flying through the air.

Amber lay face-down in the dirt. She had heard the shot, and then the four-wheeler's front-right tire had disappeared, it seemed, and she was thrown onto the ground. Her right shoulder had taken the heaviest blow, and her face—the side not already cut by the barbed wire—had slid in the dirt. As she lay there, her shoulder throbbed with a delirious sort of pain like she had never known before. She knew she had to get up, though. She put her left palm on the ground. She bent her knee toward her pelvis and planted the ball of her foot in the dirt and kicked off, once, then again, then again, each time causing her torso to roll onto the displaced shoulder and shooting pain through her arm and neck. Finally, she rolled onto her back and sat up. There was the deputy walking toward her, his dark hair a disheveled mess on his head, his face dirty, snot coming from his nose, a wicked, intoxicated sneer on his face, glaring down at her, illuminated by the still beaming light from her four-wheeler.

"You dumb bitch," he said. He pulled his arm slowly up from his hip, pointed the barrel of the gun in her face. She looked into the barrel and all hope left her. She prepared to beg for her life. Then, she watched his head explode. A ring of fire briefly illuminated the circumference of his cranium, and she saw the hair on the back of his head suddenly point up into the air, saw a sparkling sprinkle of bone and blood and brain. Little pieces of buckshot shattered through his teeth, and she felt something like the sting of sand on her neck and her forehead. His face, once a menacing glower, was now empty of all expression. He fell forward in a sickening plop, his face in the dirt directly in front of her. She turned her face, averted her eyes, scooted away with her legs and her one good arm and finally came to a stand.

There stood Lurleen Folds, an enormous double-barreled shotgun in her hand. The thing was easily as tall as she. Smoke poured from its barrel. She put it down and ran to Amber. She put her arm around her and guided her toward the house. It was several minutes later before Daniel and Michael and the rest of the cavalry arrived.

# 19

HAVING NO FAITH that 9-1-1 would get them any help, Michael called a State Patrol officer he knew from the Everett trial. She was the same officer, in fact, who had initially responded to that scene and witnessed its horrible aftermath. After Michael's call, the State Patrol dispatched to all local units, so the Sheriff lost any excuse he might have had not to respond. Eventually, the Folds' yard took on the appearance of a proper crime scene. Flashes of blue and red reflected on every surface, radios booped and crackled, yellow tape stretched between trees to enclose Russ's body, now covered by a sheet. Daniel stood in Mrs. Folds' home beside Amber, watching the paramedics take his wife's vitals and listening to Mrs. Folds tell the state officers what happened. It dumbfounded him that, not an hour earlier, he had been in his home, safe and content in the company of his friends, planning for court. This hardly seemed real.

He rode with Amber in the back of the ambulance to the Emergency Room in Swainsboro. She was in immense pain, and they had given her a morphine drip, and between that and the shock, she was almost silent, save for the occasional moan and a single groggy "I love you," which made Daniel understand how unworthy of her he was.

The next day, Sunday, Daniel's mother and father stayed with Jonathan while Daniel camped out in Amber's hospital room. Her clavicle was shattered to bits, her shoulder was dislocated, and there was an incomplete break in the humerus bone of her arm. A gnarly scab was forming on her face where it had ground against the dirt. As awful as this was, they both knew it could have been much worse. She could have hit her head or broken her neck in the ejection. She could have been shot. Despite the pain and debilitation, she was grateful to be alive.

Court was tomorrow. They could almost certainly postpone the hearing, but just in case, Michael had brought the file to the hospital, and he and Daniel sat at a small table in the corner of Amber's room reading documents and making notes as she phased in and out of consciousness.

Half-asleep from the meds, Amber heard Daniel say that they would have to request a continuance, that he needed to be here with her. This had woken her from her slumber. *"No,"* she said. "You get them now," before she fell back to sleep.

Despite everything, on Monday morning at court, Tyler was actually feeling really good. He was as calm as he'd been in months, to be honest. These events, terrible as they were, had created a perfect situation. The one witness most likely to uncover his scheme, Melanie Stewart, was missing without a trace. (As a bonus, if she was gone for good, their affair would never be uncovered). His most unpredictable wildcard, Russell Tibbits, was dead. There was still this Folds woman, but she was shaken and afraid, and besides, she had nothing more than her own paranoid suspicion about some imagined plot to steal the election. The moment was perfect to put this dispute to rest. He was surprised the Drummond boy had not sought delay. As far as Tyler could see, Michael had no witness who could establish evidence sufficient to overturn the results.

He stood from his seat behind counsel's table, buttoned his jacket, moved slowly, dramatically, toward the witness stand.

"Mrs. Folds, I want to say, first, thank you so much for being here today. We are all aware of the ghastly occurrence over the weekend. You are a braver soul than I am. I don't know that I'd be able to keep my wits about me after experiencing such a thing. I cannot imagine what went through that young man's head; he was obviously a very sick individual, but. . ."

"Mr. King," the judge interrupted. "It is already going to be very difficult to hold this proceeding today, in light of the horrific event to which you refer. I am also very grateful to this witness. But, unless it bears directly on your inquiry, I am going to ask you to stick to the events of Election Day. Let's not linger on this subject any longer."

"Ten-four, your Honor. Of course." He affected a dramatic, thoughtful pause. "May I approach the witness?" He held up a paper, indicating that he would like to hand Mrs. Folds an exhibit.

"You may."

Tyler handed Mrs. Folds a document. He then turned to the petitioner's table and placed a copy down in front of Michael. It was the affidavit that Mrs. Folds had executed, the one that had gotten them into court in the first place.

"Mrs. Folds, if you would, please take a moment to review the document I've placed in front of you. Do you recognize it?"

Mrs. Folds turned through the pages, scanning the document to ensure it was the one she had signed. "Um, yes. Yes, sir. I do."

"Can you tell the court what this is?"

"This is my affidavit."

"Is this a true and accurate copy of your affidavit?"

"Yes, it appears to be."

"Now, Mrs. Folds. You did not draft this document, did you?"

"Oh, no sir. Attorney Drummond drafted it."

"And you went down to his office to sign it; is that right?"

"Yes, sir."

"And you know that Attorney Drummond is Mr. Daniel Riley's law partner; isn't that right?"

"Um, yes. I believe I did know that."

"And you yourself, in fact, were a supporter of Mr. Riley's campaign, were you not?"

"Well, I . . ."

Michael stood. "Your Honor, I would object to that question. He's essentially asking her who she voted for. That is a private matter. That is confidential."

"Goes to bias, your Honor. Strikes at the heart of this witness's credibility," Tyler answered.

"Objection overruled," said the judge, without further comment. "You may answer the question."

"What was the question again?" Mrs. Folds asked. She looked green. She trembled with worry.

"You were, were you not, a supporter of Mr. Riley's campaign for Commissioner?"

"Well. . . I don't know what you mean by supporter, I . . ."

"Did you vote for Mr. Riley?"

Mrs. Folds hesitated. "Well, yes. I did."

"And you very much wanted him to win this election, didn't you?"

"Well, I suppose I did vote for him, so. . ."

"Now, Mrs. Folds, let me ask you this: who was the first person you spoke to about the supposed irregularities you say you witnessed on November 5?"

"Well, I spoke with Pastor Reid, and . . ."

"Pastor Reid. He is the Pastor over at Hephzibah Baptist Church, is that right?"

"Yes, sir. He's my pastor."

"Now, Mr. Riley has some connection to Pastor Reid and Hephzibah Baptist; does he not?"

"Well. . ." she looked increasingly nervous. "It depends on what you mean by *connection*. He's not a member, so far as I know."

Tyler pounced on this vacillation. "He has pledged a great deal of money to your church, has he not?"

"Yes," she conceded. "That's right. He has."

"I believe that figure is in the amount of *ten-thousand dollars*?" Tyler looked up at the judge as he announced the figure. In this context, the figure did seem excessive and somewhat untoward.

"I think so," she said.

"Now, Mrs. Folds, do you know if that money has been delivered yet?"

"I don't know."

"But Pastor Reid would know, wouldn't he?"

"I suppose."

"And I imagine Pastor Reid has a certain interest in making sure that money gets paid, doesn't he? In making sure Mr. Riley wins this election, isn't that correct?"

"Objection, your Honor. He is asking this witness to speculate . . ."

"Withdrawn," Tyler said. The question had had its impact, whether she answered it or not.

"Now, did Pastor Reid encourage you to get in touch with Attorney Drummond here?"

"Yes sir."

"And in fact you did, and Attorney Drummond drew up this affidavit, and you signed your name to it, is that right?"

"That's right."

"And was Mr. Riley there, too, when you met Mr. Drummond, and he drafted this affidavit?"

She cleared her throat. "Yes," she said.

"I see. Now, Mrs. Folds, let me ask you this: did you make any effort to contact anyone with any authority over this election? The Secretary of State's Office? The Sheriff's Office? The Georgia Bureau of Investigation? Anyone like that?"

"No sir."

"Can you explain why?"

"Well . . . Pastor Reid is someone I'd go to for counsel in any situation. So I went to him and asked what I ought to do. And he suggested I contact Attorney Drummond. So that's what I did. I don't have any other way to explain it."

"I see." Tyler moved on.

"Mrs. Folds, you have testified that you observed Ms. Stewart traveling between her check-in area and the voting machine a number of times; correct?"

"That's right."

"You did not actually observe her casting any vote; is that correct?"

"That's correct."

"And you never observed her checking anyone in to vote, other than the actual voters who had come to vote that day, isn't that correct?"

"Well, it appeared that's what she was doing. That she was checking in people who weren't there. Because I could hear her computer-mouse click, then I could see her put the keycard into the little device there, and I could hear it click. And you can't get it to click like that unless you've checked off that a voter is there. And then she'd take that keycard back to the voting machine. So it appeared to me that she was casting ballots."

"How many times did you say she did this?"

"Eight or nine, something like that."

"And yet you never said anything to her? You never asked her what she was doing?"

"She said there was a problem with the machine. Like she was trying to fix something."

"And how do you know that wasn't the truth?"

"Well. . ." she looked about her nervously. "I don't know it for a fact. It looked suspicious is all." Mrs. Folds stared at Tyler with a frown. She sighed. Her shivering became more pronounced. Then she said, "That deputy, the one who came to my house and tried to kill me, I think he somehow triggered the fire alarm. He ushered everyone out except for Melanie; she stayed behind; she could have been doing anything at all after we left that fellowship hall! And that deputy—Tibbits—he knew I saw what was going on, and that's why he came after me!" Her voice trembled with conviction. "I'm sure of that!"

"Mrs. Folds, you have no *proof* of what you allege, do you?"

"I don't, and now the two people who *would* know are *gone*." She began to weep. "All of this over a political contest," she moaned. "You people crave power so badly. I didn't ask to be a part of this." She put her face in her hands and shook.

Tyler picked up a box of Kleenex from a little table in front of the witness stand. He set the box down in front of her. "I cannot imagine what you are going through," he said. "Our entire county has been shaken by these events. But, in court, we deal in evidence, not conviction. And the fact remains, Mrs. Folds, you have no hard evidence to support your suspicions, do you?"

She heaved. "No," she said. "No. I don't."

"One final question, Mrs. Folds. You say there were a number of voters who came up to the polling place in those final minutes, but weren't able to come in and cast a ballot, correct?"

"Yes."

"About how many would you estimate were there to vote, but couldn't come in?"

"About five or six."

"Less than sixteen, correct? Less than the number of votes that delivered the election to Commissioner Darby?"

She pursed her lips. "I'd say so. I'm not exactly sure, but . . ."

"Nothing further." Tyler sat back down. Michael could see a smile forming in the muscles of Leon Darby's face, even as the man tried to conceal it.

"Redirect?" asked the judge. Michael stood. He looked at Mrs. Folds and was struck by regret. He had brought her into this. She was at her wits' end, and he saw no purpose in forcing her to stay on the stand any longer than she already had; she deserved to go home, to begin recovering. *She had killed a man*, for Christ's sake. He could not imagine the trauma.

"I have nothing further, your Honor." The judge allowed Mrs. Folds to step down. As she walked down the step from the witness stand onto the floor, it struck Michael how different the mood in the courtroom was today. Last week, it had been full of promise and revolution. Now, it was covered in a thick fog of gloom.

"Call your next witness," said the judge to Michael.

"We'll call Casey Flanagan," Michael announced. A soft murmur rippled through the courtroom. Tyler shuffled through his files. He could not recall any mention of this witness.

The bailiff went into the hall and came back followed by a middle-aged gentleman who looked like he needed a haircut and a shave. His yellowy-white hair was roughly parted to one side, but little sprigs of it stuck out in wild clumps all about his head, as if he had rolled out of bed that morning without readying himself for the day. He wore rumpled khaki pants and an old-looking, faded blue dress shirt, covered by a generic-looking beige jacket. He was the regional superintendent for elections, the one who had gathered the voting data for the Goshen County contest.

Flanagan walked up to the witness stand and faced the bailiff. He raised his hand instinctively. He seemed comfortable, like he'd been in court before. He took the oath, then faced Michael, awaited his questions.

Michael pulled from a flexible brown file three stacks of paper, each approximately an inch thick, each held together by a black binder clip. He set one down in front of the witness. He brought a copy to Tyler, who studied it carefully. He held up a third copy and looked to the judge. "Your Honor, if I may approach?" The judge nodded and held out his hand. Michael handed the document up to the judge, who took it.

"Mr. Flanagan, do you recognize these papers that I've put before you?"

"I do. This is a certified copy of the data printout from our voting machines. From the caption on the front page, it appears that this data was obtained from the machines assigned to Precinct One, in the election held in Goshen County on November 5. Right behind that, in this same stack, is a similar printout for Precinct Two."

"Mr. Flanagan, do you have any sort of training or experience in how to access this sort of data on the voting machines?"

"I do. I'm certified by the Georgia Secretary of State's Office and the Federal Election Commission to operate these machines and gather voting data."

"Your Honor, I would move to admit this document into evidence."

"Any objections?" asked the judge, and looked to Tyler.

Tyler stood abruptly. The back of his knees shoved his chair backwards, causing it to fall down on the floor with a bang. Darby leaned down to pick up the chair while Tyler sifted through the papers in front of him, trying to formulate some sort of objection.

"Your Honor, I've never heard of this witness before. I have no idea what he'll testify to."

"Your Honor, he was named in our disclosures. The documents, too. Truly, the only purpose of this witness is to authenticate and explain some of the material in these documents here."

"Eh, your Honor. These papers, eh. This is some kind of computer gobbledygook. Eh. I just can't imagine them being useful. And I don't think they are relevant. Eh, you already heard the petitioner's best witness, and there's no evidence that any fraud took place. So, um. I would object on that ground."

"Overruled."

Michael looked at the papers with admiration. Here was cool, hard data, not subject to interpretation, not reliant on emotion. Just facts, set out in black and white. Reality in its most unadulterated form. "Mr. Flanagan, each page of this document has several rows of information, do you see that?"

"Yes."

"And can you describe the data set forth in each row?"

"Um, yes. Each row represents a single vote. In the first column of each row, you see a time-stamp. That's the time the vote was cast. And in the second column, right beside that, you see the candidate selected."

"I see. So, for example, the very first line, on the very first page, says 8:01:52 in the first column. And then beside that, in the second column, it says Darby, Leon. So that means that at 8:01 a.m., with eight seconds to go until 8:02, someone voted for Leon Darby, correct?"

"That's correct."

"And then on the second line, where we see 8:02:14 in the first column, next to Riley, Daniel, that means a single person cast a vote for Daniel Riley at that time, correct?"

"Correct."

"Now, correct me if I'm wrong, but there's no indication on this sheet as to who actually cast each ballot?"

"That's correct. Federal election law prohibits the gathering of data that would show who voted for whom. That's considered confidential. We just show each vote according to what time it was cast. We also have the voter roll, which identifies who came and voted; but there is nothing to match the voter's name with an individual vote cast."

"I see. Now, if we add up all the rows here, each time-stamp, for both Precinct One and Precinct Two, how many total votes were cast?"

Flanagan flipped to the back page of the report. "Let's see. That would be 1,559."

Michael scratched his head. "But, is that consistent with the final vote tally? I believe the Secretary of State reported 787 for Darby, 771 for Riley, which adds up to 1,558. Is there any explanation for that? Where's the extra vote come from?" He sounded genuinely puzzled.

Flanagan smiled. He turned through the pages. "Page seven," he said. "A write-in for one 'Seymour Butts.'"

The courtroom erupted into laughter. It was a blessed moment of relief.

"Order, order," the judge called as he banged his gavel. He rolled his eyes, tried to conceal a smile.

Flanagan continued. "An anomaly like that doesn't get reported in the final vote tally. Write-ins have to achieve a certain percentage of the vote before they're reported. Mr. Butts apparently didn't have much of a following." Laughter once again rippled through the courtroom.

"Indeed."

"Now, Mr. Flanagan, as you observe the timestamps, are you able to make out any discernible trend as to when votes were cast most often? Any particular times in the day when there was a surge in voting?"

"Well," Flanagan answered. "There is a small surge in the morning, between 8 and 9:30 am—presumably, people going in to vote first thing in the morning before they go to work. After that, the pace is pretty slow and steady throughout the day. The frequency of votes increases very slightly around 3:30 p.m., as school employees get off work and go to vote. This is all pretty typical.

"But, something very unusual happens at the end of the day. Around 4:46 p.m., the frequency of voting goes up, all of the sudden. And then, around 4:50, it spikes even higher. Between 4:49 and 5:05 p.m., there were 77 ballots cast in Precinct One, one after the other."

"Is what you are describing depicted by the data on pages 17 and 18 of the report?"

"It is."

"During this spike at the end of the day, are there any other discernible patterns, other than the rise in frequency?"

"Well, yes. There's one other obvious pattern. Every vote cast in that small timeframe is for Leon Darby."

There was an audible gasp from the gallery. The audience murmured.

"And you say the votes continued until as late as 5:05?"

"So it would appear."

"After the polls closed?"

"Again, that's what the data shows."

"Throughout the rest of the day, in Precinct One, were there any other instances where so many votes were cast for a single candidate, within such a short period of time?"

"Nothing even close. Darby got the majority of the votes in the precinct, but Riley had a significant number as well, and the votes were pretty evenly distributed throughout the day. Until this period of time right here."

"Now, let me show you just one other document, Mr. Flanagan. And I do truly appreciate your time here today." Michael pulled out another group of individually clipped exhibits. He placed one in front of the witness, handed another to Tyler, and passed one up to the judge. "Mr. Flanagan, is this a true and accurate copy of the voter roll for the November 5 election?"

"It is."

"I'd move to admit."

"Any objections?"

Tyler scanned the document. "Um, no, your Honor."

"There being none, it is admitted."

"Now, sir, this document shows who voted that day, correct?"

"Yes."

"And the data gathered from this document comes from the check-in system, doesn't it? Where the poll worker checks a voter in on the computer after checking his or her ID, correct?"

"That's right."

Michael took a moment or two. He walked over to counsel's table and looked down at some papers. He studied them. He knew exactly the next question he was going to ask. He braced himself. He needed to deliver these next questions in a professional and straightforward manner, and not in a burst of unbridled emotion, though he could barely contain the truth that burned inside of him. He needed to catch his breath, to calm himself, his heart was beating so fast in anticipation. Even as he calmed his nerves, he relished the tense silence in the room that his pause created.

He turned back toward the witness.

"I'd like to direct your attention to page nine of this document, Mr. Flanagan, where we get into the *R*'s. Are you with me?"

Flanagan turned into the document and found the group of surnames that ended in R. "Okay," he said. "I'm there."

"If you would, please take a look at the very bottom of the page there, toward the end of the *R*'s. Do you see an 'Evan R. Roundtree?'" Michael looked up to the judge. The judge was studying the roll with great interest, his eyebrows turned downward into concentration.

"Yes," he said. "I see that."

"And that would indicate that someone by that name came in to vote that day, correct?"

"Why, yes."

Michael let the answer sink in for a moment. He smiled, ever so slightly, and looked up to Judge Roundtree, who caught Michael's eye. Michael had remembered a conversation he had with Judge Roundtree some years back. The judge had mentioned, very casually, that he did not vote in local elections; that as Judge, he believed it was his duty to remain politically neutral, and he found it improper to lend his support to one candidate or the other when it came to local matters. He *did* cast his vote on state and national questions. But Michael knew there had been no state or national question on the ballot this election. Besides, he had asked Mrs. Folds, prior to the hearing today, if she recalled Judge Roundtree coming in to vote that day, and Mrs. Folds had told him *no*.

"Take a look at page three, sir, if you would."

"Ok."

"There is an indication here that one Malcolm Everett came to vote," he said. "Is that right?"

"Yes, it would appear so."

"And then, and please forgive all the turning, if you go to page eleven, do you see an indication that one Jessie Thorpe came in to vote?"

"Yes, it would appear so."

Michael looked up to Judge Roundtree once again, this time solemn-faced. He looked back at Tyler, who looked as if he might puke.

Judge Roundtree sighed, and spoke. "Malcolm Everett is the young man who was killed out on the Dixie Beeline by the chemical truck. That was Mr. Drummond's trial.

"And Jessie Thorpe was my good friend. He died last year."

There was a profound silence, as if all the air had been sucked from the room. Leon Darby and Tyler King's faces were ashen and white. Melanie had cast votes on behalf of at least two dead voters, in addition to Judge Roundtree himself, and there it was, on paper, impossible to deny.

"I have nothing further for this witness."

Tyler's cross-examination was pathetic. His best question was, "Did you personally witness the voting as it took place on November 5?" And, "Isn't it possible that a large number of Darby supporters might have come in at the last minute, before the polls closed, to cast their votes?"

"Sure, that's possible," answered the superintendent.

Tyler made no mention of the fact that the building had been evacuated, that no one at all could have been voting in that last fifteen minutes, when 70-something people supposedly came in and cast a rapid succession of votes for Darby. Tyler had to pretend as if that testimony did not exist. He bumbled along as a man totally defeated, a lawyer forced to go through the motions of maintaining the appearance that he was still defending his client. He perspired. He wiped his forehead and his neck with a handkerchief. He pulled at his collar as if it was difficult for him to breathe. He asked some nonsense questions, such as whether the voting machines had been "calibrated," as if he was trying to take down a Breathalyzer result in a DUI case. Michael almost felt sorry for him.

Finally, Tyler stepped down. Michael had no redirect.

"The petitioner rests, your Honor," said Michael.

Judge Roundtree looked over at Tyler. "Let's take a brief recess," he said. "We will reconvene at 1:00 p.m." He banged the gavel. He looked out briefly at the gallery. Everyone there could see the hurt in his eyes.

"Counselors," he said. "I'd like to see you in my chambers."

Judge Roundtree led the lawyers to his chambers. He gestured toward the two modest chairs facing his desk. They looked like part of an inexpensive dining room set—wooden ladder-backs with thatched straw for the seat. The men sat, and the straw squeaked beneath them.

The judge took his seat behind the desk. He turned his attention to Tyler. "Mr. King," he said, "you have been practicing in my courtroom for many years now. I've seen you do a good job for your clients. I respect you as a professional. I know your father. So what I have to say to you now is going to be very difficult."

"Your Honor, I . . ."

"Just listen." The judge looked at him firmly. "Just listen to me, Tyler. What I have seen today is deeply concerning to me. *Deeply* concerning. If I was sitting in your position right now, my greatest concern would be the *criminal* consequences of all this. I cannot imagine that *someone* will not file a criminal complaint based on what we have seen today, especially after everything that happened this weekend. I would not be surprised to see the U.S. Department of Justice get involved. Now, if there is some powerful piece of evidence—something I haven't seen yet—that will absolve your folks of what appears to be clear election fraud, I'm willing to see it. But you need to show it to me *now*. Because as it stands, I don't see any way for you to win this case."

Tyler shook his head and looked down at his shoe. His face bore a look of incredulity. He looked for something to say. "Your Honor, I. . . I just don't agree with you. . . All this is circumstantial . . . I. . ."

"Mr. King. Lawyer to lawyer, let me tell you this: If I were you, I'd do what I could to save some face. You need to end this now. I'll decline ruling from the bench, and we'll announce that the parties are working to resolve the dispute. You all will go and work out a consent order of some kind that results in the withdraw of these suspicious votes, and then your client will concede the election to Mr. Riley."

Michael's heart jumped in his chest. He fought hard to hold himself still.

Tyler held his hands over his mouth and glared at the judge. "Your Honor, this is outrageous."

"Mr. King, this is your last chance. I am trying to do you a favor here."

There was a long, painful silence.

"Let me talk to my client," he said, finally.

"You do that. You let me know what y'all decide. I'll give you twenty minutes."

The men departed.

* * *

Daniel was huddled together with his mother and father, Jackie, Pastor Reid, Ed Gardner, and Jeff Jessup outside the courtroom when Tyler came around the corner and stomped away down the hallway without looking at any of them. Soon after came Michael, who strode cautiously toward them, hands in his pockets, a crooked smile on his face.

"Mind if I talk to my client for a minute?" he said as he approached. He met Daniel's eyes. "Outside, maybe?"

They turned a corner and walked together in silence down a hallway and out the back door of the courthouse. Daniel wanted desperately to know what the judge had said, and his heart raced in anticipation. Michael maintained an unsettling silence as they walked across the back parking lot toward a patch of grass, until finally he said, "let's sit on that stump over there."

They sat down side by side on a wide stump. "Remember the tree that used to be here?" Michael said. "Big old oak tree. Had to come down because it had disease. It was tall enough that it could've crushed the courthouse if it fell."

"I do remember it, actually," Daniel said. Michael's calm, his choice of such a mundane topic, puzzled him. But it also relaxed him. His friend seemed totally untroubled.

"Sorry," Michael said, detecting Daniel's puzzlement. "I think I'm out of gas. I've slept maybe four hours in the last forty-eight. Anyway," he said drowsily and gave a long sigh. "It looks like we may be about to win."

Daniel's eyes went wide. He put his hand on his friend's shoulder, laughed in exasperation. "Care to elaborate?" he said.

"Judge asked Darby to concede. Tyler knows they're toast. But there's no guarantee they'll agree. I imagine he's fighting with the Commissioner about it as we speak. If they don't, there'll be lots of work ahead. Court of Appeals, probably. But. . . there's nothing we can do about that now."

Daniel took in a deep breath, relaxed, breathed out. "Well, alright," he said and looked off into the cool day.

He sat there in the quiet and let his mind wander. He thought about his little boy. He remembered a perfect afternoon, the weekend before last, walking with him along the creek in the woods near their home. A breeze blew over their faces, and the dry, colorful leaves rustled in the trees above their heads. Johnny ran along the path, stopping to scoop up piles of orange and red leaves, throwing them into the air and laughing. In that moment Daniel's heart had swelled with pure and perfect satisfaction. The moment was transfixed in his mind now as an image of all that is good and important. He closed his eyes and drew in a deep breath and lingered on the memory.

He woke from his dream when Michael put his hand on his shoulder and said, "Look, there's Tyler walking back to the courthouse." He looked up and saw Tyler marching away from the Commissioner's office, a grumpy look on his face. Michael stood and stretched his long arms out on each side, extended his slender fingers, rotated his wrists, circled his neck. "I just hope I can stay awake long enough to see what they decide."

"Have a seat, Mr. Drummond. Mr. Riley."

Daniel and Michael each pulled out a ladder-back chair and squeaked down into the thatched-straw seats. Together, they looked at the judge with expectant silence.

"I've let Mr. King and his client be excused for the day," the judge said. "He asked me for that courtesy. They're going to agree to what I proposed. The votes will be withdrawn."

Daniel could not contain the enormous smile that was forming on his face. He sunk into deep, blissful relief. He could not muster words.

"Mr. Drummond, you'll draft me a consent order and send a copy to me and to Mr. King. Ok?"

"Yes sir. Yes sir."

"You have any questions?"

"N-no sir."

"You did a good job for your client today, young man. This county is lucky to have a lawyer like you serving its people. The court thanks you."

"Thank you, sir."

"And Mr. Riley, congratulations. I hope you understand the enormous responsibility ahead of you. I'm going to expect quite a lot from you."

"Yes sir, your Honor. Thank you, sir."

"You gentlemen have a lot of work to do. I'll let you get to it." The judge stood, extended a hand to Michael, then to Daniel.

The two emerged from the chambers to an empty hallway, each of them wanting to explode into celebration. They jogged, then ran with childlike abandon down the hallway toward the lobby. Their leather soles smacked against the tiles, echoing against the walls. Daniel gritted his teeth and clenched his fists in a mighty effort to contain the victorious scream building inside his lungs. His eyes were wide, his nose scrunched into an intense, almost-angry expression. They ran together past their family and supporters and blasted out the front doors into the sunny, cool day, which now seemed ecstatically beautiful. Daniel arched his back, held his head to the sky, and issued a triumphant, albeit totally obnoxious howl into the air.

# 20

OUTKAST announced on the Friday before Christmas that they would soon release their first new album as a group since 2006's *Idlewild*. Along with the announcement, they released a surprise single, which now played through the speakers of the Drummonds' Cadillac as they cruised along I-85 North through the lights of Atlanta. It was a wonderful welcome back to the city, Jackie thought, as she gazed around at the lights and the massive infrastructure. She turned up the volume, relaxed into her seat, let the bass wash over her, let Andre Benjamin's wordplay tap-dance on her eardrums. The song was a light, barely-there piano loop atop a deep bass kick, skittering high hats and a light fingersnap, something to move your body without overpowering the rhymes. There was nothing like the first time you heard a great song. She looked over at Michael, who was nodding modestly along to the beat as he drove. She turned to look at Zoe in her punkin' seat in the back, sound asleep. She looked at Michael once again, then forward to the city ahead.

The Georgia Court of Appeals would hear oral argument tomorrow in Darby's appeal of the Everett verdict. It had given them the perfect opportunity to come to Atlanta together as a family. Zoe would spend some time with her grandparents while Jackie came to court to see Michael's argument, and then they would stay through the holiday with Jackie's family. Normally, Michael would have balked at such an extended vacation; it was hard to pull that man away from his work. But it had been an intense year, and even he was ready for some time away.

Jackie rested her forehead against the cold windowpane and gazed out at the unreal cyclorama of brightly illuminated skyscrapers, LED billboards, radio towers, highway overpasses, and the many hundreds of cars passing them in the night. How comforting to be enveloped by her city. She missed it here. She loved the feeling of coming back. She hoped Michael might be feeling the same thing.

In the past couple of weeks, she had been encouraging him to reach out to his law school classmates, his colleagues from debate, those who were living and working in Atlanta now. Some of them had high-paying jobs at elite law firms, others were working as U.S. Attorneys on their way to judgeships, others at some non-profit or advocacy group, grinding each day to make the world a better place; and there were others like him—plaintiff's lawyers—hustling to make their mark with big cases against powerful entities. She wanted him to take another look at what it could be like here, to do the type of work he loved without having constantly to swim against the racial current that ran through Goshen County. She knew that, once Daniel assumed office in January, and once Michael was named County Attorney, it would be harder to get him to leave. She wasn't convinced that the County Attorney role would be the panacea Michael seemed to expect. The power structure of that county ran deeper than the Commissioner's post. Darby's company would remain the most powerful economic force. The wealth would remain concentrated among the same wealthy white families. Those families' tendrils in state and federal government would not suddenly unloose themselves. Sure, they had gotten their hands on one lever of power, but there were many others that would remain beyond their grasp.

If they came to Atlanta, he would have fantastic stories to tell, an amazing accomplishment to tout, and he could use that to establish a foothold here. And they would be in a place where they weren't total outsiders. They could be among others like them. They could bask in the glow of their successful peers and raise their daughter in a place where she wouldn't be so different—and probably less appreciated—than her peers.

Back in Goshen County, she still felt the same intense loneliness that led her to encourage the Rileys to come. Amber had been a good friend. Her companionship had been soothing and reassuring. And she had helped Jackie to branch out, to develop friendships with the white girls who had grown up there in the county and stayed. They were perfectly pleasant, for the most part, and friendly, but it had always been an effort. She always felt like she had to *try* to fit in with them, and she just missed being able to relax and breathe freely and speak openly among a group of people who understood where she was coming from.

Thinking of the terrible thing that happened to Amber, she felt guilty wanting to leave. She had been instrumental in bringing the Rileys to the county, had pressed Amber to support Daniel's run. Now, her friend was recovering from an operation, likely to be in pain for months more, her face mottled by scabs. But the violence of that act, the intensity of the desire to maintain control represented by it, had been what pushed Jackie to decide it was time to go. How could she raise a family in such a place? If Michael was set on fighting the powers-that-be, there would be more battles to come, more people hurt. That was no place for her daughter, no place for their future children. She wasn't willing to be constantly afraid for her safety, for Michael's safety, for her daughter's.

She would wait until Michael's argument was finished to tell him what she wanted. She might wait until after Christmas. She hoped he would listen, and she hadn't yet decided what she would do if he said no. But she would try to persuade him. She peered out at the magical lights of the city, and the life spinning around her reinforced her resolve that this should be their home.

*  *  *

Daniel drove south down Alabama State Highway 87 through woods and farmland and tiny little civilizations. He had reached his favorite spot along the familiar drive—an old, abandoned big-box retail store on the outskirts of a city called Elba. *Bargain Time* read the fading, waterlogged sign over the vast storefront. Its wall of dust-covered windows revealed a grey, blank space inside. Grass grew up from the wide cracks in the concrete of the huge, empty parking lot.

This place somehow spoke to him.

Elba was built along the Pea River in the 1800s, below the level of the river's historical crest. Its proximity to the river made it an important trading post; yet, it flooded constantly. Each time it flooded, the people rebuilt it in the same place and in approximately the same form as before. The town would remain intact for ten to twenty years, until it would of course flood again, and everything would be destroyed, and the people would just rebuild it once more, as best they could. The Army Corps of Engineers offered numerous times to relocate the city elsewhere— onto some higher ground—but each time, the townspeople refused. People left, of course, and the population dwindled over the years. Bargain Time lost its customer base and had closed long ago, its vast property not valuable or useful enough to attract a new tenant. Yet, even today, the city remained an entity, a place people called home, a place that contained lives and families, a place that comprised people's worlds.

The route through Elba was part of the Riley's annual year-end vacation. For as long as they had been married, Daniel and Amber had been driving down these rural Alabama roads to the Gulf Coast each December. The Bargain Time property remained untouched and unchanged for all that time, save for the natural, barely perceptible increase in its decay. Daniel could not explain what it was about this structure that so fascinated him. He could not describe why he felt such pleasant wonder each time they passed it. Maybe it symbolized something to him, he thought, something about time and progress and history and change; but maybe it excited him simply because it was a familiar sign that he was on vacation and soon would be at the beach.

Now, more than any time before, they needed this. He looked over at Amber, who was shifting around in her seat, trying to get comfortable, as always, her arm stiff in its sling, the bolts protruding from her clavicle. Despite her obvious discomfort, she looked relaxed, finally far away from the county and the things that had caused her this pain. They'd be back soon, but for the moment, that fact was far from their minds.

"Come on down to Bargain Time!" he said in his best carnival-barker voice as they passed the decaying property. He looked back at Jonathan. "We got everythang a boy could need! Sticks, rocks, dirt! That's where mommy and me did your Christmas shopping this year!" He looked at Johnny in the rearview mirror and grinned, and the boy gave a worried giggle, not sure if his dad was joking or not.

Amber rolled her eyes and smiled politely. She turned to look at the boy, who was glaring out at the abandoned store. "You know your daddy is pulling your leg," she said.

They passed through historic downtown Elba and looked out at its old dilapidated square, the historic homes that surrounded it. They passed through the new commercial area farther down the highway. They passed through miles and miles of farmland and timberland and forest until they reached Samson, the next small town down the line. How strange and comforting it was to pass through these places, Daniel thought, each little town its own alternate universe, each with its own history, its own story for how it came into being and how it became what it is now. Each place teeming with life, with farm league baseball teams and pageant-and-dance studios, love affairs and political scandal. How interesting it was to be in a place so similar to your own home, and yet so different in subtle little ways that you'd be hard-pressed to describe. Daniel wondered about the politics here; he wondered what sort of scandals gripped their local culture. There were a thousand fascinating stories here, he knew, in these little rural places along the road to the coast, with names like Opp, Samson, Gaskin, Defuniak Springs.

Each of these little towns, he imagined, held the things he loved about the South—the wide open spaces; the freedom of movement afforded by that space; the clean air; the opportunity for quiet; the courtesy and cordiality; the abundance of vegetables; the certainty with which people held their beliefs—even if you disagreed with them, at least they were stable, at least you knew where someone stood and where you stood in relation to them—the deer and squirrels and rabbits and foxes and skunks and raccoons and coyotes roaming freely about; the variety of birds everywhere; the expanse of sky and the forever-interesting, forever-different formations of clouds; the clear view of the stars at night. How terrible and strange that into this same fabric was woven the stubborn fact of racial segregation and white supremacy, as powerful now as it ever was; the exploitation of the country's isolation by evil men—from child abusers to the purveyors of roadside pain clinics—looking to commit their misdeeds far from public view; the preachers and politicians who used the name of God and America to seduce a people in search of moral certainty to become pawns in their own quests for money and power.

How he longed for some way to resolve the good and the bad, to have the natural beauty and the genteel culture but extract the evil that had incubated here for so long. If ever he had an opportunity to try, it was now.

The Rileys arrived in the opulence and serenity of Seaside, Florida around 6 p.m. They drove along a freshly-maintained cobblestone road and pulled up to a gleaming white three-story townhome. Daniel climbed out of the Explorer and stretched his arms into the air, grateful to be free from the vehicle. The air was chilly, but the smell of the ocean made it seem warmer.

Johnny tumbled out of the back door and ran squealing into a quad of perfectly-tended grass. Daniel made several trips from the car to the home and up and down the stairs, carrying in every bag, one armload after another, until everything was in a pile at the head of the staircase. He stood there and looked down at the pile of luggage, then looked around the main level, immaculate and clean. He looked over to a couch, where Amber was lying on a pile of pillows, her eyes closed, a neutral, satisfied expression on her face. Now, he realized, finally was the time for rest.

He walked across the room to a glass door that opened out onto a deck. He opened the door and stepped out and looked down at the grassy quad below, where Johnny was running and guiding an Iron Man action figure through the air, mimicking the sound of his roaring jetpack, frolicking amongst a patch of twisty Japanese Maples. Daniel leaned forward on the railing and stood there like that for a long time, perfectly still, his eyes taking in the declining light of the day. He breathed in the clean coastal air, listened to the faint sound of the ocean in the distance, and thought about what he had done.

*Boll Weevil*

Daniel had worked out an agreement with Darby, who would be given until January 31 to wrap up outstanding business and vacate the Commissioner's office. In exchange for a clean concession, Daniel had agreed that there would be no celebratory rallies, no gloating speeches, no disparaging remarks to the newspaper. Ed Gardner had advised him that this was a good idea: to cause a scene, to draw attention to the transition, would only shine a spotlight upon the new administration. He needed to ease quietly into power, to focus on governing and not politics. He would need space to make decisions while few were paying attention. He needed room to breathe, room to make mistakes.

He and Michael had spent the past month and a half hunkered down at the office, combing through the county code, reviewing every outstanding contract, taking calls from constituents of every nature, examining their priorities, planning policy for the year to come. Daniel met with a cannabis upstart interested in setting up shop there in Goshen County, and he brought one gentleman out to look at Jessup's tobacco warehouse as a possible site for a distribution center. The county truly had the opportunity to place itself at the center of this new industry. Other counties in the region were still struggling with the same moral concerns, the same resistance to change as his county had, but now Goshen had a government fully ready to embrace the opportunity. There was the potential for great wealth, new wealth in new hands, and that was exciting.

Daniel thought about Melanie Stewart, wondered again what happened to her. The GBI had come down to look into her disappearance, but still had not found her. They felt certain it had been Russell Tibbits—her phone was in his dirty house—but he was dead, and he couldn't tell them where she was.

Lurleen Folds was a local hero. The story of the old lady who had blown away the corrupt deputy with an enormous shotgun was catnip for popular news outlets. Some right-wing publications used her to illustrate the virtues of the Second Amendment, the benefits of gun ownership, something Daniel found highly annoying. She was interviewed on the national broadcast of 20/20, where she told the story of the guardian angel who had distracted the deputy and saved her life. The video of her interview was shared over and over again, on social media and the like, by religious folks seeking evidence of God's mercy. Amber had declined to be interviewed.

The Secretary of State and the State Attorney General's Office questioned Darby and Tyler about the voter fraud, about the disappearance of Stewart and the actions of Deputy Tibbits. The men had simply denied any knowledge and, so far, it seemed there was no hard evidence against them. Everyone in the county intuitively knew they had been involved; everyone suspected them intensely; but when it came to proving it, it seemed there was very little.

Daniel thought on this. He remembered something Michael had told him before he and Amber left for the beach. Something about Melanie's ex-husband, who had gotten into a sad, desperate drunk one night at the bar at Applebee's and was muttering that, before she disappeared, Melanie told him something about an election, about a cop, about the County Attorney.

Daniel was awoken from his thoughts by the smell of cooking inside the house, the sound of sizzling on a pan. He smelled butter, and then some kind of meat amidst some kind of seasoning. He turned and walked into the house, where he saw Amber standing before the stovetop cooking something in a skillet. Steam rose into the air. She turned back at him and smiled. "This is harder with one arm," she said.

"You sure you don't want me to cook dinner?" he said.

"I'm sure. As smart as you are, you can't cook worth a damn. Eating your cooking has been the most painful part of this injury by far." She laughed and turned back to what she was doing. "You can help me cut up these veggies, though."

"Gladly," he said, a smile on his face, as he walked inside to join her.

That evening, after dinner, after Jonathan was in bed, Daniel sat back out on the porch. The air was much cooler now, almost cold, and he was wearing a soft, comfortable grey hoody, enjoying the clean air and the quiet, looking out into the darkness, drinking a bottle of beer.

He heard Amber shuffling around inside and turned to look at her. She was looking into a mirror, holding her one good arm above her head, trying to twist her hair into a ponytail. She was wearing skin-tight black pants and a loose-fitting t-shirt.

"You look nice," he said.

She smiled. "You're a sucker for yoga pants."

"You want to go up on the roof?"

They walked up the stairs to the third floor. They peeked into the boy's bedroom to ensure he was asleep, and he was. They stepped into a little enclave off the hallway and found a steel spiral staircase. Daniel followed Amber up the twisty steps to a door in the ceiling. He opened a latch and pushed open the door and the cool, exhilarating air rushed in. They stepped out onto the rooftop and Daniel lowered the door halfway and looked up into the dark night at the millions of stars, which spread infinitely around them in all directions. The night was so clear he could discern star-clusters, galaxies even. They could hear the waves of the ocean nearby. They could smell its salty breeze.

He turned to his wife. He put his hands on her waist and pushed her slowly backward toward an outdoor couch.

"Careful," she said, smiling. "This is going to be a tricky operation with this cast." She let herself fall gently onto the couch. Daniel got on his knees and positioned his hips between her legs and leaned toward her and kissed her lips. He put his hands under her shirt and could feel the goosebumps on her skin. With her good arm, she began to unbutton his jeans.

"Mommy?"

They heard the metallic clang of little feet climbing onto the spiral stairs.

"Oh shit!" they said. Daniel pulled himself quickly away and adjusted his trousers. He rushed over to the doorway. Johnny grinned up at him through the crack in the half-open door.

"You're supposed to be in bed!" Daniel said.

"I want to go to the beach!" said the boy.

"It's late!" Daniel said.

He looked over to Amber, who shrugged. "What the hell," she said. "Let's go."

They came downstairs and bundled the boy up in his jacket. The three walked out the front door of the townhouse, and Johnny shot forward. A little ray from the boy's flashlight pulsed around the lawn in front of him as he ran.

"Stay where we can see you!" Daniel shouted.

The couple walked down a sandy path onto the beach. In the darkness with their eyes unadjusted, they could not see the ocean before them, but they could hear its roar and feel the water in the air. Johnny was many yards ahead now, his flashlight now a dot of light in the distance.

They sat in the sand, and Amber rested her head on Daniel's shoulder. She was so glad to be here. She was so glad this year was coming to an end.

After some silence, he looked at her and said, "Do you ever wish we had stayed in Rosewood?"

She thought about it for some time, then, looking out at the ocean, she said, "No. Of course, sometimes, when I look at my face, or when my shoulder is killing me, I wish we had never done any of this. But honestly, now more than ever, I'm glad we did it. I'm proud of you."

She thought for a moment more. "I'm proud of myself," she said. "I did something great. I almost died, but instead I'm alive. I've never felt so intensely before that there is a purpose to my life. After all that's happened, there must be. This was somehow all meant to happen."

She turned from the ocean to Daniel, looked in his eyes with great seriousness. "You realize you can't squander this. When we get back, you have a tremendous responsibility. You owe a great debt." She wrapped her hand warmly around his bicep as she spoke.

"I know," he said. "When I think about what you did. When I think about all that Michael did, all that everyone who supported me did, and then I think back to what led me to run in the first place. . . My ego. . . my own selfish desire to win. . . I feel. . . embarrassed."

He looked at her and tears began to well in his eyes. "I'm sorry," he said. "I'm sorry for putting you through this." He leaned his head forward and touched his forehead against hers, felt the warmth of her skin. "I'm going to work hard every day to make sure it wasn't in vain. I want you to know how seriously I take my duty to you. And to everyone who helped me."

"I know you do," she said and kissed him.

Johnny came running to them. "I found a crab!" he shouted. He was holding up a sand-white crab by its pincher. It wriggled and writhed in the air beneath his hand. "Look!" he said. He was laughing with immense pleasure as he watched the wiggling crustacean.

"My goodness!" said Daniel. "What are you going to do with him?"

"Let's cook him!" he said. Daniel and Amber burst into laughter.

"Let's let Mr. Crab live another day," said Amber. "I don't think he'd be very good to eat."

"Ok!" the boy cried. He threw his arm back and flung the crab through the air and ran back onto the beach.

They sat there watching their boy, Amber's head on Daniel's shoulder. Daniel's eyes had adjusted, and he could now discern the horizon. He stared out at it and thought about his profound obligation, the impossibility of his task to change an unchanging place, and his determination to do it.